# The Evil Within

## Magic of the Realm
### Book Two

**Kimberly Marraffino**

The Evil Within
Magic of the Realm ~ Book Two



Cover by Stefanie Saw (www.seventhstarart.com)
Copyediting by Dennis Doty
Copyediting by Enchanted Ink Publishing
Map made by Kimberly Marraffino
Symbol designed by Kimberly Marraffino and made by DRIVEN Digital Services

Second Edition June 2022
Printed in the United States of America
Published in Nacogdoches, Texas

ISBN: 978-1-7360404-8-5 (Paperback)
Library of Congress Control Number: 2022908940

www.KimberlyMarraffino.com

*To Ian,*
*Thank you for helping me name some of the*
*characters in this series.*

*I'm sorry it doesn't have dinosaurs.*

KILUEMAR
North Shores
Demetrius Desert
Arista Bay
Lunar Cave
Werewolf Highlands
Full Moon Forest
Dragon Cove
Forbidden Coast
Midnight Ridge
Dead Man's Bay
Siren Sea
Elf Beach
Centaur Forest
Dwarf Ridge
Lucien Valley
Cursed Cave
Forsaken Bluffs
Casteya Castle
Raven Lagoon
Enchanted Hills
Stoweward
Maevis Mountains
Shadow Forest
Sunset Cliffs
Valley of the Giants
Drolnogard Peak
Mystic Woods
Nymph Grove
Guardian Lake
Emrys Cave
Muse Meadow
Kitra Forest
West Shores
Caerwyn Village
Sunrise Mesa
East Shores
Cassil Cabin
Cavern Beach
Half Moon Harbor
Dryad Forest
Grotto Bridge
South Shores
Ember Cliffs
0 1 2 3
Miles
N
W E
S

# Note from the Author

Content Warning:

I want my readers to be well-informed of any possible triggers or content that might not be appropriate for some. If you would like to know if this book contains any elements that might be of concern to you, please check the back of the book for more details.

Flashbacks and Past Events:

Only events happening in the past (years, decades, and centuries) will be mentioned at the beginning of each chapter.

Pronunciation and Translation Guide:

Both provided in the back of the book.

# Table of Contents

# *Chapter 1*

Night of the Storm

*Eight years ago*

A crash erupted downstairs, and shattering glass clattered against the floor. Karramis startled awake from a light sleep, the room illuminating as multiple candles ignited. Her stomach dropped, and she sprang upright, peering through the flickering glow as footsteps echoed through the shadows of the manor. Ignoring the freshly lit candles, she scrambled to her feet, kicking the heavy comforter draped across her body and partially tossing it on the floor. She tiptoed from her bedroom and down a narrow hallway. Reaching the steps of the third-floor landing, she paused as footsteps creaked closer to the stairwell on the main floor. Her pulse raced. She flattened her body against the wall and closed her eyes, forcing herself to silence her inner thoughts.

The front door creaked as a cold breeze traveled through the manor. Karramis tilted her head, turning her ear closer to the staircase. Footfalls entered and stopped in the entryway. She held her breath as whispers carried up the stairs, masking her heavy panting from the intruders. The footsteps and voices retreated away from the stairs as the front door closed. Being careful to avoid certain steps, Karramis bolted down the stairs to the second floor as the shuffling footfalls moved down the corridor leading to the kitchen.

The door at the base of the stairs was closed. Turning the knob, Karramis inched it open. A squeak emitted from the hinges, and she paused, paying close attention as silence filled the manor. Afraid to progress any farther, she slid through the small opening and entered the softly lit room.

Two twin beds sat on opposite sides of the room, and a single two-paned window rested between them along the back wall. The moon shone through lace curtains, illuminating the faces of two children as they slept. Karramis smiled and stepped closer, taking a mental picture of the memory placed before her. Her heart was heavy and sent waves of tightness crushing her chest. She shuddered, swallowing the sadness rising in her throat. Her smile fell, and she pressed her lips together, attempting to stop her chin from trembling. She squeezed her eyes and tears trailed down her cheeks.

Karramis took a deep breath and wiped the tears from her face. Reaching one side of the room, she placed her hand on a young boy and gently rocked him awake.

"Mom?" James sat up and yawned. "What's wrong?"

Karramis kissed his forehead and faced the other bed. Leaning over Rhiannon, she brushed her fingers along her daughter's face, moving the loose strands of hair draped across her cheek.

"Rhiannon? I need you to wake up, sweetie."

A deafening crash came from downstairs causing Rhiannon to jump upright.

"What was that?" the twins asked, alarmed, both rushing to their feet.

Karramis tapped her finger against her mouth, hushing her children. She raced to the bedroom door and carefully slid her upper body through the narrow opening. Glancing both ways down the hallway, she peered through the shadows of the corridor. No one was around, and the manor was quiet again. Relieved, Karramis retreated back into the room.

Standing in front of her children, she faced the door, and with her mind blank, Karramis raised both arms and steadied them. She concentrated on the empty space in front of her, summoning her powers to the surface. A subtle breeze swirled throughout the room but faded. Her hands shook as she stretched out her stiffened fingers, clenching her teeth as she focused harder. Soft gusts appeared and disappeared again, sending an unsettling chill through the air.

James stepped back, pulling Rhiannon with him. "Mom?"

Karramis dropped her hands and groaned under her breath. "Dammit."

Spotting the bewildered expression on the twins' faces, she squatted down and gestured for them to come closer.

"I need you two to do me a favor," Karramis whispered with a heavy strain in her voice.

The twins nodded in agreement.

"I need you to go upstairs and hide . . . hide where I showed you. Can you do that for me?"

The twins nodded again as James opened his mouth to talk.

"I don't have time to explain." Karramis drew them closer and wrapped her arms around them. "Please, just do this for me, okay?" Pulling from the embrace, she shifted her eyes to James. "No questions asked." She cradled their faces. "And no matter what, do *not* come out. Do you understand?"

They gave her a single nod, quick and synchronized.

"Good. Now, do you remember which book?"

"Yes," the twins answered.

"Okay, good." Karramis forced a grin. "That's good."

Exiting the room, Karramis tiptoed down the hallway as James and Rhiannon followed behind her. She paused at the two staircases—one leading up to her room, and the other heading down to the main floor—and took hold of her children's trembling hands.

Karramis kissed their foreheads. "I love you."

"We love you too," they said softly.

James leaned in closer. "Mom, what's—"

"Shh. No questions asked, remember?"

James lowered his head as Rhiannon ushered him up the stairs, both disappearing into the darkness.

Footsteps moved around downstairs, but Karramis could not distinguish where they were coming from. She shifted side to side, rubbing her sweaty palms along her upper thighs as her lower abdomen tingled. Waves of fear surged through her chest and along her spine. She dropped her eyelids and swallowed. Planting her feet firmly on the ground, she exhaled and flung open her eyes.

"I'm tired of running," she said in a whisper. "I won't let them take my children." She clenched her hands into fists and hurried in the opposite direction down the hallway. Reaching another set of stairs along the back wall, she halted. "I'm going to stop them . . . or die trying."

Descending the narrow stairwell, Karramis came to a closed door and carefully opened it. A soft orange glow and hushed crackling filled the room, coming from the oversized stone fireplace as she crept closer to the kitchen.

A cold breeze brushed against her skin, and the smell of rain blew past her nose as she entered the dark kitchen from the dining room. Her bare feet pressed against the frigid wooden floor and forced her body to recoil. She tiptoed farther into the kitchen, and the floorboards creaked beneath her. Moving over to a small hutch standing in the corner, she blindly rummaged through one of its drawers. The cold metal of a small flashlight brushed against her fingers. Grasping it in her hand, she clicked it on and examined the room.

Pieces of glass were scattered across the counter, and small shards mixed with dirt and grass along the floor. The window over the sink was broken and flung open. Thunder rumbled in the distance, and raindrops fell outside. Stepping on something sharp, Karramis moved the beam of light down and removed a piece of splintered wood from her sole. A clank ricocheted from the corner of the room. Twisting toward the sound, she jerked the flashlight back and forth as flickering lights emerged from the cracks of the cellar door. She crept closer but stopped. The knob was gone, and a section of the doorframe was missing. She aimed the flashlight around the room. A long, splintered piece of wood lay on the floor. Picking it up, Karramis grasped it as she leaned in and listened at the door.

A creak and steady breathing materialized behind her through the silence. Her body tensed as she flinched. She forced her eyes closed as the hair on the back of her neck stood up. The breathing intensified, blowing heavily against her hair as the figure behind her inched closer.

"Hello, Karramis," a distinctively calm voice said as a set of cold hands snatched her upper arms in the darkness. "Fancy seeing you alive."

Recognizing the voice, Karramis dropped the flashlight and clutched the broken doorframe with both hands before twisting around and thrusting it into the man's chest. Pushing him away, she raced over to the archway leading out of the kitchen. The light from the flashlight bounced up from the floor, illuminating the pale-skinned man as he fell to his knees. He yanked the wood protruding from his ribs, and blood gushed from the open wound as his lifeless body toppled over and smacked against the floor.

Karramis collided with another individual as they entered the kitchen. She stumbled back, tripping over her own feet as she peered up at a man towering over her. The brawny, tan-skinned man was not someone she recognized. He hid behind a wild beard and long, dark hair reaching below his shoulder blades. Karramis rose to her feet, but the man's muscular leg kicked her back against the cold floor. She groaned as she sat up, her watchful gaze observing the man's eyes darting through thick-framed glasses toward the body positioned just a few feet away. Crawling away from him, she gasped in terror as he let out a beastly growl. With his fist tightly clenched, he scowled at her as his feet pounded against the floor, advancing closer to her.

"What's goin' on up here?" a man yelled as he flung open the door to the cellar and stepped from the creaking stairs. He bent over and picked up the flashlight, directing the bright beam at the bloody body on the floor. "Well, shit. That's not gonna end well." He turned his attention over to the others and the light lit up Karramis's face. "Hello there, love."

Thunder cracked outside in unison with a flash of lightning.

"Lucas," Karramis said blankly, sliding away from the other man. "You think you could call off this brute?"

The man grabbed her hair, yanking her head back and growling at her. "I'd shut up if I were you."

"Relax, Haydrin." Lucas gently elbowed his way between the two. "I got this."

Still holding onto Karramis's hair, Haydrin stepped back. He tightened his fist and pulled harder before flinging her backward as he let go, tossing her onto the floor.

Karramis raised her chin and clenched her jaw as Lucas bent down. Her heart pounded and chest flared as his deep blue eyes met her unblinking gaze. An unwavering sense of dominance radiated from them, both refusing to allow the other control over the situation. She crawled away from him as his menacing glare fixated on her, but he wrapped his hand over her leg and pulled her closer.

"Where are they?" Lucas asked calmly.

Karramis grinned, her voice filled with sarcasm. "Who?"

Lucas chuckled under his breath. "Where are they, Karramis? I can sense 'em, but I can't pinpoint where they are."

"I have no idea who you're talking about."

He stood up. "So, ya wanna do this the hard way, eh?"

Lucas raised his arm and backhanded her across the face. She landed hard on the floor, hitting her head against the wooden boards. The room spun as a throbbing erupted in her temples. She closed her eyes and fought against the pain deepening across her cheek as a set of hands grasped her upper body and lifted her into the air.

Karramis's eyelids twitched with resistance as she drove open her eyes. Her body bounced against Haydrin's shoulder as he crossed the threshold and descended the rickety stairs into the cellar. Distorted voices and a clap of thunder rang in her ears. The side of her face pulsated with her heavy heartbeat but was masked as her body was tossed on the floor, the pain racing along her back as the air was knocked out of her. She panted with shallow breaths as she pulled her legs into a fetal position. Her bare skin pressed against the cold stones beneath her, and she shivered, the chill piercing through her like icy razor blades. Peering through a slight haze, she observed multiple figures within the dim light of flickering candles as they cast shadows along the walls. She moaned as she pushed herself up, but her arms were kicked out from under her. Her face smacked against the floor, and she cried out as blood dripped from her nose. Her head pounded as her body trembled, the uncontrollable shaking intensifying with each shuddering breath. Afraid to move, Karramis slowed her hurried breathing, struggling to combat the agony flowing through her.

"I want her dead!" a hostile voice snapped.

Karramis winced and curled her legs tighter against her body as the familiar voice boomed over her. It was Leif—the man she had killed upstairs, or at least, had tried to kill. Unfortunately, the brazen and cutthroat vampire was still alive.

"Really, mate?" Lucas circled around Karramis and headed over to Leif. "You're gonna kill the poor defenseless witch when she's down? Where's your pride? At least wait until she can fight back."

"Defenseless?" Leif paced as he ran his fingers through his flaxen hair. "That bitch tried to kill me!"

The hostile vampire marched in circles and rubbed his hand over the bloody section of his shirt. The wound was healing, but not fast enough for the hot-tempered man, who resisted the urge to dig his teeth into Karramis, draining the life from her body and regaining the full strength of his abilities.

Leif pounded his steel-toed boots against the cellar floor and sent vibrations shaking beneath Karramis. Her muscles twitched, and she recoiled, anticipating another painful blow to her body. Regretting her inability to successfully kill the enraged bloodsucker, she was certain he would get his revenge. Luckily, Lucas was present, and he had a way of controlling Leif's ruthless and unpredictable nature most of the time.

"Exactly. If she wanted ya dead, she woulda succeeded." Lucas crouched next to Karramis. "Right, love? I mean, your powers are . . ." He tilted his head and tightened his gaze. Grinning, he pushed back the messy waves stuck against her bloody face. "Why didn't ya use your powers, love?"

"Don't . . ." Karramis groaned, lifting herself with shaky arms. "Don't call me that."

"Call ya what?" Lucas reached out to help her. "Love?"

Karramis jerked her arm away and pushed herself into a sitting position.

Scowling, he said bitterly, "Well, ya didn't mind me callin' ya that before."

"Yeah, well, that was a long time ago, Lucas . . ." She glared up at him. "And some things change."

Lucas clenched his teeth and yanked her to her feet. His tight grasp squeezed her upper arms, and she cried out as he lifted her onto her tiptoes before throwing her back. She crashed against the floor, and whimpers escaped from her as blood rose from the fresh scrapes along her arms.

Lucas turned his back to her and ran his fingers through his hair. "Gastell, get ova' here."

An enormous creature shuffled his bare feet over to Lucas, his wide eyes sitting uneven on his unusually small head, focusing on nothing in particular. A long, flat nose and crooked teeth rested against the humanoid creature's face. With his mud-colored and dingy skin, and the potent smell of dead fish and rotten eggs emanating from his hefty body, Karramis recognized the creature right away. He was an ogre.

Lucas scrunched his nose. "Go outside and patrol the area. I don't want anyone tryna escape."

Gastell's heavy footsteps pounded up the stairs, shaking and squeaking under his massive body. His booming steps faded from the kitchen and down the hallway as the storm rumbled through the manor.

Karramis crawled away from the others, her body trembling as she slid on her stomach across the floor. Leif's boots stopped inches from her face, and she cowered as Lucas lifted her onto her feet. Every inch of her ached as each muscle tensed within his grasp.

"Look at me," Lucas said calmly as she bowed her head.

Karramis refused.

Lucas squeezed her arms and shook her. "Look at me!"

She winced as she raised her watery eyes.

"Well, well. What do we have here? Look at this, guys . . . it seems the fearless and stubborn Karramis is not only powerless, but now she's scared, weak, and pathetic." He released his grip, and she fell to her knees. "You're completely useless to anyone but me." He knelt beside her, lifted her chin, and whispered, "Maybe I should just keep ya for myself."

Lucas met Leif and Haydrin by the stairs. The three men muttered to one another while Karramis ignored the hushed huddle and glanced around the room, frantically searching for a way out.

Cobwebs filled most corners of the stone room, and dusty shelves leaned against the walls. Among the wooden shelves were old books and various glass bottles filled with mysterious liquids—the labels faded or missing. Pillar candles sat on the shelves on one side of the room and lit up a small area of the cellar. Along the far back wall was a barely visible set of stairs leading up, and piles of stone and dirt were scattered along the floor.

Karramis continued to search the room but paused after meeting Haydrin's dark eyes. The menacing man folded his bulging arms across his muscular chest and continued glaring in her direction. His emotionless stare made the hair on her arms stand up. Her stomach twisted, and her insides turned cold. She shifted her body, moving both herself and her gaze away from him.

She had to get away from her captors. Her life—and the lives of her children—depended on it. But how? How was she going to overpower these men without her magic? Leif, although injured, was still stronger, and she had no idea who, or what, Haydrin was, but she did not want to take her chances with him. Lucas, however, was the only one she did not fear, nor did she question her ability to outsmart him. If it were only Lucas, she might have had a chance, but she was not feeling confident with the others around, especially without her powers. But why were they not working? When she had made the decision to suppress her powers all those years ago, she understood it might have some lasting effects, but she never thought it would be this severe. The magic inside her was still present, something she was certain of, because it was the only thing keeping her alive. However, the years of suppressing her abilities forced her active powers so deep inside her, they were proving harder to bring to the surface. Karramis had always hated her abilities because they made her different from the ones she loved, an outcast in her mind. She had spent a lifetime filled with resentment for something she had no control over, yet now was the time for her to embrace her magic and the destined path she had been forced upon. She needed to fight—fight to save her children, even if it meant she would not survive in the end.

Thunder clapped outside, getting louder as rain hammered against the exterior cellar doors. Lucas drifted away from the conversation, his attention on Karramis as her eyes scanned the room. He cleared his mind and focused. His gaze met hers and she froze, her plan quickly fading from her mind.

*"Nice try, Lucas,"* Karramis thought, her inner voice steady and calm. *"I may be powerless, but I'm not stupid. And I'm still stronger than you."*

Lucas narrowed his eyes and stormed over to her, backhanding her across the face. An uncontrollable scream erupted from her as her head flung sideways, an intense burning sensation racing across her face. Her cries bounced off the walls and traveled up the stairs, fading into the shadows of the manor.

Puffing his chest, Lucas cracked his knuckles and flicked his head to the side, popping his neck. "You made me do that!" He circled around her. "This is all your fault. If ya woulda just cooperated for once in your life."

Karramis lifted her head. *"Please Lucas, stop."* Her gentle brown eyes beamed up at him, burrowing into his soul through his vexing gaze. *"Stop this. This isn't you."*

The tense muscles along his face relaxed as he stared at her. Reaching out his hands to console her, he quickly drew back as she pulled away from him. He sighed and staggered backward, the guilt exploding inside him as the woman he loved lay injured and scared at his feet.

"Knock it off, witch," Leif demanded. "Lucas!"

A heavy thud crashed against the floor upstairs within the kitchen, and the three men jerked around, facing the noise as footsteps scurried beyond the landing.

Panic raced through her body, and Karramis quickly grabbed Lucas's leg as he moved toward the stairs. He stumbled and clutched Leif's shoulder. The vampire twisted his lean, muscular body around and kicked her in the stomach. Crying out, she gasped for air as the pain smothered her, squeezing her lungs and piercing her gut. Leif sniffed the air and rushed to the stairs, but the flames of the candles stretched high off the wicks as Karramis's magic exploded outward and tossed the three men through the air. Leif and Haydrin hurtled into the shelves, the breaking of boards and pained groans of the men ringing out like an explosion as Lucas flew in the opposite direction, colliding against the stone wall.

"Go get 'em!" Lucas yelled in a hardened tone as he hurried to his feet and over to Karramis.

Tossing the broken boards aside, Leif pushed himself up and grabbed hold of Haydrin's freshly scratched and bloody arm. The two raced up the stairs and after the footsteps receding away from the landing.

Lucas forced Karramis onto her stomach and straddled her, unraveling a rope looped around his belt and tying her arms behind her back. Removing a gray blindfold from his pocket, he wrapped it around her eyes and knotted it tightly against the back of her head.

Jumping to his feet, Lucas rammed his fist into his palm. "Fuckin' hell!" He paced the room, running his fingers through his messy, brown hair. "Dammit, Karramis! Why the hell do ya havta be so bloody difficult?"

Blinded and bound, Karramis did not answer him but instead concentrated on the sounds coming from upstairs. Loud bangs echoed somewhere in the manor before everything went quiet, the heavy panting and stomping of Lucas now resonating through the cellar and filling her ears. She shifted her legs under her body and anticipated the actions of his rage.

Lucas closed his eyes and focused on the children he sensed within the manor. Their magic was faint and hard to locate, but he knew they were close by. Karramis grew uneasy with the silence, her skin tingling as pins and needles stabbed at her nerves. Her head pounded, and her heartbeat thumped in her ears. The smell of rain, musk, and cedar filled the damp cellar as the thunder rumbled, vibrating the frigid stones under her legs. Her body shuddered, both freezing and terrified. Her muscles tensed as Lucas moved closer, sensing his towering stance as he came to a stop.

She jumped and leaned back as his hot, rapid breath blew against her face.

"Why can't I hear 'em?"

Karramis scoffed and chuckled.

He seized her shoulders. "Answer me!"

"I don't know!" she said, matching his tone. She lowered her voice. "They don't have their powers, so maybe that has something to do with it."

"Yeah, they do. That's how I found ya. I sensed their magic two days ago and tracked 'em not far from here. It didn't take long to find this place. Actually, it was ratha' easy." He laughed. "You're losin' your touch, love."

Karramis's chest burned, her hurried exhales shuddering as they escaped. Her heartbeat throbbed in her thighs, the blood unable to flow as her body pressed into her legs.

Lucas pulled off the blindfold. "Wait, ya didn't know?"

"No. No, I wasn't sure how you found us. I thought maybe I had used my powers again without knowing. But I . . . I haven't used my magic on purpose in years."

"So, that's why ya didn't use your magic. You're outta practice." He sighed. "Not a smart decision there, love. Well, I guess ya found it again, eh? Or at least, it found you. That didn't take long."

"Well, when someone is beating the crap outta you and trying to kidnap your children, there tends to be a bit of urgency and motivation involved."

"Right. Well, speakin' of your kids, why can't I hear 'em?"

"Like I said, I don't know. Maybe they're more powerful than you. I mean, I learned early on how to block your obnoxious and invasive powers, not to mention your complete disregard for privacy."

"Yeah, well, I didn't like the secrets. I was supposed to be your friend."

"You *were* my friend, Lucas. One of my best friends. But there were things . . . things I didn't want to tell you—"

"But I loved you!"

Karramis flinched as his voice bounced off the cellar walls.

The storm outside grew louder and more intense as the rain pounded against the exterior walls of the manor, the wind howling and the ground rumbling. The gentle earthquake settled to a stop, and the wind slowed, but the storm continued to roar.

"What the hell was that?" Lucas asked as he glanced around.

"It was them," Karramis whispered to herself.

Disregarding the unusual incident, Lucas lowered himself down. "I loved you . . . and ya broke my heart."

"I didn't mean to do that to you. I never meant to hurt you. I *never* would've done that to you on purpose. You have to know that. And I loved you, too . . . just not the way you wanted me to, and that did something to you. You changed. You're the one who changed things between us, not me."

"No—"

"Yes. Yes, y*ou* are the one who decided to hate me. *You* are the one who chose to be vengeful and fight on the side that wants my children dead. *You* are the one who let your feelings of revenge and hatred surpass any other feelings you ever had for me. *You* are the one who threw our friendship away all because *I* chose to love someone else the way you wanted me to love you. But I didn't see you that way. I'm sorry. You hate me because I love Will . . . because I chose him over you."

Lucas cringed at her declaration, and the seconds of silence trailed on for what seemed like forever as Karramis waited for him to respond.

"I'm sorry, Lucas," she said, secretly loosening the rope tied around her wrists. "I didn't mean to hurt you. But . . . you can't hate me for loving someone else."

Lucas leaned in, his heavy breaths brushing against her ear. "Wanna bet?"

"Fine. Have it your way." Karramis placed her cheek against his and whispered, "Let's get this over with then."

She threw her arms out from around her back and rammed her body into his, pushing through the pain and shoving him backward against the wall. Karramis sprang up and dropped the rope at her feet. Swinging her arm through the air, she drove her fist across his face before racing over to the stairs. Her body ached as she hurried up the steps. She crashed into the door, and a boom rang out as it smashed against the wall, and two of the hinges ripped from the door frame. She sprinted through Leif's blood and slipped, streaks of red smearing across the floor as she hurried to her feet. Slipping again, she skidded into the island in the middle of the kitchen, sending items crashing from the counter. Lucas slammed into her and pressed his body into her back. Pain erupted along her injuries as she was forced against the counter. She tried to regain her footing as he struggled to grab her arms. Twisting around, she elbowed him in the stomach. He hunched over as a breathless groan escaped from his body. She pushed him back and ran into the hallway, jerking open the front door and racing outside.

Rain poured from the sky, and thunder clapped, booming overhead as lightning lit up the sky. Karramis ducked behind the bushes under the front windows as footsteps boomed inside the manor.

Leif and Haydrin rushed into the kitchen from the dining room and switched on the lights. Lucas leaned against the island, clutching his stomach and catching his breath.

"Can I kill her now?" Leif asked Lucas.

"No. You're not gonna kill her."

Lucas stormed down the hall as Leif and Haydrin followed behind him.

Leif tugged at Lucas's arm, twisting him around. "You still love her, don't you?"

Lucas yanked his arm away and continued down the hall, exiting through the front door and disappearing into the storm.

Leif faced Haydrin. "I really hate that witch."

"Well, if Merrick doesn't finish her off soon, you should."

"Definitely. I still owe her for this little stunt." Leif put a finger through the bloody hole in his shirt. "That crazy bitch ruined my favorite shirt."

Leif and Haydrin left the manor through the front door, turning the corner and meeting Lucas and Gastell on the other side of the building.

Yelling over the rain, Lucas glanced over at Haydrin and Leif as they approached. "Gastell's gonna patrol the back side of the house. I want ya two to spread out and search outside. Karramis is out here somewhere."

Meeting Lucas's tone, Leif asked, "What about the children?"

"Keep lookin' for 'em, but I want Karramis. She's our ticket back. And with her powers not workin', she's defenseless, but there's no tellin' what kind of powers those damn kids have."

"How is she our ticket back without her powers?"

"She still has 'em, they're just not—Never mind, just find her!"

They all scattered, heading in opposite directions around the outside of the manor.

Karramis crouched in the bushes as the rain poured down the side of the Victorian manor, bouncing off the thick vines crawling up the side of the stone exterior. She closed her eyes and concentrated on the voices as her gut squeezed, fear and nervousness wringing together. The cold water trailed down her body as she clutched her drenched nightgown. Shivering, she folded her arms across her chest. The coldness made the injuries along her torso and face numb, and she pushed herself up from the ground.

The voices of the others faded, and Karramis hurried from the bushes and ran back through the front door. Water splashed against the hardwood floor as it dripped from her body and nightgown. Stepping farther into the front hallway, she spotted shadows moving within the brightly lit kitchen. She staggered up the stairs and ignored the second floor as she ran to her bedroom.

Karramis made her way through the candle-lit room over to the bookcase in the corner. Pulling a book from the shelf, she paused as a click sounded from the bookcase. She held her breath and heaved open the door, moaning as she exhaled. The soreness wrapped around her abdomen, squeezing and ripping at her muscles. She panted, holding her hand against her stomach as she entered the hidden room. It was empty, but the hatch door was open.

"Dang it, kids. Why didn't you listen to me?"

Karramis rushed back into her room and rummaged through a tall wardrobe across from her bed. She pulled various items of clothing from the intricate antique closet and tossed them on the floor. Reaching the back wall, she ran both hands along the detailed design on the interior wall and searched among the pattern. Her fingers swept across a noticeably deeper indent, and she quickly pressed it. A hidden compartment popped out from under the wardrobe, housing a scarlet satchel.

She removed a stunning jeweled necklace from the velvet bag. The base of the silver chain contained an eight-point silver star with Celtic knots in the middle of each point. In the center of the necklace was a hexagon-shaped deep red garnet within a gold inlay. Along the sides of the crimson gemstone were tiny black obsidian stones surrounding it. At the center of each point, among the Celtic knots, were alternating stones of tiger's-eye and bloodstone.

Karramis placed the necklace over her head and tucked it into her nightgown. "Please let this work."

Disappearing back into the bookcase, Karramis made her way through the hatch door and traveled down the stairs into the hidden room below. She staggered within the narrow and dimly lit passageway and reached a small door at the end of the hall. It was open. Squeezing through it, she tumbled to the floor, the latch snagging her nightgown and ripping it along the bottom.

The study was quiet except for the dripping of water coming from the open windows. The storm outside was calm, and the closed drapes lay flat, soaking up the rain resting along the windowsill. A bright glow flickered as shadows moved along the curtains, grunts and splashing footsteps matching the silhouettes.

"Go get 'em, ya idiots!" boomed a familiar voice.

Karramis ran to the window and flung open the curtains. Flames burned along the tree at the top of the hill as five figures ran away from the manor. Her eyes widened as her heart sank in her chest. Catching sight of movement in her peripheral vision, she locked eyes with Lucas as he staggered to his feet.

Karramis bolted from the study and into the conservatory. She crashed through the back door, exiting the manor into a calm storm as Lucas plowed into her, and they tumbled to the ground. Karramis's feet slipped across the soggy grass as she hurried upright, but Lucas jumped on top of her and pinned her arms down with one hand as he flipped her over onto her back. His weight restricted her airflow as he drove his body harder down onto her.

"Stop it!" He squeezed his legs tighter. "You're only makin' this worse!"

Karramis grunted and thrashed, the intense pain tightening around her lungs as it suffocated her. "Get off me!"

"Karramis!" He fought against her as he reached into his pocket. "Stop it! Don't make me do this!"

She ignored him, squirming and fighting against his overwhelming strength. "Get off me, you son of a—"

A sharp sting pierced through her left side, and she gasped. Her body stiffened and fell limp as Lucas relaxed. Her breathing weakened as the burn radiated along her side, rippling outward and coursing through every nerve. Sliding off her, Lucas yanked the blade of a pocketknife out from under her rib cage. Her body recoiled, the metal slicing her again as it exited. The pain immediately forced her to draw her legs inward as she whimpered.

Lucas dropped the knife on the ground and stood up, wiping his bloody hand on his jeans. "Ya made me do that! I told ya to stop, but ya neva' listen." Pacing, he curled his hands into fists and yelled, "Fuck! Dammit, Karramis!" He stopped and lowered his voice. "If ya woulda stopped fightin' me, this neva' woulda happened." Reaching down, he grabbed her arm. "Get up."

Karramis gasped as her body's dead weight fought against her attempt to stand up, sending every inch of her into an excruciatingly painful state. Her legs grew heavy, and she crashed to her knees. Her head spun as the pain pulsated like rapid drums beating in her ears. Her stomach churned, the intensity of the stab wound driving the acid in her guts to bubble over. The sharpness burned her insides as she forced herself to swallow the vomit rising in her throat.

Still holding her arm, Lucas said in a calmer tone, "C'mon, love." He wrapped his arms around her waist and pulled her up. "It's not fatal. You'll be fine."

Karramis jerked her arm away and flung herself back onto the ground, stretching out across the grass. The intentional descent pinched her injury, and she rolled onto her back. Wincing and crying out, she pressed a hand against the wound, the pressure minimizing the discomfort.

Lucas grasped both arms again and lifted her onto her feet. Karramis shoved him away and was released from one of his tight clutches. As he yanked her closer, Karramis threw her weight into him, pushing him against the exterior wall of the conservatory. With the pocketknife now in her hand, she plunged the blade into his abdomen before yanking it out and stabbing him again. Lucas let out a guttural cry as he snatched her arm. She tugged, but his hold on her was too strong for her to fight, so she drove the blade deeper into his body. A muffled yell rumbled from his chest, and he slid is hand down her arm and seized the handle of the pocketknife. He collapsed to the ground and hesitated as he jerked the blade from his abdomen.

Karramis ran, her legs heavy and weak as she scrambled away in the wrong direction along the backside of the manor. She slowed as the rain stopped, the wind faded, and the clouds vanished. Frowning, she scanned the clear night sky. The storm was gone. She continued forward as blood seeped from her nightgown, covering the dirty, wet material in crimson red. A loud boom exploded somewhere in the distance, and she halted.

A quick rippling force rattled the ground beneath her bare feet, and she bolted along the front side of the manor.

"James! Rhiannon!" Karramis called out in a panic as she rushed around the corner. Spotting the children and others at the top of the hill, she hurried after them. "Run!"

Adrenaline took over, and the pain merged into the strength she needed. She would not allow them to take her children. Karramis was not going to let them use her powers to get back to the realm. The portals needed to be sealed shut before the next full moon, and remain closed until the twins were strong enough to defend themselves against Merrick and stop the prophecy from coming true. Her ability to open a portal had to end here and now, so Lucas could not use her or control her. She was not going to be afraid anymore. She was done running. Karramis was going to stop this fight tonight and protect her children at all costs, even if it meant sacrificing herself to do so. Not being strong enough to travel through the portal with her children, she would have to send them alone—something she had dreaded for years. Goodbyes were never easy. However, saying them one final time was even harder. Her sadness overwhelmed her, and this emotional response would aid in the next step of her plan.

Stumbling from the other side of the manor, Lucas yelled, "Karramis!"

Karramis blended her pain and emotions together, weaving them flawlessly into strength, mixing it with her determination to complete this one final task. She would not only have to rely on her magic, but now, she would have to depend on her innate spellcasting ability as a witch, as well as, her most trusting and powerful skill, creating her own portal. The spell had been etched in her mind for a long time, a spell she memorized years ago but hoped she would never have to use.

With her children beside her, she clutched the necklace and uttered the words of the spell that would help guide the twins back home to Kiluemar and back to Will. Even though she could not control her active powers, she let go of all doubt and put her trust in magic, the powers hidden deep inside her, a carefully thought-out incantation, and her motivation to save her children. And it worked. The magic flowed through her body as a portal swirled a few feet away.

"Go!" Karramis said harshly before adding in a softer tone, "I know you're scared, but please just walk through it."

"Aren't you coming?" James asked, stopping in front of the portal.

Karramis smiled as her lips trembled. "I-I'll be right behind you. I love you. Now go!"

The pain of lying was far more agonizing than the actual pain pulsating along every inch of her. Karramis wanted to go, but she had to stay behind. She had always known she was meant to die for her children, but as the twins walked into the portal, her heart broke at the idea of never seeing them again.

"Karramis!" Lucas ran faster, grimacing as his own injuries burned along his abdomen. "No!"

She tilted her head and grinned at him as she crashed to her knees. *I did it.* Karramis tossed the necklace into the portal and dropped her arms. She closed her eyes and the misty vortex faded. Her limp body leaned sideways and fell into Lucas's arms as he approached her. Holding her tightly, he gazed down as her breathing slowed and life drained from her body.

# Chapter 2

## On the Other Side

*Eight years ago*

A gust of wind blew across the bed as a thump pounded from the front of the cabin. Will sprang awake, panting and peering through sleepy eyes. Muffled groans and voices whispered down the hallway. Reaching for a shirt draped over the foot of the bed, Will raced from his bedroom and paused, staring at two figures moving through the shadows in the living room. He tiptoed into the room and flipped on the lights. Two children twisted around with a yelp of alarm under their muffled cries, grasping one another's hand and pulling each other closer.

Water dripped from their muddy pajamas, each droplet splashing in slow motion against the floor. The air grew thin as Will struggled to breathe, the disbelief crushing his chest. His shoulders slouched and mouth hung open as his eyes darted back and forth between the two. Flutters filled his stomach and raced up his chest. A mix of shock and relief consumed him, drawing him to his knees.

"Kids?" he said with a slow exhale.

James and Rhiannon raced over to the man they recognized from a picture on their mother's nightstand. "Daddy!"

Crashing into him, the twins threw their arms around him, squeezing as they sobbed in his tight embrace.

"I'm here," Will said softly, blinking back tears. "I've got you. You're safe now."

~

Will rushed to close the front door as the bright afternoon sun beamed into the living room. The twins lay nestled along opposite sides of the couch, sleeping under an oversized blanket. Smiling, Will stood watch over his children, allowing himself to enjoy this moment of happiness.

The last time Will had seen them was the day they were born. Having only spent a few hours with the twins, his decision to be apart from them and their mother was not an easy one. But the only way to protect them all was to have them leave Kiluemar and formulate a story about how the three of them had died during childbirth. And the plan had worked—at least, up until now. But as Will stood over his innocent children, he pondered what to do next.

Will only had bits and pieces of what had happened, but he was sure of three things: Karramis was dead, the twins had been discovered, and the full moon was fast approaching. There was only a week to come up with a new plan to get his children out of Kiluemar undetected and figure out a way to prevent the others from notifying Merrick the twins were still alive. Based on what the children had told Will, Karramis had performed a spell and removed her magic, and in doing so sacrificed herself. He did not understand her reasoning behind this, yet, but he hoped he would be able to figure out her plan before it was too late.

Will swallowed the lump in his throat, the heartache choking him as he wiped the tears forming along the bottom of his already puffy eyes. Karramis was dead, a fate he had always feared after learning about the prophecy. However, he could not bring his heart and soul to believe it, but his mind argued with him. Karramis's magic kept her alive, and she could not survive without it. This was a fact he knew all too well.

Will analyzed the details from his children's story, determining what Karramis had planned with her final actions. Always having a backup plan, she would have come up with something if they were ever discovered, but he did not know what it was or why she had to do what she did.

"James? Rhiannon?" Will gently rocked them. "Wake up, please."

The twins opened their eyes, yawning as they sat up.

"Sorry for waking you, but I need to know exactly what your mum said in her spell."

James rubbed his eyes. "But we already told you everything we could remember."

"I know, but I need you to try and remember anything else. I reckon her spell will help me."

"With what?" Rhiannon asked. "And when are we going to see her again?"

Will's heart sank in his chest, and he hung his head, letting out a sigh and closing his eyes. Karramis was not only gone, but he had to be the one to break the news to his children.

"I'm so sorry . . . but y-you won't be seeing your mum again." He placed his hands on their arms. "She's gone."

The color faded from the twins' faces as their eyes grew red and watery. Their breaths shuddered in their chests. They stared blankly at the floor, the innocence in their eyes disappearing behind a wall of tears. Will dropped to his knees and embraced them, all three clutching one another as the twins sobbed against their father's shoulders.

Not wanting them to face the horrors of last night all over again, Will tucked them back under the covers. They quickly drifted off to sleep as they surrendered to the grief consuming them. Exhausted and overwhelmed with the heartache of Karramis's death, Will placed a few blankets and a pillow on the floor next to them and gave into his own grief. Haunted by the idea of never seeing her again, he cried himself to sleep.

A few hours later, James bolted wide awake and sprang to his feet. "I remember!"

Will jumped awake, rolling from under his blanket and onto his knees. "Bloody hell!"

"We remember!" the twins said, Rhiannon jumping to her feet next to her brother.

Will panted as his heart pounded beneath his ribcage. "The spell?"

"Yes!"

"Well, not word for word," James added, "but more of what she said."

"Brilliant!" Will pushed himself off the floor. "Let's get you over to your grandfather's whilst it's still dark so we can figure this all out."

James and Rhiannon glanced at each other. "Grandfather?"

~

Will lifted James and Rhiannon onto the back of a horse and wrapped a blanket around them. The darkness engulfed the animal beneath them, but the silky hairs tickled their exposed legs under their oversized shirts. Cuddling with each other, the twins trembled as their bare feet peeked out from beneath the thick material. The summer night was warm, but the breeze was cold and damp. Every star sparkled as they nestled high above the trees circling the area, the smell of pine blowing through the crisp air.

Will jumped on the horse's bare back and draped his arms around his children, grabbing hold of the horse's black mane.

Clicking his tongue, he tapped his heels against the horse and directed the animal over to the trees. James sat in front, grasping the horse's mane under his father's hands as Rhiannon pressed her body back into Will's chest and held tight to his arms. As they broke through the tree line on the other side of the forest, the horse picked up speed, heading straight over to a dim glow coming from a few miles away. The steady movement of the horse's stride made Rhiannon sleepy, and she yawned and closed her eyes.

"Where're we going?" James asked.

"To the village."

The horse made its way closer to Caerwyn Village, trotting effortlessly along the wide-open field. The darkness and the soft pounding of the hooves allowed Will the freedom to release his built-up emotions. Tears trailed down his face in streams as he suppressed the heavy sobs in his chest. Even after all the years apart and the fear surrounding the prophecy, Will had held out hope he would see Karramis again, and he could finally live the life he had always longed for with his family. But as he embraced his children, he knew he would have to say goodbye yet again.

Rhiannon squeezed Will's arms as she opened her eyes. "Daddy?"

Wiping his cheeks along his shoulders, Will cleared his throat. "Yeah?"

"Do you want us to tell you what we remember?"

"Oh." His voice cracked. "Absolutely. Yes, of course."

"Well, she said something about blood."

"Oh yeah," James said, "and I also remember her mentioning something about the powers she removed having to break free on a waiting night."

"Waiting night?" Will asked, confused.

"No." Rhiannon shook her head. "No, James. I think she said *waning* night."

Will cocked his head. "Waning night?"

"Yeah. And she also mentioned something about fading and falling—"

"And something about her heart," James interrupted.

"It all rhymed too," Rhiannon continued, "but I can't remember any of it. Then she said something about how we have to get home."

The sun rose along the horizon as they reached the stone archway of the village. The horse slowed and strolled into the quiet town. Traveling down a dirt path, they passed stone and wood-slatted buildings. The windows were dark, and the area was eerie, sending chills up the children's spines as they made their way through the ghost town.

"Did your mum say anything else that you can remember?"

The twins thought for a moment.

"The necklace!" Rhiannon's voice echoed down the road, and she cowered. "Oops. Sorry."

"It's quite all right," Will said in a normal tone. "What necklace?"

"The one Mom used in the spell."

"Where is it?"

"I—I don't know. I mean, she used it, and I think I remember seeing it on the floor when we arrived here. But I . . . I'm not sure. I'm sorry."

"It's fine, Rhiannon." Will kissed the back of her head. "We'll find it. If your mum tossed it through the portal, then it must be somewhere back home."

James adjusted the blanket as it slid off his shoulder and down his arm. "Speaking of that, can someone please explain all of this? The spells, portals, where we are exactly? And why this Lucas guy is after—"

"Lucas?" Will grasped the reins tighter. "Lucas was there?"

"Yeah. He was the one after us, along with a few others."

Will clenched his teeth. "That bloody bastard! I knew it. I knew that git had something to do with this."

"Who's he?" the twins asked.

"An utterly mental and loathsome bloke. He's completely off his rocker and works for people who are even worse."

The horse halted and stood in front of a large two-story gray stone structure with wooden beams along the sides. Beside the base of the building were flower beds with outstretched petals in many different colors and sizes. The windows were long and rectangular, consisting of two horizontal panes—all of which had one section open to the outside. A wide cobblestone path led to the oversized wooden door.

Jumping from the horse, Will hurried the children over to the front door as the sun crept higher in the sky. He pounded against the dense wood and waited.

Will whistled at his beautiful horse. "Callie, go to the stables and wait for me."

The black-and-white horse trotted away, and the twins' eyes opened wide as they fixated on the creature, watching the winged horse disappear around the corner.

Footsteps approached on the other side of the door before it swung open.

Yawning, Kavana stood half asleep in her pajamas. "Will?"

"Hey, Kavana." Will hurried the children through the threshold. "Close the door."

"What's—"

Kavana stopped abruptly as she closed the door and faced the others. Her breath shuddered as she gazed wildly at the two children standing in her entryway. The little girl's high cheekbones, almond-shaped eyes, and oval face reminded her of Karramis. But as she stared at the little boy, tears tickled her cheeks. Peering into his deep brown eyes, she smiled, then hugged the children as she continued to cry.

"Children," Will said softly, "go get yourself some food." He pointed down the hall. "The kitchen's back there."

He waited for the twins to disappear into the adjacent room.

"Will, what's going on?" Kavana asked with a perplexed expression on her face. "Are those who I think they are?"

"Yes."

"But I thought—"

"It was a lie. All of it."

Her eyes lit up with joy. "Then that means Karramis is alive too?" She waited for him to respond. "Right, Will?" The happiness in her voice disappeared, taken over by a grief-stricken low tone when he refused to meet her gaze. "Right?"

Will did not answer as the sadness returned to his red eyes. He turned away and quickly wiped a tear from his face.

Kavana's heart dropped against her lungs as a rush of sorrow stormed her body, raging through her nerves and leaving her numb. She let out a shaky exhale as she leaned into Will, crying against his chest.

Will widened his gaze, allowing the air to dry the tears forming in the corners of his eyes. "Where's Zarrius?"

"He and Pavian went out early to patrol. I—I have no clue where they'd be right now."

Will opened the front door and peered through the crack. "I'll go see if I can locate them. Please take the children back to my place, but don't let *anyone* know they're here."

Wiping her face aggressively with her hands, Kavana sniffled. "Okay. Do you want me to take them on the horses?"

"No. No, I can't take the chance of anyone seeing them. Can you teleport them?"

"No, we can't teleport others. I thought you knew that. Not to mention, that portal is still a few miles from your place. You can't expect them to walk that far, especially in those clothes and without any shoes." Her breath shuddered, and she sniffled again. "By the way, why are they dressed like that?"

"They were a mess when they arrived, and I didn't have anything for them to wear after they got cleaned up, so I gave them some of my old shirts. Listen, just stay here until dark. I'll meet you back there later." Will turned to leave but stopped. "Also, keep them calm. We don't need them using any powers and alerting anyone."

"Powers?"

"Yes, I reckon that's how Lucas found them."

"Lucas? But how'd he—"

"I don't know." Will shrugged. "No one knew they were alive except me."

"Do you think he read your mind?"

"I don't see how. I made sure to stay off his radar."

"Well, Lucas is a persistent man so maybe he refused to believe she was dead."

"Possibly. But it doesn't matter. He found them and now because of him she really is gone." Will walked through the door frame. "Listen, I'll see you later. Take care of them until I get back."

"I will." Kavana shut the door and leaned against it as tears began to fall down her face again. "I promise."

~

The twins rested peacefully on the couch as Kavana slept curled up on the chair next to them. Will returned home in the middle of the night. Exhausted, he lowered himself onto the temporary bed still on the floor and fell asleep.

Kavana shook him awake a few hours later. He peered up at her through half-open eyes, and she quickly placed a finger against her lips then pointed over to the sleeping children. She tilted her head in the direction of the front door before tiptoeing outside.

"Did you find my dad?" Kavana asked.

"No. But I stopped searching after a few hours."

"Why?"

"To be honest, it's probably best if very few know about the twins right now. I can't risk some telepath catching word and it getting back to Merrick."

"True, but we have to tell him eventually."

"I agree. But I've got to figure a few things out first. I need to know what Kar—" Will blinked and swallowed the lump in his throat. "I need to know what she was planning . . . what she was trying to do."

Kavana perked up. "I think I know."

"Really?"

"Yeah. After talking to James and Rhiannon, I think I might have pieced a few things together. Oh! And we found the necklace." She pulled it out from under her shirt and removed it from around her neck. "I was afraid of losing it." She handed it to him. "I cleaned it up the best I could."

He sighed, examining the blood-stained stone necklace. "This is the one I gave her . . . to help protect her. I was told these stones were powerful and were best for protection."

"They are," Kavana said reassuringly. "Very powerful. In fact, powerful enough to siphon magic into."

"What do you mean?"

"I think Karramis put her magic into the necklace. The spell she used, along with these stones, would have been powerful enough to hold her magic, at least for a short time."

"But why? Why did she do it?"

"Karramis knew there were ways for Lucas to get through the portals, even without the full moon, and she didn't want to take any chances. If she removed her magic, then he wouldn't be able to use it against her or somehow force her to use it."

"But why didn't she come with them? Why didn't she just open the portal and come through too? She didn't have to stay behind. She didn't have to remove her magic. She . . . she didn't *have* to die."

Will stepped off the porch and stopped at the base of the stairs. He exhaled and leaned over, resting his hands against his thighs as tears swelled in his eyes.

Kavana hesitated as she placed her hand on his shoulder. "I think I might know that too. The kids said something about not being allowed to leave the area around their home. Karramis must've had a protection spell around the house. And if she did that, then she would've been extra careful and stopped practicing her magic altogether."

Will turned his head toward her and frowned. "She used magic . . . but then stopped using magic? I don't understand."

"Protection spells aren't powerful enough to be sensed unless closer to the actual protective wall, so unless Lucas, or any of Merrick's other guys, was nearby, he wouldn't sense it. But Karramis's magic is—*was*—very powerful, especially the one she couldn't control."

"Her fire powers."

"Right. Not to mention, no one knows how powerful your kids are. She needed to place the spell around them, so they wouldn't be traced if any magic occurred. But you know Karramis, she never liked having magic in the first place, so she must've stopped practicing."

"So, without practice—"

"Without practice, she had no control. Everything would've been unpredictable and potentially dangerous. And she's never been able to take anyone with her through her portals. They always ended up hurt somehow or landed in some random place. You've been the only person to ever go through one of her portals without any major issues, but even you ended up miles away from her."

The wind blew through the clearing as they both stood quietly.

"Karramis knew," Will said in a low, unsteady voice. "She knew she wouldn't be strong enough to hold the portal open, focus on sending the children to me, *and* keep it open long enough to go through herself. And she . . . she would never risk someone using her magic to return to Kiluemar to notify Merrick the twins are alive."

"Exactly. If she had the spell to remove her magic ready, then she was willing to die to protect them."

Will turned his eyes to the ground. "She sacrificed herself for them."

"And you would've done the same thing. You know it. Will, she loved you more than anything else in this world. Don't forget that. But she had no other choice. She had to protect them." Kavana hugged him. "Now, what do we have to do to protect your children?"

Although the decision would not be an easy one to follow through with, Will had discovered the best plan for the safety of his children early that morning before returning home.

"We've got to get them out of Kiluemar." Will sighed. "We've got to hide them again and lock the portals to prevent Lucas from coming through."

"What?" Kavana exclaimed, her voice shrill. "Why?"

"It's the only way to stop Merrick from discovering the children are still alive. It's the best way to protect them until they are old enough to handle everything."

"But . . . but y-you guys are leaving? But they just got here."

"No," he said, disappointed. "I won't be going with them."

"Wait . . . then who is?"

Will pulled his shoulders back and flashed her a side grin. "You."

Kavana pointed to herself. "Me?" She paced. "Oh, no, absolutely not! Nope. I can't take care of two kids. I—"

"One, actually."

Kavana halted and glanced at him, waiting for him to explain.

"I discussed everything with Pavian, and he's willing to help. He'll take James, and you will take Rhiannon."

"What?" Kavana said in unison with the twins.

James and Rhiannon hurried down the steps and rushed over to Will and Kavana.

Rhiannon scowled at her father. "You're going to separate us?"

"You can't do that!" James said sharply.

Kavana's hands were on her hips. "Pavian? I thought you said you couldn't find him?"

Will shifted his head at the three of them. "One at a time, please." He glanced over at the twins. "Listen, give me a minute so I can talk this over with your aunt, and then I will explain everything to you both, all right?"

The twins nodded and returned to the porch.

Will grabbed hold of Kavana's arm and led her away from the cabin. "No, I said I wasn't able to find your father. However, I found your brother last night as he was heading to Raina's. I told him everything, and he wants to help. He's willing to take James, but I need you to take Rhiannon."

James and Rhiannon stalked by the windows next to the front door, paying close attention to their father and aunt as they discussed the plan to separate them.

The twins did not want to live apart from each other. They had already lost their mother, and now they would not only live without their best friend, but they would also be forced to grow up without their father—a father they barely knew nonetheless, but loved just as much as they loved their mother. He had been the missing piece to their family for so long, but the love their mother had for him made the children love him just as much. Through the stories she had told, Karramis made him real for them. Despite never having told the twins their father was alive, she also never confirmed he had died either. James and Rhiannon had always assumed he was dead by how often their mother cried for him.

Losing their mother had been traumatic, but having to deal with the fact she had died for them was even more agonizing. They knew the only way to make sure her death was not in vain, and the only way to stay safe, was to follow along with the plan to protect them. They would have to say goodbye and live a life without each other, the father they had just met, and a family they would never get the chance to know. Neither one wanted to face the final moments and words they would soon have to endure, but they were not the only ones who would have to say goodbye to the ones they loved if everyone moved forward with the plan.

# Chapter 3

## Goodbye

*Eight years ago*

Kavana stood outside a single-story house in the center of Stoweward. Tapping a loose fist against her leg, she rocked side to side, staring with a distant gaze at the door. Her heart palpitations rang in her ears as a twitch tingled in the pit of her stomach.

Things had not ended well with Aidan, and she had not seen him in weeks. Afraid to confront him, she was unsure what would happen once he opened the door. Their relationship ended weeks ago, but Kavana had to say goodbye. After more than a decade together, Aidan deserved that much from her. Despite being the one who had broken up the relationship, she still had a burning ache inside for one final sendoff, just one more kiss. Not knowing when she would return, she could not leave without saying the one goodbye that would be the hardest.

She knocked and waited, rubbing her sweaty palms across her pants. Footsteps approached, and her stomach fluttered, sending a rush of faintness through her body. The door opened, and her heart sank as she exhaled the breath she was holding back. It was not Aidan, but rather his younger sister, Nina.

The redhead peered out with emerald-green eyes. "Kavana?"

"Hey, Nina."

"What're you doin' here?" Nina asked with a smile, her Scottish accent less prominent than Aidan's.

"Looking for your brother. Is . . . is he here?"

Nina's face dropped into a frown. "No. He . . . he's gone. He left last night. I—I thought he would've told you."

"No," Kavana said coldly. "No, he didn't tell me." She huffed, placing a hand on her hip. "Okay then. Well, I just wanted to tell him that I'm leaving, and I won't be back anytime soon."

"Where are you goin'?"

"I'm sorry, I can't tell you that, but it's not because I don't want to. I . . . I just can't."

"Oh. Okay. Well, if—I mean, when—Aidan comes home, I'll let him know. But I have a feelin' I won't be seein' him for a while."

"Nina, do you know where he is?"

"Yes. But I, too, can't say where."

"Right. Well, take care of yourself, and when he does come back, tell him . . . tell him I said goodbye, will you?"

Nina stepped through the doorway and hugged her. "Yes, I will. Take care." As Kavana turned to leave, Nina smiled. "By the way, I miss seein' you around here."

Kavana nodded and smiled back before heading down the path away from the house. The corners of her mouth drooped, and her lips pressed together as her jaw tightened. She narrowed her eyes, scowling as she headed out of town. The nervousness and apprehension fluttering through her faded, shifting to anger and resentment. He left her. Aidan had left without saying goodbye, not a single word or even a note. Apparently, he did not have the same love, respect, and loyalty she had for him, or even the decency to let her know he was leaving. Kavana stomped off and vowed she would never forgive him.

~

Raina slept nestled under the blankets as Pavian quietly got dressed in the dark. Though his final goodbye had been said hours before, Raina convinced him to stay the night. However, the goodbye he had given earlier was not the one he wrote in the letter placed on her pillow. Unsure of when he would return, Pavian did not want Raina to live out the rest of her life waiting for him. He loved her too much to keep her bound to him and the idea of growing old together.

Pavian had always wanted to take the next step with Raina, but he worried his father would not approve. He was his father's right-hand man, the leader of the guard, and the one Zarrius relied on for everything. He was convinced his father would never allow him to step away from his duties and live a simpler life—a life with a family, and one no longer focused on the responsibilities as the next leader in the hierarchy of their magical bloodline.

Pavian pulled a diamond ring with a gold band from his pocket and held it in his hand. It was his mother's ring, something he had held on to for all these years. There was no doubt Raina was the one he wanted to give it to, but he had never found the right time to ask.

Gazing down at Raina as she slept peacefully, he questioned if he was making the right decision. He did not want to leave her. She was his everything. She was the one who made him complete and more than just a servant to this magical world. Raina was the part of him that made him better, alive. The world did not exist when they were together. How could he truly be happy without her? Not only would he have to live separated from her by a magical barrier, but he was also giving her permission to move on and find love with someone else. He was letting her go—one of the hardest decisions he had ever made. But he had to help his family. Now, more than ever, his brother-in-law needed his help. Pavian needed to protect his sister's children and do what was necessary to stop the prophecy from coming true. The time to be selfish was gone. If the roles were reversed, Karramis would do anything in her power to protect his own children.

Pavian placed the box on top of the note. By leaving Raina his mother's ring, he was giving her a token of the love he would always have for her, but it would never be a symbol of their two lives joining together as one. He kissed her forehead and headed for the bedroom door, pausing for one final mental picture of the future he was leaving behind.

~

Callie drank from Guardian Lake along the southwest side of Maevis Mountains as Will stood waiting. With the full moon a couple nights away, Will was preparing the final steps of the plan before sending his family to the non-magical realm and sealing the portals behind them.

The binding of James's and Rhiannon's powers had not worked—a plan Will and the others were certain would fail—so Will, in full agreement with Pavian and Kavana, settled on another way to make sure the twins' powers could not be tracked in the non-magical world. The solution was to permanently lock the portals so no one could travel in or out of Kiluemar. Those inside would be trapped within the magical boundaries, and those on the outside would be forced to live there until the portals were reopened.

Pavian and Kavana had finally notified their father of the twins' arrival, and the plans going forth to help protect them. Zarrius, distraught after learning the truth about Karramis and the twins, was hesitant to allow Pavian and Kavana to leave

Kiluemar and live in the non-magical world. But if the prophecy was right, like it had been about Karramis, then his grandchildren needed to stay away from this world until they were powerful enough to defend themselves. The young children did not stand a chance against Merrick and his men, and Zarrius could not guarantee he, or the members of his guard, could protect them until the time came for them to face their fate.

After being advised about the plan to close the portals permanently, Zarrius warned all the residents of the island about this spur-of-the-moment decree. Telling everyone it was for the safety of the island, he gave them only a few hours to make their final decision—stay locked inside Kiluemar with the dangers residing within the boundaries or live defenseless in the non-magical world. Most chose to leave, but many decided to stay. However, a fear lingered after many grew concerned of what would happen when the vampires, sirens, trolls, and other malevolent creatures that chose to stay grew weary of their temporary prison and became hungry. No one knew what the future had in store, but many were sure the outcome did not bode well in their favor. Without Pavian, and some of the more powerful creatures who had elected to leave the realm, many believed Kiluemar was doomed to fall into the wrong hands, just as the prophecy foretold.

Will, Pavian, and Kavana did not think that far ahead. They were only focused on saying their goodbyes, packing up a few things, and getting to the portal before the next full moon. The doorways needed to be sealed before Lucas could get through.

The rush to finish these final tasks left the three overwhelmed adults scrambling to see the plan completed.

In the soft glow of the moon, a figure soared through the night sky. The mysterious creature flew closer, its flapping wings resonating within the quietness surrounding Will. The rhythmic beating faded, and footsteps shuffled within the trees.

"Aidan?" Will whispered.

"Yeah, it's me."

"Where've you been? I was worried you might've changed your mind."

Aidan emerged from the trees dressed in jeans and a dark maroon shirt, sweeping his hands through his strawberry-blond hair. "No. I just had to say goodbye first."

"To Kavana?"

Aidan halted, and his expression dropped, his shoulders hunching over.

Will grimaced. "Not Kavana then?"

"No. I was tellin' Nina goodbye." Aidan gulped. "I haven't seen or spoken to Kavana in weeks."

"Oh. But I thought . . ."

Knowing Aidan and Kavana were no longer together, Will did not finish his sentence. He remembered Kavana mentioning she was going to tell him goodbye, but maybe she had changed her mind, and Will did not want to set his best friend up for more heartache. Maybe it was better if they did not have their final farewell. The history of the two made Will question if Aidan would be able to stay away from her if he knew where she was.

He had already convinced Aidan to do him the biggest favor by following his children into the non-magical world. Traveling back and forth between two locations, Aidan was agreeing to a tiresome and lonely journey. But in addition to the tedious task Aidan would soon have to endure, he would also have to stay morphed into his shape-shifting form the entire time. Aidan could not take the risk of being tracked. If Lucas were able to sense him, he would be able to trace Aidan's whereabouts and use his telepathy to read the shapeshifter's mind and narrow down his search for the children.

The details of Will's plan were almost perfect, but with those involved sometimes being ruled by their emotions, he needed to tread lightly on certain subjects, or they could ruin everything. He had already given Aidan all the information on what he would have to do once he sensed the twins using their magic, and there was no doubt he could trust his friend with his life. Aidan was up for the task, but Will needed to make sure he would not stray from the plan.

Quickly changing the subject, Will asked, "What did you tell Nina?"

"Oh. I didn't tell her much in case someone went askin' her questions. I just told her where I was goin' and that I was doin' somethin' important to protect the realm. She promised not to say anythin' to anyone."

Will glanced down at his watch. "We need to get you out of here. Pavian will be arriving at my place soon, and he might end up waking Kavana and the kids. I've got to get back before anyone wakes up. No one knows what we're doing."

Aidan and Will headed over to the lake. Passing Callie, they stopped at a clear substance swirling in a circle. The watery vortex was one of the portals placed throughout Kiluemar. The doorways on this side of the magical barrier were always open, and they could take anyone anywhere—to another portal on the island or through one of the five doorways in the non-magical realm. The portals on the other side had limited access and only opened during the full moon.

"Listen, about Kavana." Will paused. "I need you to promise me something."

"Absolutely. Anythin'."

"You must promise me you won't go looking for her. I know you don't have their exact location, but I also know you're a very relentless person when it comes to something you want, and if you really wanted to, you could find her. I know you still love her and that something happened between you two—I'm just unsure of what it is at the moment. I reckon I shall hear the whole story one day when you are ready to tell me, so I needn't pry, but we mustn't allow our hearts to rule us. We've got to put our love, and the things we want, aside . . . for now, at least. Can you promise me that?"

"Yes, I promise. I swear I will do whatever I must to protect yer children and keep them safe. I will watch over them from afar, and when the time comes, I will bring them back to you. You have my word."

"Thank you, Aidan." Will hugged him and patted his back. "For everything."

"Ye're welcome." Aidan nodded and smiled. "See you soon."

"I hope so. Take care of yourself."

"You too, Will."

The two gave each other one final nod before Aidan disappeared into the portal.

~

Will entered his bedroom just as the front door opened. Peering back down the hallway, Will witnessed Pavian sneaking into the cabin. The two nodded at each other before heading to a comfortable spot to rest until morning.

James and Rhiannon both woke up before the others. Not wanting to wake them, the twins made their way outside.

Today was their last day together, and they were unsure when they would see each other again. Knowing their lives now revolved around a prophecy and the imminent danger surrounding their magic, they were certain the possibility of only having to be apart for a short time was not likely. It would be years before they saw each other again. Their lives would never be the same with the broken bond of losing their best friend, losing a piece of themselves. The twins completed each other, complemented one another. They were yin and yang, complete opposites, but still of like mind. She was the calm to his chaos, the voice of reason. He was her rock, her protector, the one who understood how to counter her stubborn side. Though two separate entities, together they were one.

Pavian tapped on the doorframe of Will's bedroom. Sprawled out on top of his blankets, Will lay facedown and fully dressed as he rolled onto his side. He peered up through deep narrowed eyes, and Pavian laughed at Will's messy curls sticking out in all directions. Not having had much time to cater to his own needs over the past few days, Will was unkempt with his uncombed hair and scruffy face.

Peering down at the shoes still on Will's feet, Pavian teased, "Astral traveling?"

"Huh?" Will asked with a yawn.

"Never mind." Pavian chuckled. "You need to get up. We don't have much time."

Pavian's footsteps retreated as Will pushed himself up and sat on the edge of his bed. Glancing over at Karramis's necklace on the nightstand, Will closed his eyes and sighed.

The final phase of the plan would happen tonight. The full moon was tomorrow, and the portals needed to be sealed before Lucas could get through and alert Merrick of the truth revolving around Karramis and the children. They were alive—well, the children were. The lie Will had told all those years ago was bound to surface, but he figured he would have Karramis by his side to face the dangers surrounding that lie. He had never imagined she would not return to him. Now, he would have to face not only a lifetime without her, but even more years without his children. Will had already missed out on so many years of their lives. How many more would he have to miss out on? Would they actually return to him, or would he have to deal with even more loss? The questions repeated in his mind as he changed into different clothes.

Kavana and Pavian were sitting on the couch when Will entered the living room. They both sat silently as if lost in their own thoughts. Abandoning their inner notions, they focused on Will as he strolled by.

"So, what's next?" Pavian asked, rising to his feet.

Will headed into the kitchen. "The only thing left is doing the spell and going through to the other side." He glanced over at Kavana. "Do you have the spell?"

"Yeah," Kavana said, annoyed. "The damn thing took me days to write."

Pavian backed away from his sister. "Whoa, someone's in a bad mood. What's wrong?"

"Nothing. I just went to go tell—Never mind, it's nothing. It's not important right now. I'll tell you about it later."

Will remembered why she was upset. Aidan had left without saying goodbye, and she was not given the chance to say goodbye either. Guilt billowed inside Will for coming between their final farewells, but if he had not done it, one of them might have changed their mind. He could not take the chance on any last-minute changes. Time was not on his side. Having had less than a week to secure not one but two safe houses, requesting Aidan's help, and figuring out some way to stop his children from suffering the grief of losing their mother and being apart from each other was a challenge. Will was exhausted and overwhelmed, not to mention he had only spent a short amount of time with his children. He was cheated—given a gift but robbed of being able to enjoy it. He was angry, devastatingly heartbroken, and stricken with sadness. But his emotions would have to take a backseat to the task in front of him.

Pavian raised an eyebrow at his sister. "All right then." He faced Will. "Anyway, what else do we need to know?"

"Oh, right." Will filled a glass with water from the tap. "So, Kavana, you have the spell done, right?"

"Yes."

"Perfect. And you're both quite certain you're comfortable with losing your magic in the process?"

Kavana and Pavian nodded without any sign of reluctance.

"So, where are we going?" Pavian asked.

"I found both of you a place that meets your conditions. Both locations are isolated and away from any large cities. Now, you've got to go out and get supplies and food when you get there, and depending on how much you buy at a time, occasionally to restock. But without your magic, you shouldn't have any issues being tracked. Limit how often the kids leave, though, just in case."

Kavana stepped closer to the kitchen. "Where are these places exactly?"

"I can't tell you. I'll provide you both with an envelope with the address to your new living arrangements right before you go through the portal, along with a few other details to help you navigate the non-magical world. It will also contain enough money to get you the appropriate transportation to get to that location. You two mustn't know where each other are. It's best if I'm the only one who knows where each of you are located. Oh, and both of you will no longer be Wards, you'll need another last name whilst over there."

Pavian tossed his sister a smile. "How about Howton?"

Kavana grinned and nodded.

"All right, it's settled." Will exited the kitchen. "Now, I want the children to have a connection to this place, so James will keep Cassil as his last name. Most people here don't know my true surname anyway. Rhiannon on the other hand needs to have a different last name, but still have a connection to here as well, so how about Llewellyn, after her mum?"

"I love that idea," Kavana gushed.

A crease pressed into Pavian's forehead. "Question. How are you going to prevent them from finding each other? I mean, changing their names won't stop that."

"The name change isn't for them to not find each other, it's to protect them from having anyone else find any of you."

"Well, then how are you going to stop them from searching for each other?"

"We're going to erase their memories in the process."

"What?" Pavian said, shocked, tossing his wild gaze over at his sister. "You knew? You knew about this?" He glanced at

Will. "You can't take away their memories. What if something goes wrong? What if they never get them back?"

"They will," Kavana assured him. "I added it to the spell. Their memories will only be linked to their magic, and both will only be trapped in here once the portals are sealed. But once James and Rhiannon return everything will be restored."

Doubtful of his sister's spellcasting abilities, he asked, "And you're sure this will work? I mean, we aren't witches, so how can you be so sure?"

"Yes, it'll work. We're going to tap into the realm's magic and use our blood, plus James and Rhiannon should have witch magic."

The decision to send the children away was difficult for Will, but it was for their own good. He had to protect them. However, choosing to remove their magic had been a much easier decision. Magic was not only their link to this world, but it was the only way Lucas—or anyone else—could locate them. Living without any magic was safer. Even Pavian and Kavana would have to sever their magical ties to Kiluemar to stay off the radar. Their magic was constant—always working and never fading. The magic flowing within their blood was bound to Kiluemar, and as long as the realm contained any kind of magical essence, Guardian magic would forever be active.

"Also, about the money," Will said. "There's enough to get you to where you need to go. There are also a few things I included to help you figure out things whilst there. I know you guys learnt a lot of this in your schooling here, but I wanted to make sure you had everything you needed. Once you get there and recite the spell, you've got to go your separate ways. The farther away you get from the portal, the more their memories will fade until it seals completely. Once you get to your new homes, you'll have everything you need already there, except for food. Everything else is taken care of."

Kavana raised a hand, cutting him off. "Uhm, okay, I have a question. How'd you do all of this so quickly?"

Will smiled. "Karramis."

"What?" Pavian and Kavana said with a breathy exhale.

"Yeah, I know. I was a tad shocked at first as well. But honestly, I wasn't all that surprised after the shock wore off. I mean, it is Karramis after all. I knew she had a plan, I just needed to figure it out."

Kavana sat down. "What do you mean?"

"Well, after I started researching all the safe houses we have—there are loads, by the way—I found a note tucked in the binding of a page listing the house where Karramis and the twins were hiding out. It was addressed to me in Karramis's handwriting. She must've returned at some point and left it. But she somehow knew the two of you would be willing to help. She took care of everything. In fact, your sister knew you two so well she had both of your safe houses already picked out, matching your specifications perfectly. She just wasn't sure who would be able, and willing, to help, so she planned accordingly. All I had to do was prepare the details of things you might come across in your travels and whilst there. She even had money stashed in a book in the library in the various currencies we might need. There's even more money at each location."

Amazed, Pavian declared with a grin, "Karramis always was the overthinker and most prepared out of all of us, wasn't she? She always had everything figured out, even fixes for the worst-case scenarios. Father even wanted her on his guard just for that reason alone, but she never could master the other skills needed."

Kavana let out a breathy snicker. "Plus, she would've hated working for him. She was always more of an . . . an independent thinker when it came to magic and his ways."

All three chuckled quietly to themselves.

"Independent thinker, huh?" Pavian said. "Well, that's one way of saying rebellious."

Walking back into the living room, Will continued chuckling under his breath. He paused, staring out the window at James and Rhiannon as they strolled around the fenced-in garden just off the side of the cabin.

The vegetation was lush and in full bloom. Flowers in all shades reached toward the sky, the petals following the sun's bright rays, and various fruits, vegetables, and herbs were ready for harvest. Gardening was not one of Will's favorite hobbies, but he kept this one alive for Karramis. She had always loved spending time in her garden, and he had hoped she would one day return to it.

Will headed for the front door but waited, the tightness in his chest rising and creating a lump in his throat. In a few hours, they would be gone. His children would be taken from him once again. He would watch as they disappeared, just as they had with their mother when they were babies. They would have to grow up even more without him in their lives—now without any memories of him. The twins would know nothing about him, or what had happened to their mother. He was jealous they would have their grief taken away, and they would no longer have to deal with the loss of their mother or being separated from each other. He did not know how he was going to move on without Karramis or his children. Each day ahead seemed like an impending nightmare, playing over and over again. Will would have to face each morning just one day at a time. At least, one day, he would see his children again. If the prophecy had any silver lining, it was that the twins would, in fact, return to Kiluemar to face the dangers waiting for them.

Will turned the knob and headed outside. As he stepped around the corner, the twins noticed him and smiled. They had no idea the memories they had of him would soon be taken away or how they would be forced to live a life not knowing who they truly were or the family that would be torn away from them. All three would have to say goodbye, and Will would have to deal with not only sending his children off into the unknown but finally coming to terms with Karramis's death.

# Chapter 4

## Awake and Alive

A soft melody of a violin played in the distance, the melancholy tune whispering in the ears of a woman lying unconscious on a table. The woman shivered as the cold air blanketed her frail figure. Her eyelids fluttered, the ominous lullaby purring throughout the stone room. The blood in her veins sprang to life and warmed her ice-cold body. Her pale skin became flush, revealing her ageless complexion. She gasped awake as her lungs filled with air.

Karramis was alive.

The light burned her eyes as she struggled to open them. Blinking wildly through a dwindling haze, she observed the sunlight along the ceiling. She tilted her head, moving her eyes along the coarse gray flagstone walls, past a set of shelves, and down to the beautifully designed granite floor. The music amplified within the pristine room as she rested on a long wooden table.

Karramis pressed her elbows against the table and pushed herself up. She halted as a sharp pain pierced through her side, and she fell back against the table. Wincing, she pulled her dry lips apart as she inhaled through her teeth. She grasped at the intense pain stabbing under her ribs, but the sting forced her hand to draw back as she cried out under her breath.

Her hand trembled as she raised it, revealing fresh blood along her fingers and palm. Lifting her head, Karramis gazed down at her body. Her dry, muddy nightgown was covered in dark red stains as fresh blood seeped along her side. She darted her eyes around the room, her pulse quickening and forcing more blood to ooze from the wound. Where was she? How was she alive?

Replaying the events in her head, Karramis remembered closing her eyes as her body grew weak, the peace of knowing her children were safe, and the adrenaline coursing through her as her heart slowed. She recalled taking her final breath and dying. But somehow, she was alive.

Karramis was unable to think coherently as her mind filled with dread. *The spell didn't work.* Her chest tightened as each breath grew more difficult. Her heart hammered, sending waves of warmth pumping through her veins as her pulse pounded in her head. She squeezed her eyes shut, attempting to control the whimpers flowing from her mouth with her shallow breaths. *The kids are in danger.*

Karramis slid her dirty feet over the side of the table and sat up. The pain radiated through her body and forced her to hunch over. Grasping her side again, she pressed against the wound and panted through the pain. The sharp piercing throb was agonizing, but faded as she pressed harder, the pressure helping to slow the bleeding and alleviate some of the pain. Sliding off the table, Karramis placed her feet on the tiles, but she crashed to the floor as her knees buckled. She groaned as she shifted her weight over her legs and tightened her muscles, driving every bit of strength into her lower body, but her legs were too weak. Lowering herself down, she rested her chilled body against the granite floor. Goose bumps formed along her arms as the cold tiles dulled the pain.

Blood seeped from her nightgown, and droplets trickled to the floor as she lay on her side. She fixated on her bloody hand and the jeweled band on her ring finger, focusing on the red and black gemstones as they reflected the sunlight coming from the long, narrow windows along one side of the room. The light sparkled within the stones and sent her into a state of ease as she calmed her hurried heartbeat. She needed to focus and relax if she was going to get out of here—wherever here was. Karramis had to make sure her children were safe, but she was too weak. The power she had used the night before took a toll on her, and her magic was too hard to control. Suppressing her powers for all those years had been a huge mistake, but she had to find the strength, and fast.

Karramis gazed past the ring, concentrating on the shelves across the room. She focused on an empty vase placed directly in her line of sight. Not wanting to move, she turned her palm toward the vase. She winced, the subtle movement causing her wound to pinch as her weight shifted.

The music of the violin resonated through the room, soothing Karramis and filling her with peace as it drew her in. Closing her eyes, she listened to the melody playing. She recognized it. The unique music carried a distinctive tune, one she had heard before. Even though modern music was not popular in Kiluemar, music itself was something many enjoyed. However, most residents of the realm were not musically inclined. But Karramis knew of one individual who was not only a gifted violinist but also a talented singer.

"Lucas?" she whispered, her pulse accelerating.

The pain along her side grew, sending electrifying jolts through her body. She curled her legs into her stomach, and her hands flew to her side. Unable to stop the overpowering impulse, she moaned as her hands pressed into the bloody wound. Her body recoiled as she rolled onto her back. She moaned, the muffled cries rumbling in her throat. Both hands were covered in blood as Karramis pulled them away from her body, forcing her elbows against the floor and ramming her fists against the tiles. She lifted her nightgown to examine the wound. Blood flowed from beneath a set of amateur stitches, the roughly placed incisions barely breaking through her skin.

"That seems rather painful, no?" a nasally voice said from the stairs.

Karramis twisted and scurried to sit up, crying out in pain as she crawled backward. She slid closer to the bookshelf next to the table. Blood smeared along the floor as her hands pushed her across the tiles. She propped herself up against the large elaborate piece of furniture and groaned.

A young woman swayed her hips as she approached Karramis. "Let me take a look, chère."

"Don't touch me!" Karramis snapped, wincing as she forced her body harder into the bookshelf. "Who are you? And where the hell am I?"

The gorgeous young woman, who had flawless porcelain skin and exceptionally long, curly, and platinum-blond hair, retreated over to a door next to the stairs. A smile rose along her heavily decorated face as she pushed the door open. An even colder breeze exited the room as the woman entered. Peering through the small opening, Karramis spotted a fully stocked wall of wine racks within the dimly lit room. The petite young woman, who appeared barely old enough to drink, grabbed a bottle of wine from the back wall and closed the door behind her. She pulled the cork from the half-empty bottle and gulped down a mouthful. Leaning against the door, she stuck out her noticeably large chest as she stared intently at Karramis.

Ignoring the seemingly innocent young woman, Karramis twitched her fingers at the empty vase, but nothing happened. Despite being alive, she still could not control her active powers. She opened her hand, concentrating on conjuring a portal.

"I don't get it," the woman said with a hint of hostility in her voice, her refined French accent more noticeable to Karramis.

"Get what?" Karramis asked as she repositioned herself.

"I don't get his obsession with you. You're not very pretty."

The young woman walked along the wall next to the shorter empty shelves. She ran her fingertips along the top of the wooden furniture, avoiding the vase and a few candles as she strolled alongside it.

She took another drink from the bottle and scowled. "*Oui,* I'm definitely prettier than you."

Karramis chuckled but the pain squeezed her side, and she abruptly stopped.

"Did you hear me?" the young woman exclaimed, annoyed. "I said I'm definitely prettier than you."

"Yes, I heard you." Karramis peered over at the woman. "But what do you want from me? A rebuttal? A snide comment? Or are you looking for confirmation? Well, sorry, but"—she groaned as she pressed harder into the wound—"but you won't be getting any of those from me."

The woman's expression tightened, and she stomped over to the stairs and plopped down. She chugged the last bit of wine and grasped the empty bottle, dangling it from her hand as she leaned back into the step.

"Fine, then." The young woman flashed a devilish grin. "But I still don't get his fascination with you. From where I'm sitting, you aren't very impressive, in more ways than one."

Karramis refused to entertain the young woman's incessant need to degrade and berate her. She could tell the young woman was only trying to agitate her, but she was not sure why.

Calmly, Karramis asked, "Where am I? And who are you?"

The woman stood up and placed the bottle on the table next to the stairs. "Well, chère . . ." She flicked her hair from her shoulders. "Je suis Camille De la Rue Beaumont."

Unimpressed with the dramatic introduction, Karramis added, "And where am I?"

"France," Camille said with an overzealous and throaty enunciation.

"France? What? How did I . . . What the hell am I doing in France?"

"That's exactly what I've been wondering for all these years. You haven't . . ."

Karramis drew back in surprise, ignoring the rest of Camille's words. *Years? What is she talking about?*

There was no way this young woman was telling the truth. Maybe Camille was confused, or crazy. Karramis glanced down at the clothes she was wearing, and it was in fact the same dirty, tattered, and blood-soaked nightgown from last night. The stab wound Lucas gave her was also hurting and still bleeding. She brushed her fingers along her face, and it too was still tender and swollen from the abuse she had endured. The only thing she could not explain was, despite her overall dirty appearance and matted hair, her face and upper body were now clean, and the stitches along her wound appeared old.

Even though curiosity loomed around some of the unexplained circumstances surrounding her current situation, Karramis still wondered how she was alive. She had planned everything out perfectly, but somehow the spell had not worked.

She worried if James and Rhiannon were safe and back in Kiluemar. She had to find out, but first she had to get out of here. Karramis needed to focus on getting her magic to work and keeping Camille talking, pulling the young woman's attention to something other than what she was trying to do. But before she could come up with a plan, Camille appeared towering over her, and Karramis flinched back in surprise, causing her body to constrict as a harsh moan erupted from her.

Camille squatted just a few inches from Karramis's outstretched legs, beaming at her with a grin. The room grew quiet as the music from the violin stopped. Only Karramis's soft hurried exhales remained, as well as the heavy breathing coming from Camille.

Reaching out a hand, Camille hovered it over Karramis's body. "I can feel it." She let out a heckling laugh. "After all these years, I can *finally* feel it."

Karramis raised a brow. *Years? What the heck is she talking about?*

Lowering her hand, Camille's fingers caressed Karramis's skin.

"Cami!" a voice yelled from beyond the stairs.

Camille drew back, grumbling as footsteps descended into the room.

"What are you doing down here?" Leif asked as he paused on the bottom step.

"Nothing," Camille admitted deceptively. "J'étais just checking on her. I heard some noises and wanted to make sure she was okay."

Leif inhaled, the sweet and metallic scent of blood filling his nose. A hunger burned his throat, and he swallowed, the extraordinary appeal of Karramis's aroma accelerating his bloodlust. His towering and muscular body strutted over to Karramis as a sly grin beamed across his pale face, exposing his perfectly straight teeth.

"Look who's finally awake." Leif crouched down. "You look like shit, Karramis."

"Oui," Camille agreed.

Karramis jerked her head sideways as footsteps hurried down the stairs.

"What's goin' on?" Lucas stopped at the base of the steps as he spotted Karramis bleeding and the blood on the floor. "What the hell happened to her?"

"Je ne sais pas, mon amour." Camille batted her eyes at him. "She was like this when I found her."

Lucas frowned. "Go upstairs, Cami."

"Oui. As you wish." She ran her fingers across his chest and blew him a kiss. "Anything for you."

Karramis rolled her eyes as Camille retreated up the stairs. "She's a little young for you, Lucas, don't you think?"

Lucas gave her a boyish smirk. "Jealous, love?"

"You wish."

Leif sat on the stairs and let out a drawn-out exhale. "Oh brother, not this shit again."

Karramis struggled to push herself off the floor.

"Here." Lucas reached out a hand. "Let me help ya."

"No!" Karramis pulled away from him. "Don't touch me. I can do it myself."

"Still pissed at me afta' all this time?"

"All this time? Have you lost your mind? You tried kidnapping my kids. Not to mention, you freakin' stabbed me!"

"Yeah, but that was . . ."

Lucas did not understand why, or how it had happened, but he figured Karramis planned for it to play out this way. He had always thought it was her own magic controlling the events following that night. But by the sounds of it, she did not know the truth yet. Eventually he would have to tell her, but right now she was hurt and needed help.

Lucas reached out a hand again. "Stop bein' so damn stubborn, Karramis. Or do ya wanna bleed to death?"

Leaning against the step, Leif smiled. "I wouldn't mind that."

Bleeding out would not help her with trying to escape, so she accepted his hand. Lucas placed her arm behind his neck and reached around her backside, grabbing her waist and lifting her onto her feet. Blood covered the side of Lucas as she leaned into him.

Leif cracked his neck and drummed his foot against the floor, fighting against his impulses to tackle her as he drew in another long inhale.

Karramis held her breath as Lucas raised her onto the table. She slid back and squeezed her eyes shut, holding in the scream racing up her throat. Removing his button-down shirt, Lucas placed it firmly against her side, and she grimaced and instinctively jerked away.

"It doesn't look like it's bleedin' that much anymore, but we need to seal it up because the stitches aren't workin' very well."

"What"—Karramis inhaled through her teeth—"What do you mean seal it up?"

Leif stood up and removed a small dagger from under his shirt as he called up the stairs. "Hey, Cami! Get me a lighter!"

"Why?" Karramis's heart raced as she darted her eyes back and forth between Lucas and Leif. "What are you going to do?"

The door at the top of the stairs clicked open and a lighter flew down.

Leif caught it and headed over to Karramis. "This'll be fun."

"What is he doing, Lucas?" Karramis asked with panic in her voice.

Leif flashed her a callous smirk as he ran the flame over the blade. "Hold her down."

"Oh, hell no!" Karramis said, unsuccessfully shoving Lucas away.

Lucas pushed her onto her back and held her down. "Just relax, it'll be ova' before ya know it."

"You two are insane!" She struggled to get away. "Let me go!"

"Relax!" Lucas covered her mouth. "We're only gonna cauterize it. Just hold still."

Karramis fought against his weight, but the hot steel seared her skin, and she surrendered. Her muffled cries under Lucas's hand dwindled as her body went into shock. No longer able to fight, she closed her eyes and passed out. Waking a few seconds later, she was relieved. The stabbing pain along her side was gone, masked behind the throbbing ache of burned skin, a much more tolerable discomfort.

Lucas helped Karramis sit up. "The worst is ova', love."

"Yeah, right." She moaned. "Easy for you to say. You don't have a . . ."

She stared down at Lucas's abdomen, his white undershirt stretching along his torso. With no signs of a bandage along the stab wounds she had inflicted, Karramis placed her hand on his stomach and examined the area. There were raised sections of skin underneath his shirt but nothing resembling a recent injury. Her fingers traced along his body, and a rush of desire coursed through Lucas. She pulled up the material, exposing the lower section of his stomach and observing two faint scars embedded along his abdomen. Transfixed by the embrace, Lucas leaned his body closer to her as she caressed his old injuries.

"What the hell is going on, Lucas?"

Lucas snapped out of his trance. "What?"

"What's going on?" Karramis slid away from him, then halted, her body locking up as the pain returned. "Ow! Dammit!"

Her breath quivered. "Tell me what the hell is going on. How are you healed already?"

Lucas did not answer, but instead focused on her as her attention shifted inward.

Karramis panicked, the pain and strange events making her mind burst with confusion and fear. *I have to get out of here! I have to find my kids. I need to get home and warn Will.*

Lucas stepped back and tightened his gaze, causing Karramis to turn her attention to him. His pinched expression amplified the crease between his brows. Curling both hands into fists, he flexed the muscles along his forearms. The change in his behavior caused Karramis to fidget along the table, ignoring the soreness ripping into her. His calm and compassionate demeanor flipped, and she held eye contact with a different person, one whose body language frightened her. Lucas stood tall, his shoulders pulled back and his chest puffed out. His stance was wide, showing signs he wanted to charge at her.

Karramis made the mistake of letting him in. She let her guard down and broke her focus, allowing Lucas into her thoughts. He heard her mention Will—the one person he hated more than anything else. She had to think of something fast to rectify her mistake. Peering at the shelf behind Lucas, Karramis focused on the vase and three pillar candles. If she was strong enough to control her fire magic and light the candles or move the vase with her telekinesis then she would be able to open a portal and get home. But the pain coursing through her was not enough to send her magic into defensive mode, and the spell she used last night would not work in this instance. Plus, she did not want to surrender her magic again. She wanted her powers to work correctly, so she could get back home and warn her family.

Karramis needed time, a diversion, something to help distract Lucas while she allowed herself to refocus and draw enough inner strength to control her magic.

With a flirtatious smirk, she bashfully asked, "So, you still play? I heard you playing earlier. It sounded familiar. Have I heard it before?"

Her smile was his weakness. Lucas never could veer away from her beautiful and captivating grin. It made everything else around seem dull in comparison to the brightness it brought to a room. It was, without a doubt, her most attractive feature.

Leif tightened his gaze on Karramis. "Lucas?"

Ignoring Leif, Lucas relaxed his shoulders and loosened his fists. "Yeah, I still play. Not much else to do 'round here. I wrote that one many years ago, so I mighta played it for ya before."

"It's lovely. Do you still sing?"

"Occasionally . . . when I'm alone."

Still staring in his direction, Karramis was able to bend her gaze past him and concentrate on the vase and candles. Flicking her fingers, she bounced her attention back and forth between them, striving to ignite the candles or move the vase.

"So, who's Camille? Why's she here? And where is *here* exactly?"

"We're actually in France, not far from Spain. And Cami has been here with us for about two years now. She's waitin' to go to Kiluemar with us."

"Lucas?" Leif stepped closer to them, frustration pinching his brows together. "We need to talk."

"Waiting?" Karramis asked in a brisk tone, smiling at Lucas. "Waiting for what?"

"For the portals to reopen."

Karramis was attempting to pay attention while still focusing on her hidden agenda, but as Lucas's words set in, she stopped and locked eyes with him.

"Wait. Are we in Château Rouge?"

"Yeah. How'd ya know?"

"Oh. I, uhm . . . I did some research years ago on all the safe houses, and Château Rouge is the only one in France." She paused and her eyes widened. "Wait! The portals are closed?"

"Yeah. They were sealed shut. No one out *or* in."

Karramis drew in shallow breaths, whispering to herself, "And you said . . . you said Camille has been waiting for . . . for two *years*?"

"Karramis," Lucas said softly, moving closer to her, "how long ago did ya last see me?"

She zipped her eyes back and forth, blinking uncontrollably as her mind went fuzzy. Her heart thumped against her chest, squeezing with each beat. Refusing to give in to the agony slicing into her muscles, she swallowed, forcing down another scream and the sour taste rising from her stomach. Her eyes stopped on Lucas, and she analyzed him. Last night he had been clean-shaven, but now he had short stubble along his cheeks and chin. His hair was slightly longer, and a few gray strands mixed with the brown around his face. The laugh lines and shallow wrinkles around his eyes showed signs of years added to his life.

"Years." Karramis turned her gaze to the floor. "She kept saying years." She jerked her head up. "Years? It's been *years*? How? How is this possible? I—I shouldn't be here. Why? How . . . *how* am I alive?"

"I'm not sure, love. All I know is when ya collapsed that night, I thought you were dead, but ya weren't. Your heart continued to beat—slowly, very slowly—but it was still beatin'. Everythin' else about ya stopped, though. Your breathin', your agin'. It was like ya were frozen in some kind of magical stasis."

"That night?" She paused. "How long ago did this happen?"

"Eight years."

"Eight! Eight years? I-I've been dead—or whatever that was—for *eight* years?" Karramis rubbed her forehead and whispered to herself. "What the hell is happening? I—I shouldn't be here."

She scooted off the table and her legs shook under her weight. Grasping the edge of the wooden furniture, she leaned into it.

"I removed all my magic," she continued in a normal tone. "I was supposed to die that night." She lowered her voice again. "I have to find the kids. I have to find Will."

Karramis closed her eyes as her frantic rant came to a halt. She had done it again. She had mentioned Will's name, but this time it was out loud. Will was the one thing that always sent Lucas into a state of rage. He became a person Karramis did not recognize—a man lost within the idea of an 'if I can't have her, no one can' mentality. There was no denying it now, or even trying to hide it. Glancing over at Lucas, she observed the pain and anger racing across his face.

*Dammit.*

"Bravo, Karramis," Leif said mockingly as he clapped his hands. "What a fabulous performance. Up until now, that is. I see you are still spinning your deceptive web of lies and manipulation. Some things never change, do they?"

Karramis rolled her eyes. "Aren't you tired of not having a life, Leif?"

Leif stood inches from Karramis, their eyes locking in on each other. Uncomfortable with how close he was to her, she slid along the side of the table away from him, progressing closer to the bookshelf. Leif refused to blink as he followed her continual escape. She reached the end of the table and paused, afraid to let go. The pain in her side was no longer the problem, but her legs were. The muscles in her thighs were tight and burned, battling against her aching knees as they trembled. The soles of her feet ached with a stabbing pain, each nerve slicing open as if filled with shards of glass as she stood up. The pain was manageable, diminishing with each slow and steady breath, but the weakness was not something she could fight. She would never be able to outrun Leif or the others, let alone escape her stone prison through a portal without one of them following her. She needed to find a way to get herself alone with one of them. It did not matter who, as long as she was strong enough to overpower them. Karramis was not only formulating a plan, but now she was consciously fighting the invasive eavesdropping of Lucas's telepathy. Luckily for her, her mental strength was much stronger than her physical and magical capabilities at the moment.

Still locked in on Karramis's dark brown eyes, Leif leaned in and placed his face directly in front of hers. His blue irises burrowed into her soul as he listened to her heart beating steadily. The blood in the veins along her neck pulsated, making his pupils dilate as he drew in a long inhale. He lifted a hand, and Karramis pulled back, jerking her head away as she maintained eye contact. Rubbing his hand across her stomach, he wiped the blood from her nightgown and licked his fingers. He closed his eyes as he swallowed, an exhilarating rush sending every inch of him into a state of ecstasy. Her pulse remained steady as the black of his pupils expanded outward past his irises and into the whites of his eyes. The veins around his eyes swelled and the blood within them turned black, matching his darkened gaze. His smooth, pale skin was even fairer against the harshness of his eyes. The gruesome appearance did not seem to intimidate or frighten her, and Karramis held her ground as he opened his mouth, exposing his sharp fangs.

"You don't scare me," Karramis said confidently.

Leif growled through his teeth. "Yes, I do."

"No. Not anymore."

"Oh, I highly doubt that."

She gently pushed him away. "How's the hole in your chest? Too bad I missed."

Leif let out a taunting laugh as he grasped her hand and squeezed it. "Careful, Karramis. You're treading in dangerous waters." He breathed into her ear. "Öga för öga, witch."

With her voice calm and unyielding, she whispered back, "Well, it's a good thing I'm a fantastic swimmer."

Leif's face and eyes returned to normal as he took a step back. "We'll just have to see about that."

He turned away, pausing before twisting and ramming his fist into her stomach. Karramis let out a choking gasp as he shoved her into the table, the intense pain weakening the muscles in her legs. The candles along the shelf behind Lucas ignited and the vase flew across the room, glass scattering as it crashed against the wall. Leif faced the noise and released Karramis, and she collapsed to her knees and grasped her stomach, whimpering in pain.

Camille hurried down the stairs. "Ca c'était quoi?"

"English, Cami, please," Lucas said, startled by her unexpected arrival. "No one understands you."

Leif yanked Karramis off the floor and pushed her onto the table. "Christ, Lucas, we've been here for years and you still can't fucking speak the damn language? And, I understand her just fine."

Camille smiled at Leif. "*Merci.*" She stepped from the stairs and made her way over to Lucas. "I asked what that noise was?"

Karramis pulled her legs into her stomach and cradled her abdomen.

"It was her." Lucas pointed at Karramis as he stepped over to Leif. "Did ya havta hit her so hard?"

Leif scoffed. "Well, as a matter—"

"Her magic is getting stronger, no?" Camille inched her way between Lucas and Leif. "I felt it earlier. It was very powerful, but now it's even more intense."

Lucas scowled at Leif. "We'll finish this some otha' time, mate." He strolled over to the shelf. "Yeah. I sensed it too when I came downstairs. It's gettin' stronger by the minute." Licking his fingers, he extinguished the flames of the candles. "We're gonna havta restrain her or somethin' before all her magic comes back."

Karramis winced as she sat up. "Wait . . . I—I didn't have my magic this whole time?"

"Shut up!" Leif lifted his chin at Camille, motioning her over to Karramis. "Go."

Camille swayed her hips closer to Lucas as she made her way over to Karramis. She ran her hand down his arm, caressing his fingers as she strolled by. Lucas scoffed and jerked his hand away.

"Cami!" Leif snapped. "Focus!"

"Très bien." Camille clutched Karramis's leg. "Jeez, I can't have any fun."

Karramis slapped her hand away. "Get away from me!"

Disregarding the feisty request and abrupt smack, Camille snatched Karramis's wrist. "Oui, her magic is powerful . . . very powerful. But it's hard to control. I can feel it fighting against me. There's a fire raging in her. Tell me I get to use it, s'il te plaît! This magic will be fun to play with."

Questions emerged in Karramis's mind. Everything she had learned since opening her eyes did not make sense to her. How had she been alive, but not really, for eight years? Had she been frozen in a magical stasis? And how? She had never heard of anyone ever being trapped within their own body unable to die. Why had her magic not returned to the island? Had it been trapped all this time within the magical barrier, and only now returned to her? But why? Why now? Karramis pondered the many questions, but the one that stood out was why her powers were finally restored. Unable to answer the questions herself, she drew her attention back to the task still in play. She needed to get out of here, but doing so would take a miracle or a clever plan, maybe even both.

Karramis focused on Camille, who now stood next to Lucas and Leif. She did not know what they were discussing and did not care to eavesdrop. She needed to center her thoughts and summon the magic deep down. Her powers had never been easy to manipulate, but her magic—despite her hatred for it—never let her down in the past when she really needed it. Even after all this time, her magic had kept her alive somehow, and now it had returned to her. She was not going to give up. She was going to get out of here, one way or another.

Karramis's thoughts transferred back to Camille. "Wait, she's an Echo."

Not hearing her, Lucas asked. "What?"

"She's an Echo, isn't she?"

"That's none of your business," Leif announced bitterly.

Never having met one in person before, Karramis was unsure exactly how an Echo's powers worked. She had read stories about them when she was in school, but Echoes had not lived in Kiluemar for centuries. They were not a rare creature, but most did not know they even had magical abilities. Echoes could only use their powers on other magical creatures. Their only ability was to siphon the magic of the one they touched. They did not steal it but simply duplicated it. But with many magical creatures living inside Kiluemar or in hiding, most Echoes did not know their powers even existed.

Karramis refused to accept Leif's elusive reply and questioned Lucas. "You were planning on using her to open a portal, weren't you?" She exhaled, shaking her head in disbelief. "You went searching for an Echo just to get through, didn't you? You were hoping she'd be able to tap into my powers and open one of my portals to get you back."

Lucas let out a heavy breath. "Yes. We'd been stuck here— "

"Lucas!" Leif rolled his eyes and crossed his arms. "This is getting ridicu—"

"Give me a minute, Leif."

Leif's shoulders dropped, and he scoffed through his nose. "I'm not leaving you alone with her."

Lucas peered up at the sullen vampire. "Listen to me, I can handle her. Go upstairs. And take Cami with ya."

"Are you insane, Lucas? You can't be serious. You know she has a way of manipulating you. You can't control your—"

"I got this, Leif!" Lucas narrowed his eyes. "Leave."

"Fine! Fy fån! Your fuckin' funeral." Leif stomped up the stairs, uttering Swedish profanities under his breath. "Nu går vi, Cami!"

Camille shrugged her shoulders. "What did he say?"

"Let's go, Cami! Now!"

Karramis filled with delight and fought back the urge to smile. Her adrenaline surged, sending warmth flowing underneath her clammy skin as the door at the top of the stairs slammed shut. This was it. She would be alone with one of them. This would be her only chance to get out of here, but she had to be careful not to ruin her one opportunity at escaping. She had to play her cards right or she would lose. Luckily for her, Lucas was the one staying behind.

"Did you only keep me here to use me?" Karramis asked softly. "To use my powers to get back to Kiluemar?"

"No." He edged his way closer to her. "I brought ya here because you were still alive. Well, sorta. I hoped ya woulda opened your eyes or showed more signs of life, but ya didn't. You just laid there—frozen, barely alive. I searched for years for an Echo and finally found Cami here in France. Lucky, eh? I told her all about Kiluemar and magic, and she didn't hesitate to come along. When she got here, she confirmed my suspicions.

Your magic was gone. I couldn't sense it, but she was unable to feel any as well."

"But you only searched for her so you could go back, right? Back to Kiluemar? Back to your obedient responsibilities and obligations to Merrick?"

"Yes and no. Yes, I wanted to go back. But it wasn't just for the things I had to do for Merrick . . . I wanted to go home. Kiluemar is my home. It's all I have left, the one constant in my life. But I also wanted to see if ya had your magic because if ya did then that meant you were still truly alive. Magic only leaves us when we die. But ya had nothin'. No traces of anythin'."

Karramis thought for a moment. "But my heart was still beating?"

"Yes. That was the confusin' part. No one could understand it. Everythin' about ya stopped except your heart and pulse."

Analyzing the mystery surrounding her unexplained state, Karramis whispered, "They must've sealed my magic inside."

Lucas moved closer. "They what?"

"My magic. It's been trapped in Kiluemar this whole time. When they sealed the portals, they trapped my powers. When it was supposed to be released from the necklace, it was meant to go back into the island, but it didn't, and I don't know why. And I have no idea how I am alive. I mean, I should be dead right now."

Her time was running out. Leif would be back down any minute to check on Lucas, and she could not guarantee he was not already listening to their conversation. Karramis had never trusted their friendship, especially after Leif recruited Lucas to help Merrick. Lucas was never the same after she rejected his affection and moved on to Will soon afterward. Leif had taken advantage of his vulnerability. In fact, Karramis had always wondered if Merrick had his sights on Lucas from the start, and the only thing he needed was a way to swoop in and manipulate Lucas into joining him. Leif, being a vindictive and vile creature, worked for Merrick for many years. Leif was, at the time, like a father figure to Lucas after Karramis left him heartbroken. He had always wanted to protect Lucas, or control him, but she was never sure about which one, though.

The time for pleasantries was over. Karramis needed to find her inner strength and conjure a portal so she could return to Kiluemar and her family. However, the power behind it would be nearly impossible to call upon in her present state. She was too weak and lacked years of practice, even more so after eight years of being trapped in a magical coma. She had to do something drastic to jumpstart her powers.

Seeing how her magic had worked moments ago, Karramis accepted the next step in her plan, coming to terms with what she would have to do to make her powers work. But it would involve an exhausting amount of mental control and strength, as well as an exceptionally painful experience, more than she was already undergoing. There were only two guaranteed ways to bring one's magic to the surface. One was an emotional trigger, and the other was by having an excruciating pain inflicted upon oneself. Emotions were not something she could easily control, so the latter was, unfortunately, the route she would have to take.

Karramis was certain she could alter the current conversation and move forward with her foolproof strategy. All she had to do was summon his inner demons, something she was all too familiar with. She was going to have to manipulate his emotions and force him to abandon the love he had for her. She was going to have to piss him off.

# Chapter 5

## Home

Karramis tumbled onto a grassy clearing as the portal closed behind her. The hard and inept landing added even more agony to her heavily beaten body, and her muscles quivered with weakness. The fresh cuts and bruises along her cheeks and left eye burned, her face having suffered a majority of the damage from her harrowing escape. The red marks along her neck ached with her hurried heartbeat. Blood seeped from her nose and split lip. Each shallow exhale rubbed against her raw throat. But despite all her new injuries, nothing was more grueling than the wound along her side, now accompanied by a bruise left by Lucas's steel-toed boot. The intense and penetrating pain squeezed along her left side, sending nagging jolts deeper into her body.

The courageous but reckless brawl she had suffered moments ago at Château Rouge left her begging for some relief, anything to dull the pain she now tackled. Struggling to lift herself up,

Karramis's arms started to tremble. She questioned whether her frail body could handle any more as she fought through the agonizing pain of moving.

Her body was unsteady under her own weight, her arms trembling as she pushed herself up, but she collapsed and smacked against the ground. Lying with her cheek resting against the dry, leaf-covered ground, Karramis wanted to fight, but it was a losing battle. She closed her eyes and gave into the fatigue taking over.

The leaves rustled and crunched around her, growing louder as pounding footsteps sent the earth vibrating beneath her fragile body. Falling further into darkness behind her eyelids, she grew deaf, no longer able to hear the footfalls advancing over to her. A figure hurtled to the ground beside her, filling her with both joy and fear, but Karramis was too weak to react.

"Shh, you're okay," a familiar voice said, distorted and seemingly miles away. "You're safe now. I've got you, Kare."

A man carefully rolled Karramis onto her back and swiped the strands of hair off her bloody face.

"Oh, my gosh. What happened to you?"

Recognizing the voice, Karramis said weakly, "Pavian?"

"I'm here."

She pried open her eyes. "Kids?"

"They're here." Pavian lifted her into his arms. "They're safe."

Karramis's breath shuddered as a sigh of relief fell from her lips. She closed her eyes, giving in to the pain and falling unconscious as Pavian rushed by the others, hurrying in the direction of the abandoned cabin.

James was baffled by the sight of her. Not only was she alive and badly beaten, but she was exactly how she had been the last time he saw her—wearing the same bloody nightgown and not a day older. His confusion was overwhelming, but his concern about her condition was more powerful than the reasoning behind her miraculous return.

Rhiannon crossed her arms and shuffled her feet as she strolled behind everyone else. Her eyes faced forward but did not focus on anything. She was lost within her mind, rationalizing the event playing out, unable to comprehend an explanation. Shock and denial took over, increasing as her anxiety tapped against her nerves, creating an uncomfortable twitch throughout her body. Her mother was alive, but was it real or just a manifestation of wishful thinking? She did not remember falling asleep, but she was afraid it was a dream.

Aidan walked with his arm around Kavana, who was stuck in a blank trance. Soft sobs shuddered in her chest as the tears along her face dried. The arrival of her sister was surprising and pulled her into another place—an emotional blend of curiosity, disbelief, confusion, and happiness. But knowing Karramis had been alive all this time and witnessing her now clinging to life overwhelmed Kavana with guilt and unease. The pain and fear her sister must have suffered all these years was hard for Kavana to accept. The thought of what Karramis must have gone through was daunting and sickening.

~

Karramis sprang awake, her eyes bolting open as she gasped for air. The nightmare of her final moments with Lucas played back within her dreams. She panted and darted her eyes around the room. Staring up at the ceiling, she recalled her escape—every moment, every mistake, every injury. She shuddered and caressed her neck, sensing his fingers wrapping around her throat and restricting her airflow. Her cheek ached as visions of her face crashing against the rough stone wall behind Lucas's powerful blow flashed behind her closed eyes. Running her shaky fingers over the bandages along her cheek and temple, she recalled every strike. The bruises on her stomach tightened, the pain surging as she experienced his foot ramming into her again.

Karramis gazed around the room, trying to erase the terrifying memories. Her tense muscles relaxed. She twisted the corners of her lips into a smile, a pinch pulling beneath the bandage sticking to her cheekbone. A sigh of relief released from her body. She was home. She was back in the cabin she had lived in all those years ago with Will. It was the home where her children were born, a place of comfort and peace. Still smiling, she closed her eyes. She was safe. She was finally able to relax and allow her body to recover from the hell it had endured. But as her body sank into the couch, Karramis sprang up, a loud groan exploding from her as she fell back, driving her body into a fetal position.

"Son of a bitch!" Karramis buried her face into the pillow. "Dammit! Dammit! Dammit!"

Kavana burst through the front door. "What happ—Oh my gosh, you're awake." She hurried over to the couch. "Are you okay?"

Surprised, Karramis said, "Kavana, what—" Her tone shifted to panic. "Wait, where're the kids?" She tried to sit up but paused, the pain spreading through her like a wildfire. "Are"— she groaned as she lowered herself down—"are they here? Are they okay?"

"Shh, calm down." Kavana grabbed her sister's hand. "They're okay, I promise. They are both here and safe."

Karramis relaxed, grimacing as she sank deeper into the cushions.

"But are you?" Kavana asked sympathetically. "How are you feeling?"

"Like shit." Karramis moaned as she adjusted herself. "I feel like I was trampled by a herd of elephants . . . or worse."

"Definitely worse," Kavana said without hesitation.

Karramis frowned at her. "How bad is it?"

"Oh. Not . . . not that bad."

Karramis scoffed. "Yeah, right. You know, you've never been a very good liar, K."

"No. I—I didn't mean it like that. Honest. It's just—What I meant to say was you already look much better than when you got here."

"Right." Karramis slid her legs sideways and slowly lowered them off the couch. "Anyway, I'm guessing I have Pavian to thank for that?"

"Yeah, he's been tending to you. Luckily for us, there were already some medical supplies here."

Karramis slowly sat up and cradled her side. "Pavian really should've been a doctor instead of working for Dad. He definitely has a healing hand, that's for sure. By the way, where is he?"

"Outside. He and the kids needed a distraction, so they went for a walk."

"How are they? The kids, I mean?"

"Okay . . . considering the circumstances."

"Good." Karramis glanced down at her nightgown. "K?"

"Yeah?"

"Why the hell am I still wearing these damn clothes?"

Kavana caught a chuckle in her throat. "Only you would care about how dirty you are, even after everything else you've been through. Well, I *was* going to change you, especially with how much you stink, but—"

"Hey! Thanks a lot!"

"Well, you do."

Karramis inhaled, sniffing the air before quickly scrunching her nose. "Eww, I do."

They grinned at each other before letting out a thunderous chuckle.

Abruptly ending her pained laughter, Karramis pleaded, "Ow. Don't make me laugh. Anyway, you were saying?"

"Once Pavian got you inside and evaluated your injuries, he didn't want to move you again, at least not until your breathing and pulse returned to normal. He said we needed to wait until you either woke up or were healed more."

"How . . . how long have I been out of it?"

"Three days."

"Three days?" Karramis said in disbelief.

"Yeah. You were in real bad shape, Kare. I mean, it was *bad*. None of us were even sure if you'd wake up, let alone survive, honestly."

Karramis glanced at the medical supplies scattered around the room. "Where'd all this come from? These aren't the usual medical supplies we store here."

"The village. Pavian and Aidan—"

"Aidan?"

"Yeah. He's the one who helped us get back here. Will—"

"Will?" Karramis interrupted frantically. "Where is he? I need to see him. Is—is he here? Why haven't you mentioned him?"

"Calm down, Karramis, or you're going to hurt yourself. Just breathe."

Karramis drew in a long inhale, releasing it and asking in a calmer voice. "Where's Will?"

Letting out a heavy sigh, Kavana twisted toward the front door, unable to face her sister. "We can't find him."

"What?" Karramis jumped to her feet but fell back down as she cried out.

Kavana rushed over. "Oh my—Are you okay?"

"Yeah." Karramis paused and drew in shallow breaths, driving the pain from her body with each exhale. Calmly, she asked, "What do you mean you can't find him?"

"No one has seen him, and this place has been abandoned for a while. Based on a few things we found around the place, he hasn't been here in years. I'm sorry, Kare."

"No. That can't be right. There has to be an explanation. Maybe he's in the village?"

"He's not, we already looked there."

"What about Stoweward?"

Kavana shook her head. "We checked there too."

"No. I refuse to believe he's just gone . . . or—or worse. He's got to be here—Wait." Karramis widened her eyes. "You all went looking for him? And Pavian's been to the village?" Her voice was stern but filled with worry. "Kavana, who knows we're back? No one can know we're back yet. It's too dangerous. If Merrick finds—"

"Relax. No one knows we're back. I'm assuming Dad probably does because the portals are open, but no one has gone to see him yet. Pavian and Aidan went in the middle of the night to get the medical supplies and some food for us. We've done everything to make sure no one knows the kids, or you, are here. And Aidan was the only one who went out looking for Will."

"Do the kids know yet? About Will?"

"No. We were still holding out hope of finding him, but Aidan has searched the village, Stoweward, and even tried seeing if he could find him on the other side of the island, but nothing. He's just not here."

Karramis thought for a moment before smiling and rising to her feet. "I know where he is." She headed over to the hallway. "I need to get changed."

"Wait," Kavana said disapprovingly as she blocked her way. "What're you doing?"

"I can't very well go out looking"—Karramis inhaled—"or smelling like this. Plus, I really have to pee."

"Go out? Go where?"

"To get Will."

"No, you can't. You can't go out like this. I mean, you're still hurt and . . . and you almost died. You're in no state to—"

"I'm *going*, Kavana. Now, you can either help me get cleaned up, or you can move aside. Either way, I'm doing this. I need to find him. He needs to know I'm alive and that his family is back."

There was no arguing with Karramis once she made up her mind. She was a free spirit and did not take kindly to being told what she could and could not do. She did what she wanted and made a habit out of challenging those who told her not to do something.

"Fine," Kavana said with a heavy sigh. "I'll help you, but you better tell Pavian I fought harder with you on this."

"Deal."

Reaching the hallway, Karramis asked, "Hey, don't you want to know what happened?"

"No. I'll leave the interrogating up to Pavian. I'm not going to question it . . . I'm just glad you're back."

~

The warm shower helped dull some of Karramis's nagging pain, and she strolled casually into the living room wearing clean clothes with her damp waves springing against her upper back. The jeans and shirt she wore were outdated but fit perfectly against her average hourglass figure, while the fresh bandages on her face clashed with the black and blue bruises.

"Feeling better?" Kavana asked from the kitchen.

"Yeah. A little. The pain is more annoying than anything. It only hurts if I move too fast."

"Well, don't move too fast then."

Karramis winced as she sat down. "Easier said than done."

The front door opened, and Pavian walked in.

Pausing in the doorframe, he beamed at Karramis. "You're awake."

"Hey, Pavian," Karramis said with a smile.

He sat down and carefully hugged her. "I've missed you, Sis."

"I've missed you too."

Pavian leaned back. "How are you feeling?"

"Better. Thanks." Karramis glanced at the door. "Pavian, where're the kids?"

"Still outside. They're fine though." He exhaled. "You had us all scared there for a while."

Kavana entered the room from the kitchen. "That's an understatement."

"What happened to you, Kare?" Pavian asked. "You look like you had the shit beat out of you."

"Well, I did."

Kavana glared at her with a serious expression. "What?"

"Who did this?" Pavian added, his face pinched with anger.

"Lucas."

"Lucas?" Kavana and Pavian said, shocked.

Pavian shook his head in disbelief. "Why? I thought . . . Why would he do that?"

"It's a long story, but he's not the same person anymore. And . . . and well, I kind of pushed his buttons and set him off. I admit, it wasn't the best idea, but hey, it worked."

Kavana frowned. "You did it on purpose?"

"Yeah. Kinda."

Pavian and Kavana narrowed their eyes at each other and then at Karramis. "Kinda?"

"Well, I didn't really have any other choice. I needed to get the heck out of there. My powers weren't working right, and I needed to force them to the surface. My emotions weren't strong enough to trigger them, and the pain I was in just wasn't enough either, I guess. I wasn't expecting him to get that many hits in before I was able to conjure my portal. His rage was unlike anything I've ever seen before. It was crazy. *He* was crazy."

With his forehead deeply creased, Pavian asked, "Kare, where've you been this whole time? I mean, I'm happy you're here and all, but how are you alive?"

"I don't know exactly. This is all new to me as well."

"What does that mean?"

"It means that for the last eight years I've been unconscious in some kind of magical coma in southern France. My body—dead, but not dead—was being watched over by Lucas and the other lunatics who work for Merrick. My magic was gone, but not really. It kept me alive somehow, despite having been removed. And I woke up thinking it had only been a day or two, but it turned out almost a decade had passed. I don't know why I'm here. I mean, I shouldn't be. I can't explain it. None of it makes sense to me. And I don't really care, honestly. I don't care why I'm alive, or why I'm here. Why should I? Why should I question it? What I do care about is seeing my kids and finding my husband."

Pavian and Kavana did not understand it either, but then again no one truly understood how or why magic worked. Magic was unpredictable, elusive, and, at times, unexplainable. Therefore, like Karramis had said, why question it? Why challenge the miracle in front of them? Without a word, the three siblings decided to let the subject go. The answers they wanted would not be answered today, or possibly never, so they chose not to dwell on it any longer.

However, Karramis did have some questions about her children and the last eight years. What had happened when she sent the twins through that night? Was the strategy she had planned out helpful? What had the twins been up to the last eight years, and why were they back now? Were they in danger? The time would present itself soon enough to get all her questions answered, but she too would eventually have to go into further detail about everything that had happened at Château Rouge. And now, with the portals being unsealed, Lucas would again be coming after her and the children.

All the questions and concerns disappeared as James entered the house, followed closely by Rhiannon. The twins spotted their mother awake and halted, the three of them staring at each other.

Rhiannon mirrored her mother's emotional response as tears filled their eyes, both smiling at each other. The sight of her sent Rhiannon's body into a combative struggle between overwhelming delight and a powerful sense of disbelief. Her knees trembled as warmth filled her chest. With gentle eyes, an infectious smile, luscious wavy hair, and a kind, welcoming presence, Karramis was exactly how she was eight years ago. But now, she was even more beautiful to the young girl who yearned for her mother's embrace more than anything else in the world.

James gasped, his breath catching in his throat, afraid she would disappear if he exhaled. His heart fluttered with joy but ached as he caught sight of her appearance. He stared into her eyes, and tears trailed down his face as he became lost in the happiness and love emanating from her loving gaze. He let out his trapped breath, and warmth raced through his body. He smiled, the relief taking over and sending him into a state of tearful and consuming excitement when she did not disappear.

Karramis held back the sobs rising in her chest, the fear and concern for her children's safety diminishing with each quivering exhale. Her chest pounded, her heart racing uncontrollably with anticipation and love. There was nothing more powerful than the love a mother had for her children. All her sacrifices were worth it as she gazed into her children's eyes. Every decision she had ever made was for them—to protect them—and nothing else mattered. Her children were safe, and home. It was something she had always wished would happen. Knowing she would do it all again if she had to, Karramis released all doubts and heartache linked to her past decisions.

James took a step, then stopped, taking hold of Rhiannon's hand before continuing forward. Karramis pushed herself onto her feet, the pain veiled by the happiness flowing through her body. The twins hesitated as they approached, unsure if they would hurt their injured mother.

Karramis hugged them. "My babies."

The three cried, tears falling without reservation as the twins embraced their mother. Karramis quietly winced but ignored the pain as they squeezed harder. She matched their tight grasp, refusing to allow her injuries to take away from the moment.

Karramis glanced up at her children, both standing taller than her, and cradled their cheeks. "My babies aren't babies anymore.

You two are so grown-up now." She sighed as another tear fell from her eye. "I've missed so much."

Removing her hand from his face, James held it. "We'll fill you in."

Rhiannon smiled, pulling them all back into a hug. "We have plenty of time now, Mom."

~

The reunion was filled with tears, laughter, and reminiscent conversation. The three sat discussing their lives at the manor and what the twins had been up to the last eight years. Kavana and Pavian had retreated outside, giving their sister the privacy she deserved as she became reacquainted with her children.

Despite the talk about what the twins had been up to living within the non-magical world, none of them brought up where Karramis had been all this time. The twins knew the details of those years would eventually come up, but for now, all they cared about was that she was alive and finally back home with them.

Karramis was overwhelmingly happy being reunited with her children. Everything she had planned for, everything she had been willing to sacrifice, was for James and Rhiannon. She was happy, grateful, and finally able to relax knowing the twins had survived all these years. They were back where they needed to be. They were home, and they were safe—for now, at least. But she still had to find Will. He needed to be here with them.

Karramis grabbed her side and groaned as she lifted herself off the couch. "I need to go."

"Go where?" the twins asked, baffled.

"I'm going to go get your dad." She paused, taking a deep breath. "He needs to know we're back."

"You can't go like this," Rhiannon said, observing the pain her mother was trying to ignore.

Pavian entered the cabin with Kavana trailing behind. "What's going on?"

Rhiannon placed her hands on her hips. "Mom thinks she's going to go find our dad like this."

Pavian scoffed at Karramis. "You're what?"

In a serious but sympathetic tone, Kavana said, "There's no talking her out of it, Pavian. She's going to do it one way or another, so you might as well just let her go."

Pavian tossed his stern gaze between his sisters. "Fine." He folded his arms over his chest. "But on one condition."

"What?" Karramis asked flatly.

"Someone goes with you."

The twins raised their hands. "We'll go!"

"No." Karramis shook her head. "Absolutely not. You can't. It's too dangerous."

"Nonsense, Mom," James said with a grin.

"Yeah," Rhiannon added. "We've proven many times— okay, maybe not *many* times—but at least the one time—"

"We can handle ourselves," James concluded.

Pavian and Kavana smiled. The twins were just like their parents, in more ways than just their physical appearance.

Pavian laughed. "Stubbornness must run in your blood, Kare."

"Yes, it does, *Brother*," Karramis declared with a snarky tone. "I get it from father's side of the family." She sighed, peering over at the twins. "Okay, fine. But if at any time I think you two are in danger, I'm going to send you back here immediately. I will not have you two hurt or in any kind of trouble, especially since I'm guessing you don't have control over your magic yet."

"Deal!" the twins said excitedly.

James and Rhiannon mounted two of the three horses Pavian and Aidan had brought back from the village. James sat atop a black stallion and caressed the horse's mane as the chilly winter breeze blew the tail of the brown mare in front of him. With a jet-black tail and mane, the chocolate-colored horse waited patiently as Rhiannon adjusted herself in the saddle. Covering her legs with the skirt of her dress, Rhiannon held tightly to the reins of the bitless bridle.

"You're going to be cold again," James called up to Rhiannon with an authoritative tone.

"I'll be fine." Rhiannon patted the bag tied to her horse. "I brought a thicker jacket this time."

Pavian lifted Karramis up onto another horse, a palomino with a stark-white mane. The twins frowned as their mother moaned, her body plopping onto the tame and gentle stallion's back. Karramis was in no condition to be out of bed, let alone riding a horse, but they understood her need to find their father. They wanted to find him as well. Ever since they had returned to Kiluemar, the twins' memories of their father had resurfaced, and they remembered the time they had spent with him when they were here before. Though the period of time they had here was not nearly enough, they still valued the little memories they had. They needed their family back together—something they never had experienced before but had longed for their whole lives. James and Rhiannon had always wanted a family—a mother *and* a father. Now, they would finally have that chance, but first they had to find him.

Pavian and Kavana waited as the three disappeared into the forest on the eastern side of the cabin. Both fearful of where Karramis and the twins were heading, they worried their sister would not be able to protect them, or herself, from the dangers waiting for them just beyond the trees.

# Chapter 6

## Uncovered Magic

*Twenty years ago*

The news of Karramis's magical abilities had not surprised Will when he found out the morning after they first met. In fact, he was pleased to learn his mother's bedtime stories were real.

Will's favorite pastime as a boy had been getting lost in a world of fantasy. Magic, faraway lands, monsters, heroes, and adventurous journeys were a captivating escape from the real world. There was nothing more thrilling to the adolescent boy than the wonderful stories created in the fantasy genre. He had always dreamed of a magical world—a place where magic existed and mythical creatures roamed free, a world filled with vampires, witches, werewolves, mermaids, and all the creatures he read about. But nothing interested Will more as a boy than the stories about dragons.

Dragons were his mother's favorite too. An expert in the subject with her facts and knowledge, Meredith Cassil would talk about these flying beasts as if she knew about them firsthand. To her, dragons were majestic misunderstood creatures. In her stories, they were friendly, intelligent, kindhearted, and one of the most powerful creatures to ever exist.

There were four types of dragons, each representing one of the natural elements of Mother Nature with their own unique appearances and magical abilities.

The Earth Dragons were the smallest, roughly nine feet tall from the ground to the tip of their horns. Their bodies were similar to that of a Komodo dragon but much larger. These were the friendliest and gentlest of the dragon species. The powers of these creatures were unknown, but legends said they could control the tectonic plates and magma below the surface of Earth.

Air Dragons were the largest, standing almost fifty feet tall, not counting their outstretched wings. These solid white creatures had feathers instead of scales covering most of their short bodies and extra-long tails. Despite their size, Air Dragons were the most docile. They controlled the wind and moved the clouds.

Fire Dragons were the most unique of the four. Changing color as they aged, these creatures were born red, but turned gray, and eventually black as they got older. They were also the only land dragons to have two legs instead of four, using their wings to help stabilize themselves when standing. These creatures, like Air Dragons, were enormous, reaching twenty-four feet tall. They were the most dangerous and territorial of all the dragons. Having the ability to breathe fire, they were also the most feared.

The Water Dragons were Meredith's favorite and the ones she most often discussed in her stories. They were unrecognizable as a dragon to most people. In fact, the Water Dragon was frequently mistaken as a prehistoric long-necked marine animal. However, aside from the long neck, rounded midsection, and front-end fins, these dragons had a different appearance than the extinct creatures of long ago. Being over forty feet long, this species had a mix of dolphin and serpent features. They were the smartest and fastest, and they had the ability to control all water.

Will's parents had encouraged his love of books, and his admiration of the magic and unknown within those stories. They pushed for him to accept the unbelievable, never question the unexplained, embrace the unexpected, and look beyond the unimaginable. Will lived by these notions and rarely deviated from these powerful ideas. But he wondered why his parents thought this way. Both set in their ways, his parents had never been the type to believe in magic.

Meredith was a strong supporter of the Catholic church, choosing to live by the words written in the Bible, yet she told Will amazing stories that often made him think they were her family's legacy told to each new generation. And Will's father, Clark Cassil, was a firm believer in facts over fiction. Being a historian, his father seldom picked up a book or watched a movie not relating to an actual event in history. But despite these strong traits, Meredith and Clark had always valued the excitement, respect, and acceptance Will had when it came to believing in the possibility of something more than what this world held.

Will finally understood his parents' strange behavior many years later after meeting a shy but lively twenty-year-old while working in a pub just a few weeks after his twenty-second birthday. Karramis's arrival had not only left him wanting to know more about magic and her world, but it made him want her. There was not only a physical connection but also a mental and emotional one. The magnetic pull tugged at him every time she was away. She not only made him whole, like everything in life made sense, but with her he was calm, happy, and experienced something unlike anything he had ever felt before. He loved her.

After four months of only seeing Karramis for a few hours a week, Will grew even more anxious each time she left. They would meet in various locations in the countryside just outside London to help minimize the chance of being spotted or followed by magical or non-magical spies. Karramis was paranoid her father would discover her secret and figure out a way to bind her magic or send Will off to some random location in the non-magical realm.

On the day of her twenty-first birthday, Karramis followed through with her plan to meet up with Will later that evening. She did not want to celebrate her birthday without him, so she formulated a foolproof idea to avoid getting caught. After a quick dinner with her family, Karramis told them she was heading over to Lucas's place in Stoweward and was unsure when she would return. Lucas Fraye was one of Karramis's oldest friends in Kiluemar, and she considered him one of her best friends, valuing his advice and companionship. Having spent the morning with him, she knew he would be home the rest of the evening, and no one would question her whereabouts if she were with him.

Karramis left through her portal and arrived outside the western part of London where Will was waiting. They spent the remaining hours together in a secluded area before saying their goodbyes as the sun rose. But as Karramis disappeared, Will took the plunge, doing something wild and spontaneous. Refusing to wait until the next time they would meet, Will secretly jumped through the portal just as it started to close, and it spit him out on the other side.

Stepping out of the portal and into her bedroom, Karramis kicked off her shoes and crashed onto the bed. She drifted off to sleep, unaware Will had followed her and was now wandering around a dangerous part of the island.

Will made his way north across Sunrise Mesa as the sun rose higher along the cloudless sky. He walked for a few miles, the curiosity of the strange location running rampage in his mind. He was unsure of where he was, let alone how he was going to get back home to London. Karramis was nowhere in sight and the rocky mesa made him uneasy as strange voices echoed in his head.

A roar erupted from the mountain in front of him and sent thunderous shock waves across the terrain. Will halted as terror rose from the pit of his stomach. Glancing around, he spotted a large opening within the base of the mountain. Another roar rang out, and Will stumbled back. Regaining his footing, he stood frozen as an enormous black-and-red winged creature emerged from the mouth of the cave. His muscles tensed, and his posture was rigid. His heartbeat hammered in his ears, the pain of his rapid pulse restricting his airflow.

"Will!" Karramis exclaimed, her eyes popping open as she jumped to her feet. "How the hell . . ."

She concentrated on Will before running straight into a swirling misty vortex. Landing against the stony ground, she stumbled over various rocks as a Fire Dragon took flight, soaring from the cave and straight after Will, who was standing a few yards in front of her.

"Will!" she yelled as she ran over to him. "Run!"

Will twisted and called back. "No, wait!"

Karramis slowed down, wincing as her body weight forced her feet into the rocks. She stopped next to him, his calmness and vacant expression making her uneasy. The creases along his forehead and the bridge of his nose were prominent as he gazed sternly at the creature.

"Will, we need to get out of here."

He did not take his eyes off the dragon as it circled overhead. "I can hear him."

Karramis cringed. "What?"

"I can hear him—his thoughts, I mean. He's talking to me."

"You can *hear* him?"

Will nodded. "It's strange. He's actually thinking in some kind of odd language, but I can hear his thoughts and somehow understand them."

"Well, what's he saying?"

"He's telling me not to be afraid of him. He isn't going to harm me. I can trust him."

Karramis had grown up terrified of dragons. They were unpredictable and only did things to benefit themselves. Doing as they pleased, dragons had not been on the side of good or evil for many years. They were territorial, mean, and deadly if provoked—at least, that was what she had been told. But as Karramis stood there, she gazed up at the creature she had once feared. She was unnaturally relaxed, safe even.

"Wait," Karramis said, stepping in front of him. "What's your name?"

Will exhaled a sharp snicker. "What do you mean? You know my name."

"Yes, I know it's Will Cassil, but what's your full name? What's your mother's maiden name? What about your father?"

Will raised an eyebrow. "Why?"

"Just humor me."

"Well, my full name is William Drolnogard Cassil. My mum's maiden name was Drol—"

"Drolnogard?"

"Yeah. Why? What's going on?"

Karramis did not answer but stood peering aimlessly into Will's eyes, flashing him a side smirk.

"Karramis? What's happening?"

Her gaze widened. "That's why I was able to sense you that first night—The night we met. All these months I could sense your magic, but you never brought it up. I never even thought to ask you more about your mother's stories or anything about your family. I just assumed she had met someone from the realm or someone with magic. I never imagined *she* was the one with the powers."

"But my mum didn't have powers."

"Yes, she did. She was a Drolnogard. She never knew about her powers because all the dragons live here."

"What does being a Drolnogard have to do with magic?"

"Drolnogard isn't just a last name, Will. It's a magical ability, a power."

"So . . . I can hear Harkin because I'm a Drolnogard?"

Karramis glanced up at the dragon and back over at Will, tilting her head. "Harkin?"

"Yeah, that's his name." Will shrugged as Karramis scowled playfully at him. "What? I didn't name him."

~

*The present*

James was uneasy the closer they got to Emrys Cave, zipping his eyes in all directions as his stomach hardened. He shuddered as his body became cold and a chill raced up his spine.

"James?" Rhiannon sensed the panic rising in her own body. "What's wrong?"

Karramis turned her attention to James, his face pale as his eyes searched the sky frantically. "James, what's wrong?"

"I've been here before. I remember this place."

"You've never been to this part of the island," Karramis assured him. "Not unless your dad brought you here."

"No." Rhiannon shook her head. "He never brought us here. In fact, we barely left the cabin."

"No," James admitted. "No, not with Dad."

Rhiannon gasped. "Your astral projection!"

James nodded.

Karramis pulled the reins back, and her horse stopped. "You can astral project?"

He nodded again.

She turned to Rhiannon. "Can you?"

"I think so. I did it the one time, but I wasn't able to control it like—"

A massive white creature roared overhead, appearing from above the top of Maevis Mountains. Its powerful outstretched wings sent a rush of air crashing down into Karramis and the twins as they glanced up, watching the creature traveling among the clouds.

"That's it!" James yelled. "That's the thing that chased me!"

Karramis held tight to the reins and kicked her horse. "Go!" She hunched over at the sudden jolt, the pain piercing her torso. "Get to the cave!"

James urged his horse forward and raced behind her.

"Wait!" Rhiannon called, her voiced muffled by the galloping as she hurried her horse after them.

Witnessing his mother folding over in pain, James shouted, "Mom, are you okay?"

"I'm fine! Just keep going!"

Karramis and James directed their horses through the entrance of the cave before pulling back the reins and forcing them to halt.

Grasping her side, Karramis let out a muffled cry.

James jumped from his horse. "Mom!"

"I'm fine," she said with pain in her voice. "I'm okay. Just help me down." She groaned as she slid from the horse, James catching her and lowering her down. "I think I'll just keep my feet on the ground for now. That was definitely not part of the plan."

"What was that thing anyway?" James asked nervously.

"It was an Air Dragon."

"Was it about to eat us?"

Karramis chuckled, grimacing from the pain of laughing. "No, he wasn't trying to eat us. Dragons don't usually eat people. But they can be dangerous if they think we're a threat to them. Without Will—without your dad here—we have no way of telling them we mean them no harm. And I'm not sure if they will remember me."

James gulped. "Did you just say *usually*?"

"You don't have to worry, James. As far as I know the dragons here have never killed anyone on the island, let alone eaten them. They usually keep to themselves and everyone stays away from this side of the island."

James searched for his unusually quiet sister, who was sitting on her horse at the entrance of the cave. Her pale complexion against the darkness of the cave was prominent, her body stiff and eyes open wide, but she was smiling.

James focused on his sister, but her mind was filled with distorted voices. "What's wrong?"

The horses staggered back toward the entrance, snorting as they tossed their heads wildly in the air.

"You can't hear them?" Rhiannon whispered, keeping her eyes focused on something behind her brother.

James followed the direction her eyes faced, observing two large reptilian creatures hiding among the shadows of the cave.

James lowered his voice and leaned over to his mother. "What. Are. Those?"

The creatures were tall and stood on all fours. Their light brown coloring mixed with dark green along the top of their smooth backs were reminiscent of boulders. Stepping more into sight, the creatures' faces broke through the darkness, showing the others their rounded snouts and horns on the top of their heads and along the back of their cheeks. With a smooth, scaly underside and a long tail, the creatures were similar to a lizard, except they had large leaf-shaped wings folded along their sides.

"Those are Earth Dragons," Karramis answered.

"Are they"—James stepped back—"dangerous?"

"All dragons are potentially dangerous, remember?"

"These aren't." Rhiannon disembarked from her horse, making her way over to one of the dragons and petting it. "This is Raeth." She stroked the other creature. "And this is Oakley."

Karramis rested against her horse, trying to alleviate the pain still throbbing in her abdomen. "You can hear them?"

"Yeah." Rhiannon moved her eyes over to James. "Can't you?"

James focused for a minute. "Yeah . . . through you."

Confused, Karramis asked, "*Through* her?"

"Yeah," Rhiannon said. "James and I can hear each other's thoughts as we think them, and he must be—"

"Hearing them through her," James finished.

Raeth moved over to Karramis and sniffed her.

Curiosity pulled Rhiannon's brows together as she stood next to Oakley, observing Raeth's odd behavior. "He can smell dragon blood in you." She shifted her head upward, meeting Oakley's gaze. "In fact, they can smell it in all of us."

James's expression matched his sister's inquisitive glare. "What're they talking about, Mom?"

"I'll have to save that story for another day, just like this whole being able to read each other's mind thing." Karramis sighed and smiled at Rhiannon. "Well, I guess you're a true Drolnogard, just like your dad."

"But why can't I hear them by myself?" James asked, disappointed. "I mean, I'm a Drolnogard too, right?"

"Yes, of course." Rhiannon strolled over to him. "Maybe my ability to hear them is just stronger. Or maybe our connection is stronger than your Drolnogard powers are right now." She faced her mother. "Right?"

"Possibly. Drolnogard is a natural ability, but it's still magic, and magic must be learned, mastered. It comes easier for some but not others. Even after all these years, I still have issues controlling most of mine. It's not just a physical ability, but it's also psychological. Most magic is mental, emotional, and physical, all working together. Maybe your fears are overpowering your ability. Or maybe it's like what your sister said. We can figure all this out later, sweetie, but right now we need to find your dad."

"He's not here." Rhiannon stopped next to Raeth. "I mean, he *was* here. He's just not here now. He went out earlier with some of the other dragons. Raeth said he's most likely—"

"I know where he is," Karramis said with delight in her voice.

"Where?" James asked.

"The Lookout."

"Where's that?"

"A few miles from here. It's one of his favorite spots on the island."

"Raeth said they can fly us over there," Rhiannon said hesitantly.

"No, that's quite all right," Karramis declared. "I've had enough riding adventures for today. I'm going to keep my feet on the ground for now."

Rhiannon nodded with a relieved chuckle. "Yeah, me too. Gravity isn't my friend. But how are we going to get there then? Especially before dark."

"My portal, of course."

"No, you're not!" James objected.

Karramis scoffed. "And who's the parent here?"

"Mom, James is right. You're still hurt and you aren't strong enough yet."

"I'm fine. I promise. I can muster up enough strength to get myself over there. The events a few days ago helped bring my magic to the surface again, and portals are the one thing I'm actually good at . . . most of the time. It should be easy enough for me to handle, especially with such a short distance."

"Okay then," James said, unconvinced, "and what will you do to get back? Are you going to be strong enough to come back through? And what about Dad?"

"Probably not. But I will worry about that later. Anyway, listen, you two stay here." Karramis paused. "I mean it, kids. Stay. Right. Here. Do not, under any circumstances, leave this cave. Do you hear me?"

They started to argue. "But—"

"I mean it. Just stay here. It's not safe out there."

The twins let out an exaggerated sigh. "Fine."

Karramis kissed their foreheads. "Okay, that's just weird. I'm going to need the full story the first chance we get." She headed for the cave entrance, but paused, turning back and pointing at the ground. "Stay."

They nodded as their mother exited the cave.

James tossed his sister a stern glare. "She's got two hours."

Rhiannon folded her arms. "Agreed."

# Chapter 7

## Will to Survive

Karramis waited outside the cave, concentrating on the strength needed to conjure her portal. Having lied to her children, she did not want to use her powers in front of them. She was right about one thing: her portal was her easiest ability, but it still took physical strength, something she was limited on at the moment. She did not want her children to see her struggle, let alone suffer through the pain she would have to fight through. Karramis was determined to get to Will, and nothing was going to stop her, even if she had to walk the whole way.

Leaving the children behind was not only for their safety and her inability to bring them in her weakened state, but there was another reason as well—a selfish one. She wanted to see Will first. Alone. She wanted to be in his arms again and have her body pressed against his. She wanted to smell him, kiss him, feel his touch. She needed this.

Karramis did not know for sure how Will would react, but she did not want to scare him by opening a portal right in front of him. She decided to exit her portal inside Kitra Forest, a few yards from the clearing along the southeastern cliffs.

The Lookout rested beyond a dense mix of trees, which made it difficult to travel through. But a small clearing at the edge of the cliffs opened, creating an amazing view, especially during sunrise. This was Will's favorite place on the island. He loved going there to think, watch the dragons fly around, and communicate with the Water Dragons. Being a Drolnogard, Will could, if he focused hard enough, telepathically converse with the dragons from miles away.

Karramis caught herself against a nearby tree as she stumbled from the portal. Her magic was returning to its original state, but her body still suffered from the injuries inflicted on her. Her legs were heavy, and everything above her waist ached with each step. Every movement was challenging against her bruised muscles and damaged tissue. Luckily, she did not have far to go. She remembered every inch of this area and could navigate it blindfolded. She and Will had spent many hours here after he moved to the island, and even more after they got married. The seclusion, breathtaking views, and complicated trek through the trees made this place ideal for the young couple to enjoy their privacy.

She moved along the makeshift trail, continuing closer to the edge of the forest. Entering the clearing, she paused as the Air Dragon she had seen earlier emerged from the clouds, flying over the ocean with two Fire Dragons. She stared for a moment, remembering the three creatures from years ago.

The Air Dragon, who she now recognized as Phosmeratae, was the one she had only met a few times before. Not being a social creature, he rarely left the cave at the top of Maevis Mountains. But Will must have convinced the feathered creature to come down from his home and socialize more with the other dragons. The larger Fire Dragon, with more ash and black color than red, was Harkin, while Ignara had a mix of red and subtle gray along her scales. The three dragons danced across the colorful sky as the sun descended closer to the horizon behind her.

Sitting on top of a boulder on the edge of the cliff was Will, glancing out at the ocean below. Karramis shuddered, catching it in her throat as tears fell from her eyes. She wiped her face as flutters rose in her stomach. Her love for him burned, a love which had not faded over the years but had only grown stronger. Yearning filled her insides, her heart steady as the fluttering intensified. Euphoria rose inside of her, a rush of awareness forcing every nerve to tingle. Warmth spread throughout her body, the increased blood flow causing the pain to return, throbbing and pulsating. Her knees trembled as she fought against the ache.

Karramis took a deep breath and shuffled forward, the grass rustling under her shoes. An Earth Dragon next to Will twisted, huffing as it caught sight of Karramis, both locking eyes on each other. Recognizing the dragon as Terramina, Karramis stepped forward, her legs weakening beneath her. She grunted as she collapsed to the ground, her weight forcing her down.

Will jumped from the boulder and bolted around in her direction. He advanced forward as his narrowed eyes centered on the figure on the ground. He paused, locking in on Karramis as his soul pulsated back to life. They stared at each other and the world around them disappeared.

"Hi, Will," she said softly, the cuts and bruises pinching as a smile spread across her face.

Will's alarmed expression dropped, shifting to confusion as she spoke. His mouth cracked open as a heavy breath escaped from his lips. He refused to blink, moving closer with a cautious stride.

Karramis could not take her eyes off him, tracing his body and rediscovering every inch of him. Broader in the shoulders, Will had more muscles along his arms and chest. His hair was wild and shaggy, his curls falling against the top of his ears and across his forehead. It was still the same shade of brown but with a few added silver strands mixed in. His once clean-shaven face was covered with a short, bushy beard. She focused on his eyes, unable to escape his hypnotizing gaze. They were the same deep sky blue, matching the ocean behind him. She was lost in them. Her favorite feature, Karramis could stare at them forever.

"Karramis?" Will whispered in disbelief. "Is . . . is this real?"

Her chest grew warm as her heart pounded against it, racing as the voice from her dreams was even more captivating in person.

"Yes, it's real," she said, unconvinced by her own words as she summoned the strength to stand up.

Karramis fought against the desire to run into his arms, knowing the results would end with her back on the ground.

Guarded, Will progressed closer. "How? Is this magic? Are you really here?"

"Yes." She smiled. "I'm really here. I'm real."

Will paused as he caught sight of the severity of her injuries.

Spotting his distress, Karramis carefully stepped closer to him. "It's okay, Will."

He continued toward her. Reaching out a hand, he hesitated.

"You can touch me," Karramis said with a comforting tone as she craved his embrace.

"And I won't hurt you?"

"No."

"And you won't disappear?"

"No. I'm not going anywhere, I promise."

Will's fingers brushed across her wrist, and his palm trailed slowly up her bruised arm. Karramis quivered with exhilaration, her knees becoming weak again. She leaned her body closer as he traced his hand along her shoulder.

Will exhaled, staring into her eyes. "You're real."

Karramis breathed a giggle. "I told you."

His gentle touch traveled up her shoulder and along her neck. Cradling her cheek, he slid his fingers through her hair and leaned in. His lips touched hers, the electrifying elation surging through them as they drew each other closer.

A new twinge throbbed under her skin, transmitting a burning passion radiating through her body as the pain she once felt faded. Time stood still, erasing all traces of the years apart from her mind. Every heartache, every sacrifice, and every moment of longing melted away, disappearing behind a wave of passion and complete connectedness. Memories of happiness, love, intimacy, and friendship took over. All emotions linked to the last fifteen years vanished, leaving behind a fully healed heart, and a soul rising from the ashes.

Will pulled away, a smile emerging across his face. "That was better than I imagined it would be."

Karramis chuckled with a bewildered expression. "You imagined I'd come back from the dead and . . . and you'd kiss me?"

"Well, when you put it that way it sounds creepy and not at all romantic," Will said with a playful tone and a handsome grin. "But yes, I quite often dreamt you'd come back to me. I never truly believed you were gone, but as time went on it became more real. But every dream, every kiss in those dreams, was amazing. But this—this right here—exceeds them far more than I had ever expected."

They kissed again.

Will pulled away and held her face as he drew his brows together. "By the way, what the bloody hell happened? Who did this to you?"

"It's a long story. I'll tell you about it in a bit, but first . . ."

She clasped her hands around the base of his neck and pulled him in for another passionate kiss.

~

The two rested on the grass not far from the cliffs as the sky grew darker. They were lost in each other's company. All four dragons flew around, brushing the calm waters below with their wings as stars appeared across the dark blue sky.

Karramis told Will everything about the night she sent the children through the portal, what had happened when she woke up at Château Rouge a few days ago, and what she had to do to get away. He did not take the story of her desperate escape and Lucas's violent attack on her lightly. Will was furious and vowed he would get his revenge. This act of Lucas's was the final straw, drawing Will into an even deeper hatred for the man who aided in ripping his family from him and ruining fifteen years of his life.

She informed Will the children were back together, how their memories and some of their magic had been restored, and how Pavian, Kavana, and Aidan were with the three of them at the cabin, awaiting the right time to notify the others of their return.

Will explained his decision to leave the cabin and why he had ended up living in the cave with the dragons, as well as why he had stayed hidden the last two years.

Karramis learned Merrick had killed many on the island over the years—some for their powers, while others had been victims of his bloodthirst. When Merrick finally decided he wanted Will's magic, he sent everyone he had left in Kiluemar after him. The cabin was not safe for him anymore, so he moved into the village. But after a while, he grew to miss the dragons, and with no active powers, he was never able to leave and still stay safe. He did not want to abandon the dragons, so he decided to move into Emrys Cave with some of them. There was a decent-sized alcove not far from the main entrance that provided a suitable living space for him. It even had a small freshwater pond and enough room to make an outhouse. It was not luxurious or the best way to live, but Will was determined to stay alive for his family.

Karramis held his hand, rubbing the wedding band along his finger. "I'm sorry we lost all that time."

Will interlocked his fingers with hers. "The past is irrelevant now. You're alive. You're home. The children are home. That's the only thing that matters to me now. The years lost no longer compare to right now and the years we have been given."

Karramis leaned in and kissed him, groaning as the pain returned.

"Are you all right?" Will asked, pulling from the passionate embrace.

"Yeah," she said deceitfully as she pressed her hand into her side.

"I beg to differ. I need to get you home and into bed."

Karramis tossed him a teasing grin.

"To *rest*," he added with a snicker, mimicking her mischievous smirk as he stood.

"I'm fine. Really."

"I see you're still as tenacious as ever." Will scooped her into his arms and carried her over to Terramina. "Let's get you home."

"No. We have to go to the cave first."

"Why?"

"Because that's where James and Rhiannon are."

Will lifted her onto Terramina's back. "You left them alone with the dragons?"

"Relax. They're Drolnogards." Karramis grimaced as she glided her legs over the dragon. "Can't I just use my portal?"

"Absolutely not. You're clearly still in pain. You need to rest and heal."

"Yeah, but I'm not a fan of—"

"I would never allow you to fall." He mounted the dragon. "You needn't worry so much."

"Did you forget who you're talking to?"

"My mistake." He wrapped his arms around her. "It's all right, darling, I've got you."

Leaning back into his chest, she smiled. "Good. Don't ever let go."

"I won't." Will nudged Terramina forward as he held Karramis tighter. "So, the kids are true Drolnogards?"

"Yeah," Karramis answered with strain in her voice, gripping tightly to Will's arms as the dragon outstretched her wings.

Will beamed from ear to ear as the Earth Dragon took flight, delight rising in him as he held his wife again, and the thought of his children sharing his ability filled his mind.

His mother's legacy—his legacy—would not end with him. The dragons, his companions for the last fifteen years, would still have a connection to this world long after he was gone. His magic would live on through his children, and the Drolnogard bloodline would continue into future generations.

# *Chapter 8*

Dragon Lady

*Centuries ago*

Dragons were not only the most powerful magical creatures to ever exist but also the oldest. Being the first species created by magic, dragons had been around long before the arrival of humans. They roamed the lands, took to the skies, and swam the waters along with prehistoric animals of the past. They lived without fear, dominating the world with their elemental power, intellectual mindset, and magical blood. But as time went on and their primeval counterparts died, the immortal winged creatures fled, taking refuge and hiding from the disasters around them.

Air Dragons disappeared high above the clouds in the caves along mountaintops. Fire and Earth Dragons descended into the deep caverns, hiding within the shadows and heated crevices of Earth's crust. The Water Dragons dove into the trenches of the oceans of the world, where light faded and only darkness surrounded them. For many millenniums they remained hidden and dormant, forced to live in a hibernating state, alive but asleep until the world grew calm and they could once again thrive.

When the dragons woke, the world was a much different place. The lands were divided. Climates had changed. The strange new world was altered, and a new species had emerged—humans. Mysterious beings on two legs roamed the earth, making the newly awakened flying giants fearful of the unknown. Dragons were reborn into a completely unfamiliar world, a place so different and unusual, they no longer felt accepted or powerful.

The stories of dragons throughout history could be traced back as far as Mesopotamia, ancient China, and the ancient civilizations of Central and South America. Tales of the ferocious beasts exaggerated the truth about these peaceful and majestic creatures. Humans feared them, and time did not change their perspective over the years. Even though the dragons never showed signs of danger or aggression at first, hundreds were still hunted down and killed out of spite and panic. Many dragons fought back, killing thousands of humans—both innocent and not—in the process. But most retreated back into hiding, choosing to live a more secluded, quiet, and passive life. Coming out to indulge in simple pleasures or stretch their wings, dragons only left their homes during the night, avoiding the chances of being seen. The Water Dragons were lucky enough to have the whole ocean to hide within, but the others found concealing themselves much more difficult. As the world's population grew, it became harder to remain a secret to the individuals who misunderstood these magical creatures.

Dragons were created by magic in a time when all other living beings were massive, fierce, and strong. They had been equals to the others they lived alongside. However, unlike other prehistoric animals, dragons were not born in the usual manner. They were not hatched from an egg or born from a mother, but rather they were created from the element they represented with the magic from another source. Like a seed sprouting from the soil, the Earth Dragons emerged from the ground during an earthquake as a wildfire raged across the land. The combined elements brought to life a creature of destruction and life. Air Dragons were the rarest. Being the only one created when the combined powers of all four elements join together as one, these creatures delivered a source of rage and calm. The Water Dragons were the most common but were unlike the others. Created when a bolt of lightning struck the water of a powerful wave, these dragons had wings but could not fly. Having smooth rubbery skin, they lacked scales on most of their bodies and lived underwater. These creatures were the bringers of peace and distress. The most feared were the Fire Dragons. Magically conceived within a fire tornado, they were born from flames as the air swirled together. They were the only of their kind to breathe fire and change their appearance as they aged. These dragons bestowed death and rebirth upon the world.

Over time, dragons became scarce and obsolete. Slowly fading from the stories and disappearing entirely from the world, dragons became extinct in the eyes of humans. The immortal creatures could not survive the slayings and mistaken identities forced upon them, so magic abandoned them. Magic gave up hope that these creatures would be accepted in the new world and by the humans now ruling it. Therefore, the creation of dragons ended. For many centuries, no new dragons were born, and the ones left vanished from the known world.

However, in the mid-fourteenth century, the tales of dragons took an unexpected turn when a benevolent and courageous twelve-year-old girl stumbled upon one of the magnificent creatures in Scotland. Margaret Dagley had been out fishing when she came across an injured Earth Dragon. Despite its immense size, Margaret was not frightened but rather charmed and, after observing its distress, deeply concerned.

The brave girl stepped toward it and studied the rare creature. The smooth, uneven brown-and-green coloring along its body resembled mossy boulders covered in mud. Its body was about twelve feet long, and its tail curved around, adding another seven or eight feet to its length. Pointy horns protruded from its head and angled upward, and another set of smaller horns pointed straight back off its cheeks. Its large almond-shaped eyes were a beautiful shade of dark green with a thick brown circle around them. All four of its feet were nestled beneath its rounded body, but its maple-shaped wings were outstretched and resting against the ground.

Margaret moved cautiously and placed the basket she was carrying on the ground before removing two fish. The dragon stared at the young girl and slid backward along the grassy field, pressing itself up but crashing back down. A boom rippled across the ground, but Margaret continued forward, making eye contact with the scared creature. She raised both hands and motioned for the dragon to take the fish. The creature sniffed multiple times before snatching them from her hands and swallowing the fish whole. Margaret laughed as she stroked the creature, who was now devouring her family's supper.

The dragon playfully nudged its snout into her stomach, letting out a long exhale through two small slits. Margaret chuckled as it knocked her to the ground. Standing up, Margaret caressed the gentle creature. She worked her way over to the right side of its body. Blood covered most of the wing and the bottom half of its back leg. Multiple holes were along the membrane of the wing and three arrows stuck out from the dragon's leg. Being a butcher's daughter, Margaret knew the injuries were not fatal. But as she tugged at one of the arrows, the dragon jerked, a low roar growling in its throat. Unaware the dragon could heal, she worried the injuries would get infected and the creature would die.

Margaret hummed an old Gaelic lullaby her mother had sung to her when she was little as she leaned into the dragon. The creature exhaled and relaxed as the young girl's body pressed into its side, emitting the soft vibrations of her song. The pain would be intense, but Margaret needed to remove the arrows. She slid her hand down the dragon's thick skin and curled her fingers around the base of one of the arrows. Grasping it, she held her breath and yanked the arrow from the bloody flesh. The dragon thrashed side to side and bellowed a muffled roar. Margaret leaned in, hugging the dragon again as she resumed humming. Observing the other two arrows, both deeper than the first, she hesitated to remove them. Margaret did not want to put the creature through any more distress, but she refused to leave the wounded animal helpless with festering injuries. The pain she would inflict would only last a moment compared to the arrows stuck in its leg. Moving quickly, Margaret grabbed hold of both arrows and yanked. The dragon shifted under its massive weight, letting out another roar before pushing itself onto its feet.

Still holding the two arrows, Margaret gazed up at the enchanting and unusual animal. She had never seen a creature like this before, but it reminded her of the stories she had been told when she was a little girl. Her grandfather would tell her legends about the dangerous beast with wings who ravaged the villages and kingdoms throughout the world. However, he always ended the adventurous tales—which were told to him by his grandfather as well—with how his family never thought the creatures were monsters or even a threat. The creatures simply acted in response to the slayings, doing what was necessary to survive. Generations before her had named these mythical beings draconem, but over the years the word was lost in translation, and they were simply referred to as dragons.

Margaret was curious about where the dragon had come from, and she wanted to know more about the gentle giant, but communicating with it was impossible. She wrapped her arms around the dragon's wide neck and hugged it, and the dragon lowered its head and rested it against her back.

*"Thank you,"* a voice said behind her.

She gasped and jerked her body around. No one was there. She scanned the area, but there were no signs of anyone nearby.

Facing the dragon, Margaret tilted her head and raised her eyebrows. "Di' ye say somethin'?"

The dragon perked up, slanting its head to match hers. *"You can hear me?"*

"Aye," she said with a smile.

Although the two spoke different languages, they could somehow understand each other. But the most astonishing thing was that Margaret could hear the dragon telepathically.

~

The truth of the matter was magic had never really abandoned the dragons. It had only stopped creating new ones. Instead, the magic which would have given birth to more dragons had been used to generate a new species of magical creatures, ones who were created to aid in the livelihood of the dragons. Elemental giants were the first, but their unusual proportions made them even more of a threat to the non-magical world. These oversized humanoids were born in deep caves within the depths of Earth, rising from the hot springs where the wind howled within the stony walls. Not having their own magic, their elemental characteristics came from their size and appearance. Each giant represented a different element corresponding with each species of dragon.

The giants created for the Air Dragons were the tallest, standing almost thirty feet, but they were thin and lacked body mass. Their skin was pasty white, with even whiter feathers covering parts of their bodies. Their hair was the color of storm clouds with a mix of gray and silver.

Earth Giants were the thickest of the species, carrying extra weight in their large muscular legs and beefy upper bodies, as well as the shortest, reaching only a few feet taller than the average man. Their skin was rigid, dry, and the color of mud, and patches of moss and stone covered their perfectly proportioned bodies. The females had wavy hair with shades of hickory and juniper mixed throughout their flowy strands, while the males were either bald or had long and thick brown locks brushing against their upper backs.

The Fire Giants had charcoal-colored skin and hair the color of raging flames, with hues of orange, red, and yellow blended perfectly together. Placed along their nearly fifteen-foot bodies were remnants of ash, soot, and charred coals. They were the most athletic of the four species.

The Water Giants were the most unique, just like the dragons they had been created for. They did not live within the oceans, but they could breathe underwater. These creatures had similar features of the Air Giants, but their smooth skin was light blue and rubbery, and they were about half the height. These giants did not have anything covering their bodies, so they wore loose, flowy garments made of rags and seaweed.

The giants, confused by their creation, unfortunately never found the dragons all those centuries ago. They were placed within an unknown world and never given an explanation as to why they existed. The calm creatures simply roamed the lands, trying to find purpose. But their massive size was difficult to hide from the non-magical world, and, like dragons, they were soon feared and killed due to their uniqueness. Some were forced into servitude, slaves to the mighty and rich. Compelled into a life of chains, imprisonment, and torture, they were used as machines to further the growth of different civilizations, aiding in the development of many unexplained structures found around the world. Refusing to fight back, the giants disappeared from the world, taking shelter in the valleys and caves far from the cruel, judgmental humans.

With the unsuccessful first attempt to help the dragons, magic needed to devise a new plan, a foolproof idea, and one not involving another magically created creature. Magic would instead give powers to someone. Giving a person the ability to possess a power was not something magic took lightly. Magic was skeptical of this era and learned from past experiences not all humans used their gifts with good intentions. It needed to be sure the one chosen would be compassionate, brave, loyal, fair, and protective. This individual would have to perceive the dragons as equals and friends. They also had to be a person who did not fear them. They would have to come from a family that accepted the magical creatures and viewed them as righteous, regal, and harmless.

Magic found the person it had been searching for in the young Margaret Dagley. She was exactly what magic longed for to help bring peace, understanding, and love to its firstborn creation. So Margaret was the first, and only, individual to possess a magic for which they were not born or cursed with.

~

Margaret's heart pounded in her chest as she sat next to the young dragon. "I'm Margaret. What shall I call ye?"

The dragon cocked its head. *"I do not know. I do not have a name."*

"I dinna ken how to address ye then."

*"Would you like to decide what name I shall be given?"*

Margaret grinned. "Aye!" She thought for a moment. "Are ye a lass or a lad? Ye sound like a lass, but I canna be too sure."

*"I am neither. My species does not have reproductive parts. You shall be the one to decide."*

Margaret's eyes turned upwards, and her lips puckered. "Now then, do ye fancy Mina or Nova?"

The dragon's eyes narrowed. *"I rather prefer Mina."*

"Then henceforth ye shall be referred to as Terramina. Is that an acceptable name for ye?"

*"I believe it will suit me just fine."*

~

The stories of Margaret and Terramina spread throughout the non-magical world, and the fear surrounding these flying monsters faded. The young girl's amazing abilities were considered a gift, and the dragons were no longer hunted. Margaret's powers gave life back to the dragons and connected them to the people. Trust, acceptance, and cooperation were formed, allowing the dragons to come out of hiding and live without restrictions. They traveled across the various terrains, soared amongst the clouds, and splashed against the waves of the ocean's surface again. They were free and at peace with everything around them.

At first, Margaret could only hear Terramina's thoughts, but as she got older, her powers matured, and she was able to communicate with all four types of elemental dragons as more emerged from their hideouts. By the time she was a adult, the dragons and Margaret could sense each other and even hear one another from miles away. The dragons flocked to Europe, and Margaret was given the name Dragon Lady for her noble and remarkable abilities.

The magic did not stop with Margaret, but it continued through her bloodline. Soon after she married, she gave birth to a son, Peter. He, too, was given the gift of dragon telepathy. Peter was born with his powers, and the dragons could communicate with the young child from an early age. With

Terramina's help, Margaret knew what Peter was thinking before he was even able to speak.

Peter loved the magic he possessed. Once he was an adult, he abandoned his given surname and adopted his mother's maiden name—the one associated with power and prestige. Like his mother, he was also given a name to honor his magical abilities: Dragon Lord. The Dagley family line was deeply respected and considered royalty for many generations.

The Dagley lineage, however, soon disappeared from the world. War, plagues, and famine swept through Britain and many relatives of the magical family died. By the beginning of the sixteenth century, only two members were left—Nikolas and Charlemagne.

The brothers lived in London as official lords among the hierarchy of the royal court. Their powers pushed them into high society, and they lived comfortably behind the riches handed to them. Never concerned their magic would bring danger to their family, they expressed their powers openly.

The youngest brother, Charlemagne, regularly discussed his extraordinary gift. He was obnoxious with his desire to impress the people he casually mingled with, especially the women. Every maiden knew of Lord Charlemagne, the Dragon Lord of Westminster, and his arrogant attitude and exaggerated tales. Though his stories were embellished, Charlemagne truly loved and valued the ability to converse with dragons. It was Nikolas who withdrew from his magical calling and veered more toward an aristocratic standpoint. Being a lord was not enough for him, and he aimed for a much higher status, one with political and lawful power. Dragons were unimportant, outdated, and simply not necessary in societal and economical scenarios, and this made Nikolas rarely discuss his magical ability. The flying creatures were of no concern to him. Even as a child he had chosen not to befriend any. Nikolas wanted nothing to do with dragons or magic, so he never grew into his full potential.

Eventually, as rumors and stories of dark magic and witches spread across Europe, the Dagley brothers became targets. Magic hunters sought them out, determined to catch the two lords and earn a substantial reward. Nikolas and Charlemagne fled London and began the long journey back to Scotland. But Nikolas never made it home.

Magic hunters set a trap just north of the city, and the brothers were ambushed and captured. They sat in the Tower of London for weeks before they were convicted of witchcraft and sentenced to death by beheading. On the day of their execution, Charlemagne was saved by his childhood companion, a Fire Dragon named Emrys. However, the dragon was not able to save Nikolas, and he was killed by the guards as he tried to escape.

Charlemagne and Emrys returned safely to Scotland, adapting to a simpler and quieter life far away from the villages. The last of the Dagley line was certain that if magic hunters found their way to Scotland, he would be the first one on their list. Afraid his friend would get caught, or worse, Charlemagne sent Emrys to live far away from the unjust slayings spreading like wildfire throughout the land. Soon after the dragon left,

Charlemagne chose to change his name so no one would associate him with dragons ever again. It was too dangerous to keep the name Dagley or ever be referred to as Dragon Lord again.

The decision was hard for the young man because being a Dagley and Dragon Lord meant everything to him. He was erasing his family's legacy with this heartbreaking choice. But he understood the sacrifice outweighed the consequences of being discovered by magic hunters. Continuing the family line was more important than the name he wanted passed down through the generations that would follow him. Although his lineage would fade from the world, the legacy of Dragon Lady and Lord would live on through stories, something he vowed he would bring to life.

He thought of many new last names, including Nikolas to honor his brother. But after careful consideration, Charlemagne realized he could never part from his famous status. He wanted to retain the magical title and keep the Dagley bloodline alive, far beyond the legends he would tell. Dagleys had been linked to dragons for centuries now, but the title Dragon Lord or Lady was what most of this family before him preferred to be called. Even Charlemagne and Nikolas were rarely referred to as Dagley, and neither was their mother, who had also been known as Dragon Lady, just like Margaret.

Charlemagne sought to create a new name still reminiscent of Dragon Lord, his given and once honorable title. He wanted a name that would provide him with a connection to the magical creatures he loved and the powers flowing inside of him. So, he wrote the name backward. From then on, the Dagley line was forever known as Drolnogard.

# *Chapter 9*

## One Step at a Time

Life on the island may have been old-fashioned and outdated to many, but it still had some modern amenities. Over the years, most of the magical individuals who came to Kiluemar were regular mortals with magical abilities. Coming from a world with advancements in technology, science, and new inventions, the residents required a few adjustments to the living conditions on the island. Electricity, plumbing, and especially warm running water and toilets were a necessity to most in the realm. This was something James and Rhiannon had grown fond of, so they opted out of the more primitive lifestyle in the cave with their parents as Karramis continued to recover.

James and Rhiannon enjoyed this time alone together, seeing it as an opportunity to get to know each other and ignore the tension surrounding the others. It was the perfect occasion to get reacquainted, a pause from a much larger storyline, and find a connective bond with one another. It had been a long eight years apart, and much had happened in their lives, but most of it had occurred with a lingering ache tugging at their hearts. They reminisced about important moments in their lives and how they knew something, or more specifically someone, was missing from that memory. Despite not being able to remember each other for all those years, James and Rhiannon had sensed a piece of them was missing. Their connection went far beyond magic and only grew stronger the longer they were together. The powers they possessed were not the only thing pulling them closer—it was something much more powerful.

No one was sure what would happen once they announced their return, but hiding out for much longer would prove to be impossible. With the portals now open, Lucas's unwanted homecoming would hinder any chances of remaining hidden. With his magical tracking abilities, no one would be safe anymore. In addition to the concern surrounding Lucas's arrival in Kiluemar, Kavana and Pavian were positive their father was aware of their return as well. The plan they had followed through with all those years ago would only allow the portals to reopen with their blood and magic, so Zarrius would be wondering why they had not gone to see him yet, considering it had been over a week since they had returned. In fact, Pavian was surprised his father had not sent someone out looking for them. Zarrius, persistent in his ways, was adamant about knowing everything happening around the realm, and rarely did anything get past him on this side of the island.

The uneasiness involving his father was not the only thing stirring inside of Pavian. He was nervous about seeing Raina again. When he had first found out he was coming home, he did not want to see her. He was reluctant to return, but coming home proved to be even more challenging than he had thought. A gnawing tightness twisted in his stomach and filled his chest. Would Raina still be mad, or had she taken his advice and moved on? Either way, Pavian was content with staying at the cabin for as long as possible.

Kavana, on the other hand, was ready to leave. Having to deal with mixed emotions revolving around Aidan was starting to take a toll on her. She wanted to talk about it with Karramis and fill her in on all the heartache surrounding her relationship, but she would have to wait a bit longer. Rhiannon wanted to hear the story about her and Aidan, but Kavana hesitated every time it was brought up. Kavana did not want to tell her niece because it involved a secret, one filled with guilt and one she had never told anyone before, including Aidan. The tension from unspoken words between the two was evident, and they both avoided each other most of the time. It was clear to everyone, including Aidan and Kavana, the two still loved each other, but something had happened between them that caused a rift in their relationship. Not even Pavian knew why the two had broken up all those years ago, and to be honest, he was too caught up in his own life to stress on the matter.

~

The bruises and cuts along Karramis's body started to fade. The only visible and predominantly noticeable injury was the one along the side of her face. The powerful blow to the wall at Château Rouge had left a nasty black eye and a lasting mark on her cheek. Her side was healing well, and she was able to move about the cave without any major issues. Her broken ribs were healing nicely, the pain unnoticeable most days, and the outer part of the stab wound finally sealed internally and started to scab over. Still having to take it easy, Karramis was required to rest. Will refused to let her out of bed most days after witnessing the severity of her injuries. But after a few days of being bedridden, she ignored her husband's incessant concern and went about life as usual. The fact she had been beaten nearly to death did not seem to stop her tenacious and resilient mindset.

Karramis lay in bed, fiddling with the ruby and black sapphire ring on her finger and pondering the thought of Lucas's return. He would surely arrive back in the realm on the next full moon and notify Merrick of how she and the twins had survived and returned to Kiluemar. Lucas's abilities would confirm his suspicion when he was able to sense them and access their exact location. Even though Lucas could not read the twins' minds, and Karramis was consciously and continually blocking his powers, he could still locate them by sensing their magic. Will would also no longer be safe hiding within the cave once Lucas arrived back on the island. The vindictive man would be determined to get his revenge on Karramis for the wicked mind game she had pulled on him in France. Her actions had placed a target on Will's back and put the ones she loved on Lucas's personal hit list. Bound and determined to not let anyone get hurt by him, Karramis would stop at nothing to protect her family.

As Will slept beside her, Karramis removed the blankets draped across her legs and slid out from under them.

"Get back in bed," Will demanded with his eyes still closed.

She sighed. "I thought you were sleeping."

Will peered up at her. "I was."

"Well then, go back to sleep."

Will tossed the blankets aside, pushing himself up and leaning against the cave wall. "What're you doing?"

Karramis disappeared behind a low hanging sheet. "Getting dressed."

"No, you need to get back in bed. You're not quite healed yet."

"No, I need to get dressed. And we need to get back to the cabin and figure out what we are going to do next." She paused before emerging from behind the sheet. "And I'm healed enough. In fact, I feel good as new."

"Have you always been this stubborn?"

"Yes," she said with sass, not a hint of regret in her voice.

Will grabbed his shirt from a small table next to the bed and pulled it over his head as he stood up. "So, what's the plan?"

"First, we need to get back to our kids."

"Agreed."

"Then we need to figure out how we are going to tell everyone that the kids and I didn't die all those years ago, how I actually died but then didn't, and how Lucas will be here on the next full moon to stir up problems. We need to tell them that we now have to face Merrick, that the prophecy is starting to play out, and how we—"

"Maybe we should just start by telling everyone you and the kids are alive and go from there. It may be best to deal with one shock factor at a time."

Karramis exhaled and leaned into Will's chest. "Yeah, let's just start with that."

Will grabbed a bag filled with a few belongings and exited the cave with Karramis, stopping just outside the entrance.

"What are we waiting for?" Karramis asked. "Please don't tell me you expect me to ride one of the dragons back to the cabin."

"Not at all." He smiled at her. "Something much better."

Will whistled, and the high-pitched screech echoed across the stony mesa. A black-and-white figure soared from the trees on the east side of the cave entrance.

Karramis smiled as she spotted the creature. "Finally got yourself a pegasus, huh?"

"Yeah," he said with a boyish smirk.

The flying horse landed a few feet in front of them and tucked its wings back against its sides.

Will reached out and pet the creature. "This is Callie. She's been with me for almost ten years now. Isn't she lovely?"

Karramis stroked Callie, caressing the creature's black face and neck before moving on to her black mane. The silky black coat continued halfway down her back before white covered the rest of her body and feathered wings.

"Nice to meet you, Callie. Thanks for keeping him company while I was away."

Callie lowered herself to the ground as Will lifted Karramis onto the creature's back.

Will mounted the horse, wrapping his arms around Karramis. "Ready?"

"Wait!" Karramis grasped Callie's mane with one hand and Will's arm with the other. "She's walking, right?"

"Really," he teased, "this again?"

"Oh, hush," she said playfully. "I just woke up after being dead for eight years *and* survived a near-death experience. And after all of that, I'm finally feeling better. Even damn right lucky, if you ask me, so let's not tempt fate. At least, not anytime soon."

Will kissed the side of her cheek and nudged Callie forward. "Good idea."

James and Rhiannon met their parents outside as they arrived at the cabin.

"Wow!" James ran down the steps. "A pegasus!"

"They're rather marvelous creatures, aren't they?" Will asked, helping Karramis off Callie. "I've always wanted one."

Rhiannon approached them. "Well, it isn't actually a *pegasus*. It's just a winged horse. Pegasus was the name of the winged horse born from Medusa's neck when she was beheaded. The *real* Pegasus was solid white and belonged to Bellerophon before Zeus took the horse to carry his lightning bolts."

The three others turned their heads, their brows deeply creased.

Rhiannon shrugged. "What? It's true. Pegasus is a name, not a creature. Winged horses are commonly mistaken as the mythical animal."

"Anyway." James shifted his attention over to Karramis. "How are you feeling, Mom?"

She hugged her children. "I'm fine. Much better, actually."

Pavian and Aidan walked out the front door, making their way over to the others as Kavana emerged from around the side of the cabin.

"Thanks for taking care of them," Karramis said to them.

"Anytime," Pavian and Kavana said together as Aidan nodded.

The twins laughed. "Hey! You two sound like us now."

"How'd you do that?" Will asked, baffled.

Aidan stepped from the porch and hugged Will. "I think we have a wee bit to fill you in on, eh? It's great to see you again, although I barely recognize you. Ye're huge and . . . and—"

"Scruffy," Karramis finished for him as she observed Kavana standing with her arms folded and a distressed look on her face.

Will rubbed his chin. "You don't like the beard?"

"It's not that I don't like it, it's just I can't see your handsome face very well." Karramis smiled and kissed him. "Plus, it tickles."

Changing the subject, James asked, "So, what's the plan? What happens next?"

"Well, first," Will said, "we've got to tell everyone we're back. Then we'll go from there."

"I've already got that covered." Pavian stepped off the porch. "I sent Aidan out earlier to tell my father and get everything ready for our arrival."

Petting Callie, Rhiannon shifted her eyes over to her uncle. "When do we leave?"

"As soon as possible. The horses are ready to go, but bags still need to be packed. I'm not sure how long we'll be staying in the village, so it's best to be prepared."

"Speaking of that . . ." Rhiannon glanced over at Kavana. "How did we get our stuff if no one knows we are back yet?"

"I went and got everythin' for you," Aidan answered. "I went back a few days ago and took care of the rentals and retrieved all yer belongin's."

"Oh. Thank you, Aidan. That was very nice of you."

The discussion about Aidan made Kavana shift back and forth, squeezing her arms tighter around her body.

Karramis ushered everyone closer to the cabin. "Hey, why don't we all go inside and get everything situated before we go? Let's leave in an hour."

Karramis was one of the few who knew when something was not right with Kavana, especially since Pavian was oblivious to any form of emotion when it came to his sisters, choosing to ignore any signs of female distress. He was more of the protector, not the therapist. Despite the sadness on Kavana's face, no one else seemed to notice, or they chose to avoid the situation. But Karramis and Kavana were best friends, the ones who relied on each other over the years, the ones who knew each other's secrets and never judged the other for how they thought, felt, or the choices they made, no matter how crazy they might have been. Karramis missed her sister. She missed the bond they had, the laughs they shared, and the years of lost memories together. Maybe the years apart were not just hard on her, but also her sister. Kavana had not only lost her but had been forced into a life without any advice or reassurance she was going to be okay. Karramis had to make it up to her sister and let Kavana know she was there for her no matter what. She was going to try and fix whatever was bothering her sister.

Karramis grabbed hold of Kavana's hand and led her over to the garden around the side of the cabin. Entering the newly replaced fence, Karramis sat down on the bench along the front gate and patted the seat next to her. Kavana sat down and leaned over, crying into her sister's shoulder.

Karramis held her as she wept. "I'm so sorry."

"For what?" Kavana asked quietly as she sniffled.

"For whatever is making you so upset. And for leaving you."

Kavana leaned away. "I never held that against you. You know that, right?"

Karramis wiped the tears from her sister's cheek. "Well, I do now."

"You did what you had to do to protect yourself and those kids. I mean, it's not like you wanted to. You even left Will behind, which I know wasn't easy for you."

"No, it wasn't. That was the hardest decision I've ever had to make." Karramis ran a finger across Kavana's face, removing another tear. "So, what's wrong?"

"I can't . . . I can't tell you."

"Why?"

"Because I'm ashamed."

"Ashamed?" Karramis frowned. "Ashamed of what?"

"Of the decisions I made. For ruining something amazing."

"You mean with Aidan?"

Kavana nodded, shuddering again as she inhaled.

"K, look at me," Karramis said as her sister avoided eye contact.

Kavana raised her watery gaze.

"I've never judged you. I have never ridiculed you for your choices in life, and I sure as hell am not going to start now."

Kavana exhaled. "But what if you are ashamed of me once you find out? What if Aidan hates me? What if I disappoint Rhiannon?"

"Disappoint me?" Rhiannon asked, walking around the corner. "Aunt K, you could never disappoint me. You've been there for me when I thought I had no one. You've been the role model in my life. You're not only my aunt, but you're also my friend. And friends don't turn their backs on each other . . . no matter what."

Kavana was overwhelmed by the love and support, but she was still hesitant to tell them everything. For years she had kept not one but two secrets—secrets filled with guilt and self-pity—carrying them around since the day before her twenty-fifth birthday. She hated herself for not being honest with not only her family but also the one she loved.

"Aidan deserves to know the truth," Kavana declared as she wiped the tears from her face. "He deserves to know why I pushed him away, why I was scared to take the next step with him." She paused and slowly exhaled. "He deserves to know that he was going to be a father . . . twice."

Karramis and Rhiannon stared at Kavana, eyes wide and their mouths hanging open.

Karramis blinked as she cleared her throat. "What do you mean Aidan was going to be a father twice?"

Removing another tear from her cheek with the back of her hand, Kavana answered with an unsteady voice. "I was pregnant twice. The first time, I didn't even know I was pregnant. And the other time, I was only a few weeks along."

"What happened?" Rhiannon asked caringly.

"I lost them."

Karramis wrapped her arms around her sister. "I'm so sorry."

Kavana hugged her back, talking over her shoulder. "I found out I was pregnant with the first one while I was miscarrying. I wasn't that far along, but I lost the baby a day . . ." She drew herself out of the hug. "A day before my twenty-fifth birthday."

"Oh my—You mean the birthday Aidan proposed?"

"Yeah." Kavana bowed her head. "And I lost the other baby two weeks before he proposed again."

"Oh, K, I'm so sorry." Karramis closed her eyes and released a heavy breath through her nose. "Talk about bad timing."

"Yeah, no kidding." Kavana forced a chuckle. "He was never really good at the timing thing."

Rhiannon wiped the tear trailing down her face, her voice cracking as she spoke. "I'm sorry, Aunt K. But why would you think I'd be disappointed in you? Or that Aidan would be mad? I mean, it wasn't your fault."

"Yes, it was." Kavana hesitated. "I didn't want them. I mean, I never wanted children. I never wanted to get married and start a family. I did this! I cursed myself. When I miscarried the first baby, I didn't even cry. I was just wandering around, confused and in a daze. And then when I found out I was pregnant again, I never told anyone because I still wasn't ready. I did this to myself. The universe punished me for not wanting those babies, and now I'm being punished for being stupid and not telling Aidan. I didn't want them at first, but after I lost them, I felt empty. Incomplete. Like a part of me had died with them."

Karramis pulled Kavana closer, squeezing her as her sister sobbed. "You didn't do this. It's not your fault, K. You weren't and *aren't* being punished. These things just happen sometimes. Nothing can stop this kind of thing from happening, not even magic. Is it fair? No. Is it something we can explain? No, not usually. But is it your fault? Absolutely not. Whether you wanted the babies or not, they were, and are, a part of you . . . and Aidan. They are something special that no one can ever take away from you. You may not have wanted those babies at first, but you would've loved them—you both would've. You both would have accepted the challenge and embraced it. There's nothing in this world that would make me think that you deserved this. It was simply an accident. No matter what, you *are* their mother. And though you never got to hold them, raise them, or see them grow up, you'll always be their mother, and every mother deserves to have that moment of happiness, even if it's short. Let go of the guilt. Let the resentment toward yourself go. Let the pain release back into the world, and let the joy and love prevail."

Kavana smiled as her crying slowed. "You've always had a way with words." She chuckled. "I guess you got the brains, and I was blessed with the good looks."

The three of them laughed.

Kavana stopped. "But what . . . what do I tell Aidan?"

"Start with the truth," Karramis said. "Tell him about the babies. Tell him about the bad timing and why this was the reason you turned down his proposals. Tell him how you were scared."

"Sorry to interrupt," Rhiannon interjected, "but can I ask you something, Aunt K?"

"Yeah, of course."

"What happened to you guys before you left Kiluemar?"

"Well, two weeks after I lost the second baby, Aidan proposed again. But I was just in a completely different place—both emotionally and mentally. So, I turned him down again. He wanted to know why, and I told him I wasn't suited to be a wife and that the women in this family are cursed, and he shouldn't want anything to do with me. I pushed him away."

"Why though?" Rhiannon asked.

"Because he deserved better."

"Aunt K, you're an amazing person, so why would you think that? And he clearly still cares for you."

"But I couldn't give him what he wanted. A wife. A commitment. I couldn't guarantee I'd live past thirty."

Karramis flashed her a perplexed glare. "What do you mean?"

"The women in this family don't have the best of luck with staying alive for very long. I mean, look at our mothers. I wasn't willing to let him suffer."

"K, it doesn't matter if you were married or not. He would've suffered if anything happened to you. He loves you."

"I know." Kavana lowered her eyes. "I guess I never really thought everything through back then."

"Well, do you still want to be with him?"

"Yeah. I mean, I love him. I've always loved him. I never wanted to break things off, but I was scared and stupid. I was afraid and lost in my own self-pity. I didn't want him to have to deal with everything I was going through. I loved him too much to do that to him."

"So you pushed him away instead?"

"Yeah," Kavana said resentfully. "I guess I really screwed things up, huh?"

Karramis stood up and pointed over to the front of the cabin. "I think you need to tell *him* all of this."

Footsteps rustled behind them as Aidan came to a stop, smiling over at Kavana.

Twisting back toward her sister, Kavana whispered, "But how? How can I face him after lying to him, especially about this?"

"You do it one step at a time. A journey cannot begin without the willingness to take the first step."

Kavana sighed, kissing her sister's cheek. "Thanks, Kare. You definitely have a way with words." She walked away, pausing and flashing Karramis a side grin. "But I definitely got the good looks."

Kavana headed over to Aidan and slid her hand into his. "I'm ready to talk now."

He smiled, interlocking his fingers with hers. "I'm ready to listen."

# Chapter 10

Reunion

Pavian led the group out of Kitra Forest, escorting them into the meadow southeast of the village. With a couple miles to go and dusk steadily approaching, he tapped his heels against his horse's side, urging the animal to move faster. Though he had traveled outside the village many times before in the dark, it was not the smartest idea. Kiluemar was no longer safe, and it had not been in a while, especially at night. Dangers lurked in the shadows and roamed around every corner. The realm was not the peaceful and friendly place it had once been. It was a free-for-all outside the boundaries of Caerwyn Village and Stoweward. No one was protected anymore. Anyone outside the safeguards placed around both communities was fair game to the creatures and animals craving fresh meat or blood.

"Let's go!" Pavian called over his shoulder. "Stop dillydallying!"

Behind him, atop one of the other three horses taken from the village, were James and Rhiannon.

James laughed at his uncle as they caught up with him. "Dillydallying?"

"What? It's a word."

Callie trotted forward, carrying Karramis and Will.

Leaning against Will, Karramis said with a chuckle, "Pavian might be in his forties, but his soul is about a hundred."

Pavian scowled lightheartedly at his sister as Kavana and Aidan emerged from the forest. They, too, were sharing a horse, preoccupied with their own conversation.

Pavian twitched his head in their direction. "What's going on with those two?"

Karramis glanced back. "They're working things out. Hopefully."

"What'd I miss?"

"I'm sure Kavana or Aidan will tell you about it later."

Pavian raised an eyebrow. "Right."

The horses moved through the tall foliage, their hooves pounding against the ground as their legs brushed across the grass.

"So, James," Rhiannon said, interrupting the silence. "I've been meaning to ask you something."

"What's that?"

"Where'd you get these from?" Rhiannon rubbed the faded scars along his arms as he clutched the reins. "It looks like you got into a fight with a cat and lost."

"I got them from, uhm . . . What are they called again, Uncle Pavian?"

"Sirens."

Will's gaze widened. "Sirens? You were attacked by sirens? Why were you even in the water? And when did this happen?"

"It happened when I astral projected."

"Wait!" Rhiannon exclaimed. "The *sirens* attacked you?"

"Yeah. The second time I astral projected, I landed in the water, and they attacked me—clawing at my arms and biting my chest and shoulders."

"*Water*? Why were sirens in the water?"

Pavian narrowed his eyes. "Well, where else would they be?"

"Uh, not in the water. Sirens are half-woman, half-bird. I mean, at least they are in Greek mythology."

James chuckled. "What are you, a walking encyclopedia for Greek mythology?"

"What?" Rhiannon shrugged. "I like mythology, and Greek just happens to be my favorite."

"I don't know about all that," James continued, "but these things were definitely in the water. They were hideous and vicious." He shuddered. "And they were trying to kill me."

The sirens of Kiluemar were far from the half-bird, half-woman beings described in the myths of ancient Greece. The ones from those stories were not the cursed creatures haunting the waters on the eastern side of the island.

Marryn, Mariska, and Malena were sisters born into a family of Water Witches. Though their family had elemental magic, the sisters wanted more. Wanting power and beauty, they would stop at nothing to get it, so they decided to sacrifice their husbands in a ritual to gain all their true desires. However, magic was never meant to be used for dark and selfish reasons, so some believed magic cursed them as punishment for their heinous acts.

Drowning their husbands in the ocean seemed like a simple plan, but using an element as a murder weapon with dark magic was never a good idea. Many others also fell victim to the consequences of using magic for the wrong reasons. Magic was loyal to those who possessed it, but it still had a way of making those pay for using its essence for evil purposes, especially taking a life.

The three sisters woke the next morning, gorgeous and young but unable to breathe. Drowning as oxygen filled their lungs, the sisters were dying. Rushing out to sea, the sisters threw themselves into the same waters they had drowned their husbands in, turning into hideous and frightening creatures.

Outside of the water, they were confident, beautiful, and enchanting, luring anyone around them with their breathtaking appearance. But they were bound to the sea, unable to survive out of the ocean waters for long, forced to return to their monstrous side if they wanted to live. With the bottom half of a shark, dark fish scales covering their upper human half, and a face so terrifying it could stop a heart, the sea sirens were born, stalking the waters and hunting for their next victim.

Rhiannon rubbed her furrowed brow. "Wait a minute. How is it possible these creatures were visible in our astral projections but people weren't? I mean, James saw the Air Dragon the first time and then the sirens. And when I was in mine, I saw winged horses and . . ."

Rhiannon held her breath and closed her eyes, her body tensing up.

Unable to hear her thoughts as her mind went blank, James asked, "And what?"

"I, uhm, I'm not sure what it was, actually."

"Describe it," Kavana said as she and Aidan came up beside them.

"Yeah, okay." Rhiannon gulped. "Uhm, well, it was a large black dog, or maybe it was a wolf. It had these glowing red eyes and crazy sharp teeth. It—"

"Raamko," the three adult siblings said in unison.

Rhiannon jerked her head between Pavian, Kavana, and her mother. "Wh-what's a Raamko?"

Karramis shifted her weight and readjusted herself. "It's a who, not a what. He's Merrick's pet."

The twins glanced over at their mother. "Pet?"

Kavana cleared her throat. "Yeah. We aren't really sure what the creature is exactly, but he's lived in Casteya Castle for centuries. We think Merrick found the creature and brought him here."

"All we know about this *thing*," Karramis went on, "is that he can only see at night. His eyes seem to be sensitive to any kind of light. He also eats anything and everything he can sink his teeth into but seems to prefer magical beings over animals. I'm guessing he's some cursed being who has a grudge against magic. But that's only a theory."

"Okay, so to get back to my other question," Rhiannon said curiously. "Why were they able to see us, and we were able to see them, but no one else was visible?" She paused, aiming her next question at James. "Did you see anyone in your astral projections?"

"No, actually, I didn't. Well, aside from you."

"Okay, see what I mean? Explain that."

Pavian puckered his mouth to the side and dropped his gaze to the ground. "Hmm, well, I'm not really sure. The only people I've ever known who could astral project or travel did it completely. When they created an astral body and jumped into another place, they were there a hundred percent. I've never met anyone who only did it partially. I mean, if you two did it, then I assume it's possible, it's just I've never met another person who could. You either astral project completely or you don't."

Aidan joined the conversation, directing his question over to Pavian. "Could it have had somethin' to do with them not actually havin' their powers?"

"Maybe. We still don't know why they were able to astral project to begin with, so maybe once we figure that out, we can figure out the rest."

Rhiannon scoffed. "I sure hope so because"—James joined in, the two voices echoing together—"this is getting weird."

"Getting weird?" Will forced a chuckle. "I reckon we've passed weird and have bloody well arrived at extraordinary and downright eerie. I'm not quite sure if in that order, though."

"What do you mean?" James and Rhiannon asked.

"That! That right there. You two being able to communicate simultaneously, and the powers you possess even without having magic. I mean, I've always been apprehensive and terrified of the prophecy, especially after learning about the part regarding your arrival, but this . . . Seeing it all firsthand is extraordinary. I fancy our odds with Merrick once you two learn how to control your powers."

A crease formed between Rhiannon's eyes, a section of her father's words pulling her attention. "Wait, the part regarding our—"

"Speaking of our magic," James said in a deep tone, his voice billowing over his sister's, "when will all our powers fully arrive? I know some are back, but we can't just have some simple elemental magic and the ability to talk to dragons, right?"

Pavian kept his eyes on the sun as it dipped behind the horizon. "It will take time for all your powers to fully arrive at the surface. Your magic most definitely returned to you as soon as the portals opened—something I personally witnessed firsthand. But pinpointing each power and trying to control them is going to take time. It won't happen overnight."

Growls and wails of animals erupted, bouncing off the ground and echoing across the dark blue sky. Everyone scanned the area, searching for the source of the bone-chilling commotion.

"Wh-what was that?" Rhiannon asked, forcing herself to swallow the fear rising in her throat.

Kavana grasped the reins next to Aidan's hands. "I'd rather not find out."

Pavian kicked his heels against his horse. "Agreed!"

All the horses raced toward the soft lights coming from Caerwyn Village, entering under the stone archway as everyone pulled back on their reins and slowed to a stop.

Karramis hunched over, squeezing her midsection and pinching her eyes and lips together.

Feeling her body tense up as she buckled over, Will asked with a heavy tone of concern, "Are you all right, darling?"

The others faced them and awaited her answer.

Karramis took a few shallow breaths. "Yeah."

Will slid off Callie. "No, you're not."

"No, really, I'm fine. It's just that was a rough ride." She reached her arms out. "Help me down please."

Will aided her off the horse. "Are you positive you'll be able to walk the rest of the way?"

"I think walking might do me some good because sitting like that was starting to hurt."

"Why didn't you say something?"

"It wasn't that bad."

"You know, Kare," Pavian said, jumping from his horse, "it's okay to admit when you're hurt. You don't have to be strong all the time."

"Ha!" Kavana exclaimed. "That's the pot calling the kettle black." She grabbed Aidan's hand and dismounted. "She gets it from you, ya know. Well, you and Dad, of course."

"Uhm, sorry to interrupt . . ." James threw his leg behind him, his feet landing against the ground. "But are we all going to ignore what just happened back there?"

Pavian turned to him. "With what?"

"What do you mean 'with what'?" Rhiannon leaned over as James helped her down. "Those noises. What were those noises?"

Kavana wrapped her arms around her niece's shoulders. "Like I said before, I'd rather not find out."

"You're not at all scared of whatever is out there?"

"Nope, not in here."

"We're safe here," Will added. "The village has a spell around it. It only allows humans through and certain magical creatures like elves, dryads, and pega—I mean, winged horses."

He winked at Rhiannon, and they both smiled.

James glanced up at the open sky above them. "Yeah, but what about *over* the village?"

"The spell is a dome. The magic rises up from the ground and covers the whole village. The same for Stoweward."

"That's good. Uhm, but what classifies as a human? I mean, are werewolves humans? Wait, are werewolves real? What about vampires? Are they real? Do the two really have a rivalry going on?"

The five adults laughed.

"What?" James glanced around at them. "Hey, these are valid questions."

Kavana grabbed Aidan's hand. "I think we should get going. Dad is expecting us."

Pavian nodded. "Yeah. I think if Karramis is walking, we all should."

"Agreed," Will and the twins said.

Karramis pulled her shoulders back. "Guys, I'm fine." She winced, grasping her side. "Okay, maybe I'm not fine."

James followed behind Pavian. "How far is this place? I don't think she should walk too far like this."

Kavana turned to Aidan. "Where are we meeting them?"

"Yer father told me to bring you all to the Grand Hall."

"Why there?"

"I'm not sure."

"Well, that's good," Will said, wrapping his arm around Karramis's waist. "That's much closer than Zarrius's place."

"How far do we have to go?" James asked his father.

"Not far. Just up the road."

The seven of them made their way down the dirt path as it curved through the center of the village. Buildings with cobblestone exteriors and dark wood pieces along the walls lined the streets. Warped shingles lay precariously against the gambrel-shaped roofs as smoke billowed from some of the chimneys reaching high above the rooftops. Glimmers of yellow light beamed through the small rectangular cathedral-style windows.

James stared wide-eyed at the beautiful medieval architecture. "Wow, it's like we stepped back in time."

"Pretty cool, eh?" Aidan slowed down, allowing James to catch up with him. "And to answer yer questions, yes, werewolves are real, and yes, they're human. In the magical community, a human is someone who has blood pumpin' through their veins, a heartbeat, one who must eat to survive, and someone who can reproduce."

"That's pretty specific."

Kavana hurried in front of the twins, turning around and facing them but still moving forward. "Well, that leads us to your other question. Vampires are, in fact, very real. We actually have quite a few here—at least I think we do. Now, contrary to what you may have read in books or watched on TV, vampires are very much still alive. They have to die to become vampires, but once reborn they still have a heartbeat and blood pumping through them. They can even be killed, but they can live forever if they feed. Therefore, they need to eat to survive. The one thing they can't do, however, is reproduce. Vampires no longer have the reproductive *internal* elements to create new life." She lowered her voice. "They still have the means to satisfy their . . . carnal needs though." Her voice returned to normal. "And no, werewolves and vampires are not natural rivals, but some of them here are. Although, most of the time they try to avoid one another."

The group stopped in front of a massive stone building. A wide set of steps climbed up, stopping at a pristine white marble archway. The shallow entryway led to a rounded wooden door decorated with large iron hinges and inlaid with bronze studs. The structure towered above them, built out of smooth gray stones and whitewash plaster. High above the door was a long horizontal and rectangular stained-glass window adorned with the five elements: white swirls circling around each other, a lush oak tree, gray-and-dark purple clouds, raging flames, and waves.

The door squeaked as it opened into an extra-long room that stopped at a wall housing an enormous marble fireplace. The stone room was cold and dingy, and a draft swept through the hall and over an exceptionally long table and various wooden chairs. The ceiling rose high above them with its decorative arched wooden beams. Along both sides of the room were more stained-glass windows, but these were long and vertical, stretching from the bottom of the beams and ending a few feet off the floor. Each represented the four natural elements, similar to the window at the front of the hall.

"Where is everyone?" Kavana asked Aidan.

"I don't know. They should be here."

"Maybe we're late."

"No, I told Zarrius we'd be here around dark."

Pavian wiped his finger along the dusty table. "Well, then we must be early. What happened here? This place hasn't been used in years."

"Your father stopped the meetings a few years ago," Will said.

"Why?"

"I never asked."

James pulled out a chair for his mother. "What meetings?"

Pavian rubbed the dust from his finger. "The guard meetings."

Rhiannon wandered around, oblivious to the discussion filling the empty hall. Reaching the fireplace, she walked inside of it and glanced up through the chimney. She traced her fingers along a sizeable carved imprint along the back wall, analyzing the strange symbol imbedded into the stone.

The emblem was square and leaning on one of its points. Positioned along the east and west sides were two ovals. A diamond sat in the middle of the square, cutting through a portion of each oval. Two smaller diamonds lay next to the tips of the center diamond, each nestled between the two ovals. Four half circles rested next to each point of the square, and two half diamonds were positioned at the top and bottom of the diamond in the middle of the symbol.

A rush of calm filled Rhiannon's body, and she smiled, placing her fingertip in the carved lines again. The symbol radiated a warmth to it, bringing her a sense of peace and comfort but with a lingering sadness. There was something about this strange and unique symbol that filled her with these contradicting emotions.

"Hey," Rhiannon said quietly.

A gust tore down the chimney, blowing a bone-chilling breeze through the hall. It traveled up her spine like hundreds of tiny spiders scurrying along her back. She moved away from the fireplace as her expression fell and the hair on her neck stood up. She swallowed, unable to finish her thought as her stomach tightened.

"What's wrong?" James asked, making his way over to her.

The doors of the hall swung open and crashed against the wall.

Rhiannon jumped, meeting the deafening boom as a fire erupted along the small pile of logs still in the fireplace.

James narrowed his eyes at her and pointed at the raging flames. "Did you just do that?"

"I—I don't know. I mean, I don't think so." She paused, staring at the fire. "No, I couldn't . . ." Frowning, she shrugged. "Maybe?"

"Sorry about that," Zarrius announced as he entered the hall. "I forget my own strength sometimes."

Pavian stood up straight, drew out his chest, and presented a hand. "Hello, sir, it's good to see you again."

"Hello, Son." Zarrius shook his hand before pulling him into a hug. "It's great to see you." He patted his son's arm. "You look good, Son. Real good."

Kavana squealed, excitement forcing her to fidget.

Zarrius's attention moved to his impatient and animated daughter. He drew out his arms, and Kavana crashed into his chest.

"Oh!" Zarrius exclaimed as a chuckling grunt exploded from him. "Someone's missed me."

"Of course, I missed you, Dad."

Zarrius grasped her face. "My beautiful daughter." He kissed her forehead. "I've missed you too." His loving gaze moved between Kavana and Pavian. "Why didn't you tell me you were back sooner?"

Pavian knitted his brows, his posture domineering. "We had to wait for Karramis to recover, sir. We—"

Lifting a hand, Zarrius cut him off as his eyes stopped on Karramis. His shoulders sagged, making his posture slouch, the muscles in his body overwhelmed with relief. His stride was steady as he made his way over to her, dropping to his knees and grasping the sides of her face.

Karramis met his watery gaze, the emotion in her eyes matching his as tightness pulled in her chest. "Hi, Dad."

"Oh, my girl," Zarrius whispered, choking back the urge to cry. "My little girl. You're alive." He wiped the tears trailing down her bruised cheek. "Don't cry." He hugged her. "You're home now."

Karramis squeezed him. "I've missed you so much."

"I've missed you too. More than you know." He gently pulled her away from him. "I can't believe it. It's a miracle. How? How are you alive? How did this happen?"

"I don't know. I'm still trying to figure that out."

"Don't. Don't question it. I know that's hard for you to do, but just think of it as a miracle. You're alive. You're home. That's all that matters."

"That's what he said," Karramis said, smiling up at Will.

Zarrius stood up and presented his hand. "It's good to see you, Will."

"It's a pleasure to see you too, sir."

"We all thought you were dead."

"Hey, Dad." Kavana stepped closer. "Where's everyone else? Aidan said you were going to invite a few others."

"I didn't want to overwhelm you all, so it's just a few people, but I told them to wait a bit first."

"Why?"

"Because there are a few people who should get priority when it comes to this homecoming."

"Like who?" Pavian asked curiously with a brow raised.

"Like her," Zarrius answered, twitching his head in the direction of the door.

A slender woman with long black hair and beautiful bronze skin entered the hall. Stopping in the entrance, she fidgeted with her fingers as her big brown eyes searched the room. An enchanting grin fell across her face as her gaze stopped on Pavian.

Pavian gasped. "Raina?"

The corners of his mouth rose, a deep smile pressing his cheeks into his beaming eyes as he rushed over to her. He passionately clasped his hand around the base of her neck and kissed her, drawing her body into his.

Kavana grinned. "Well, that didn't take long."

"Shh!" Aidan whispered as he nudged her.

She raised a shoulder and flashed him a playful grin. "What?"

"Mommy?" a little boy called as he entered the hall and grabbed Raina's hand.

Pavian jerked his head down at the boy, letting go of Raina and stumbling backward. Staring down at the small boy with dark brown hair and eyes, Pavian's heart sank, crashing into the pit of his stomach and making him nauseous. He moved his eyes over to Raina and back to the young boy, his shoulders dropping as a heavy sigh fell from his lips.

Pavian backed away. "Mommy?"

Raina stepped after him. "Yes, this is—"

"Oh! I'm sorry. I didn't mean—I thought since you—Since my father—"

"Pavian," Raina said, urging him to stop.

"I didn't mean any disrespect to you, or your son—"

"Pavian!" Zarrius yelled. "Would you let her talk, Son?"

Pavian shifted his eyes to the ground. "Yes, sir."

"Pavian . . ." Raina paused, hoping he would meet her gaze, but as he stared at the ground, she continued, "I'd like you to meet Liam—"

"You named him after me?" Pavian asked, narrowing his eyes and shaking his head dubiously. "Why . . . why would you give him my middle name?"

"Because he's *your* son."

Surprised, James blurted under his breath. "Well, I didn't see *that* coming."

"Shh!" Rhiannon insisted quietly.

The hall went silent as everyone stared at the new and reunited family. With their eyes glossed over in shock, they watched quietly.

A heavy gasp escaped from Pavian as his pulse quickened, an overwhelming wave of delight and surprise rushing over him.

"Liam, sweetie," Raina said, lowering herself down to her son's level, "I'd like you to meet your daddy."

Pavian knelt beside her, and the young boy crashed into his chest, throwing his arms around his father's neck. Holding his son, Pavian smiled at Raina, tears welling up in his eyes as he spotted his mother's ring on her finger.

"See, this takes priority, don't you think?" Zarrius asked, placing his hand on Pavian's shoulder. "Congratulations, Son."

Pavian lifted Liam into his arms and glanced over at Raina. "How?"

Raina laughed, amused by his question. "What do you mean how? Do you really need a lesson in how this happened?"

"No, that's not what I mean. I know *how*, it's just—"

"I found out I was pregnant a month after you left. After your dad found out I was pregnant, he asked if it was yours."

Pavian shifted his attention to his father. "You knew about us?"

"Of course, I knew. Did you really think I wouldn't find out about you two? I make it my duty to know all the goings on in the realm, especially when it involves my children."

"How long did you know about us?"

"I found out about a year after you two started dating. You hid it pretty well, but I put the pieces together."

"Why didn't you say anything?"

"The same reason I let Karramis go on her escapades to London for so long and why I never confronted Kavana about her random trips to Stoweward at the beginning of her relationship with Aidan. You were all old enough to make your own decisions, and I had to let you choose your own lives. As long as you were safe and happy, that was all I needed."

Pavian hugged his father. "I'm sorry I kept it from you. I just thought—"

"It's okay, Son. I know why you did it. That's the reason I never brought it up. I can be a little . . . overprotective and overbearing at times."

Kavana let out a guttural laugh followed by an exaggerated cough as Zarrius glared in her direction, making his way over to her.

"Sorry, Dad, I didn't mean—"

"Yes, you did. You and your sister"—he gazed over at Karramis—"have never shied away from speaking your mind."

Two figures shifted next to the fireplace, causing Zarrius to glance up. James smiled and waved at him awkwardly.

"My goodness," Zarrius said. "Is this them? Is this James and Rhiannon?"

James playfully wrapped his arm around his sister. "Yep, it's us, the one and only." He leaned his head over and lowered his voice. "Or is it the *two* and only? Never mind, not important."

Zarrius met them by the fireplace. "You two are perfect." He hugged them. "My first grandchildren are alive. I can't believe it, it's another miracle." He examined their faces as he cupped their cheeks. "You two look so much like your parents. I can't believe you're here, and that I'm meeting you for the first time. I mean, you're both practically adults now."

Karramis twisted in the chair to face the twins and her father. "You didn't see them when they were here eight years ago?"

"No," Will answered. "The only ones who saw them were Kavana and Pavian. He knew about them being here, but he never got a chance to see them before we sent them back through."

"It was probably for the best," Zarrius admitted. "There's no telling what would've happened if Merrick had found out they were here."

The flames in the fireplace raged and sent waves of heat through the stone room as the air grew thick and dry.

Pavian fanned his shirt. "Wow, it's getting hot in here."

Aidan glared curiously at the flames. "Who started the fire?"

James announced proudly, "Oh. Well, that would be my awesome sister . . . and her *magic*."

Voices erupted and overlapped as the various tones echoed with surprise. Rhiannon remained quiet, attempting to understand her newfound powers, the awkwardness she was experiencing with all eyes on her, and the delightful reunion unfolding inside the hall. Her skin was pale, but her cheeks were rosy. Her anxious expression did not match the smile on her face. Everyone stared at her, waiting for her to say the words lingering on the edge of her lips.

James addressed the others, his voice lively and robust. "Okay, so Rhiannon is stuck in a perplexed state of mind at the moment, but once she organizes her chaotic thoughts, she'll be right back with us."

Zarrius peered between the twins and scowled back at the others. "What the heck is he talking about?"

Changing the subject, Rhiannon shifted her attention over to the fireplace. "What's that symbol on the back wall?"

Karramis slid her chair back, the legs scraping against the stone floor. "That's the symbol of the prophecy."

"What does it mean?"

"No one knows for sure. The young boy who drew it isn't alive anymore. He was the one, along with his mother, who foretold the first verse of the prophecy."

"The *first* verse?" the twins exclaimed, alarm racing across their faces.

"Yeah," Will said. "Didn't you two know there was more to the prophecy?"

"No!"

Pavian and Kavana shrugged as the twins stared mystified at them, both flashing an embellished grin.

"Well, we never got that far," Pavian admitted.

"Yeah," Kavana added, "and I only told Rhiannon the paraphrased version of the first part because . . . well, to be honest, because I kinda forgot it."

Rhiannon made her way over to her parents. "Okay, someone needs to start talking about this other verse. Like now." She turned to her father. "And I also want to know what you meant earlier when you said the prophecy predicted our arrival."

# Chapter 11

### The Created

*Centuries ago*

Days after Mikel Dorrasa uttered the same warning as his mother, Sadora, he caused an even more puzzling mystery to the ordeal plaguing the realm. A strange symbol believed to be the emblem of the prophecy—a full representation of destiny unforeseen—haunted his mind, cursing the young boy with visions of this image.

Forcing him to heed caution to the dangers soon arriving in the realm, an unknown source placed Mikel in a trance on many occasions, compelling him to draw the forewarning linked to the prophecy. Unfortunately, no one understood what the symbol meant—not even Mikel. He drew hundreds of pictures throughout his life but never knew what the symbol signified, nor did he ever remember drawing any of them.

Once Mikel died in his old age, the residents of the realm forgot about the prophecy and the symbol, tucking his drawings away, never to be seen again. But centuries later, the prophecy would return, and with another verse.

~

*Over fifteen years ago*

Karramis had never believed the prophecy was about her. Although she had been born among ashes and soot, she was far from a savior. And despite being alive among the smoke and having powers beyond the average folk, her magic was nowhere near strong enough to stop the evil destined to take over and ruin the realm. She was only twenty-three—not exactly the prime age to be fighting evil—and had a troublesome inability to control most of her powers. However, just two months after Karramis and Will married, an incident occurred, creating a domino effect and confirming the theory about Karramis and the prophecy, but in a way no one could have predicted. The events following this fateful accident would prove to be a blessing and a curse to the young couple.

Forced to continue with her training, Karramis arrived early one morning with Will, who was required to obtain physical training since he had no defensive powers. Guardians were not the only ones who needed to learn to fight so did those who could not defend themselves from physical threats.

Tenarick was most in favor of all creatures in the realm having more than just magic to guard themselves in case things took a turn for the worse. Elves were fond of being prepared for anything and never backed down from a fight. Originally created with the power to enhance the natural flow of an element, these gentle creatures had thrived among nature for thousands of years, hidden in plain sight within the non-magical world. But as other magical beings, like nymphs, mermaids, and witches, became more abundant, elves became less powerful. Eventually, the elves' magic weakened and faded from the bloodlines.

Training was a necessity to the elves, and Tenarick pushed Zarrius to make it a requirement for all Guardians, as well as all humans unable to use their powers to fight off the dangers living within the realm.

Pavian was a master at fighting. He preferred a long sword over the other weapons but never had to use it on another creature. Kavana enjoyed training because it allowed her to blow off steam, but she preferred hand-to-hand combat over weapons. She was a supporter of women being able to defend themselves with the sheer power of their physical strength. Karramis agreed with her sister but was never able to master the coordination needed to fight back with her fists. In fact, Karramis was awkward and clumsy when it came to any type of fighting. Guardians were supposed to be natural fighters, but unfortunately, Karramis lacked that gene.

Instead of fighting, Karramis practiced her magic during training days, focusing her attention on mastering her ability to control her telekinesis, which was her strongest defensive power, minus her fire magic. But again, her witch abilities were wildly unpredictable, and using them scared her, so suppressing them seemed like a better idea than trying to control the intimidating power.

Will did not agree with fighting at first. He was a pacifist, a true advocate of live and let live. However, residing in a world filled with vampires, sirens, ogres, trolls, and other deadly creatures made learning how to defend yourself a priority, especially to a man who had no physical powers, only mental. Will could not rely on the dragons to defend him if a problem should arise, and he did not want to live in a world where he could not protect Karramis as well. She was more powerful, but he never wanted to let her down if it came time for him to protect her. And that morning he would come face-to-face with his fear, thus having to prove to her, and himself, he would do anything to keep her safe.

The morning sessions commenced like all the others, everyone choosing a partner and picking their weapon of choice. Will teamed up with Caleb Kittleman, a new arrival to the realm. He, too, was not much for fighting, but only having the ability to protect himself to the full extent of his powers once a month was not reassuring to the young man or his two younger brothers. Their instructor for the day was a hefty but agile young dwarf named Quinian. Being the tallest dwarf in the known history, his average height and menacing appearance intimidated the more reluctant students. Quinian did not seem like the type to put up with excuses nor go easy on his students. Working next to Will and the others, Karramis practiced her powers with

Pavian. Never trusting anyone more when it came to sharpening her magic, she always worked with her brother.

Pausing for a break, most of the students and instructors waited around, drinking water and chatting with each other. Karramis and Will stood with Kavana, Pavian, and Tenarick, discussing next week's schedule and location as the water in Guardian Lake sloshed along the muddy shores.

The area was quiet, and their low voices were inaudible outside the huddled circle. Karramis erupted in a loud chuckle, her contagious laughter infecting the others as they mimicked her volume. She caressed Will's arm and stepped in front of him. Leaning in for a kiss, she lurched forward in shock, her body jerking in panic. An unexpected pain pierced through her back and chest like a bolt of lightning.

Will's brows drew together, the predominant crease between his eyes pinched with concern as her eyes glazed over. "Karramis?"

She gasped, choking on a mouthful of blood as it shot out from her lips with a gagging cough. Blood flowed from her body and soaked her shirt as Will peered down at an arrow sticking out of the left side of her chest. Karramis's body grew cold, the life draining from her as every inhale grew shallow and the pain started to fade. Her pierced heart thumped against the wood of the shaft, slowing with each beat. She closed her eyes and fell into his arms.

"Karramis!" Will shook her in a panic as he lowered her to the ground. "No, no! Don't close your eyes! You hear me? Stay awake!"

Tenarick knelt beside them as another elf, Alfina, rushed over, both ripping pieces of material from their clothing. Rolling Karramis onto her side, they pressed the torn sections of cloth against both sides of the wound as a stream of blood poured from her mouth. Quinian and Pavian ran in the opposite direction and raced into the trees.

"Where're they going?" Will exclaimed, terror exploding in his voice.

Kavana crashed to her knees and held her sister's head. "To get the horses!"

Tenarick tapped Alfina's shoulder and pointed over to the trees. "Get the medic bag!" He forced the compress harder against the wound. "We have to do something or she's going to die!"

Will panted, observing the color draining from Karramis's face and pulling a vial from his pocket. "She needs to drink this!"

"What is that?" Tenarick asked, carefully breaking a section of the arrow off and tossing it aside.

"Dragon blood."

"Why do you have that?"

"In case of an emergency."

Tenarick was reluctant but quickly nodded in agreement.

Will poured the contents of the vial into her mouth. "Drink this, darling."

She choked, gagging as droplets spit from her mouth.

Forcing her lips together, Will whispered, "Listen to me, you're not dying today. You hear me? Not today. Come back to me. Please, just swallow it."

The blood burned as it traveled down her throat, reminding Karramis of the first time she had alcohol. It bubbled as it reached her stomach, the acid and blood battling it out against each other as the gassy remnants flowed up her chest and esophagus. Her weak body twitched, her muscles convulsing as the magic within her shot outward. Waves of electricity erupted inside her as a powerful jolt shocked her heart, the magic fighting against the dying organ.

"She swallowed it," Kavana said, letting out a sigh of relief as she cried. "Is it working?"

Will glared down at Karramis, cradling her as she lay unconscious. "I . . . I'm not sure."

Tenarick checked her pulse. "She has a heartbeat. It's faint, but it's still there. But we need to get her—"

"Get her on!" Pavian yelled, his horse galloping across the open field.

Kavana, Will, and Tenarick lifted her off the ground, Alfina helping after dropping the medical bag as she reached their sides. Pavian grabbed hold of her as they lifted her up.

"Watch out for the rest of the arrow," Tenarick said, letting go of the bloody material.

Pavian wrapped his free arm around her and resumed compression, holding onto the horse with his legs as the animal took off. "Got it!"

"Will!" Quinian called, sliding from another horse as it skidded to a stop. "Get on!"

Will leapt onto the back of the horse and raced behind Pavian.

Karramis was alive, but barely. The arrow had pierced her heart, leaving behind significant damage that could not be repaired by magic or surgery. However, the dragon blood aided in keeping her alive as she slipped into a coma. It had not healed her but had maintained her heartbeat and stopped the bleeding. Despite the phenomenon of Karramis's unusual situation, no one was sure if she would ever wake up again.

Days dragged on, but Will never left her side. He wanted to be there when she woke up, something he was certain would happen. Remaining positive, he never allowed the fear to take over. He believed the miracle of her surviving was meant to happen, and she would eventually wake up. Will never doubted Karramis and her ability to fight. She could not give up now, especially since she was not only fighting for her own life but also for the life of her unborn child.

Alfina had discovered the pregnancy a few days after Karramis fell into the coma and notified Will right away. His joy was overcome with dread, fearing the repercussions of his actions. What if he was banned from his home? What if he would never be allowed to see his child born or get to raise it? Would using dragons' blood to save Karramis cause him to be ripped away from her? But despite this worry building inside him, Will was thankful. His decision to use the blood saved his wife, and his choice to use the blood of all four elemental dragons had most likely protected his child as well.

After learning Karramis was part of a prophecy, Will did not want to take any chances and lose her like Zarrius had lost Keya. Therefore, if he was going to break the rules, he would shatter them in a big way. By placing the blood of each elemental dragon into the vial he carried around, he had accepted the consequences linked to his actions.

~

After two harrowing weeks, Karramis woke up a few days before Christmas, unaware of the events following the arrow to her chest. In fact, despite the bandages, and grogginess lingering in her head, she deemed herself perfect—sensing no pain or ill effects of the injury.

Karramis was surprised by the news of her pregnancy, but even more shocked to find out she was expecting twins. But, like Will, her happiness was masked behind fear. Still suffering from a hole in her heart, Karramis was somehow still alive despite her body being unable to heal the injury. The dragons' blood inside her was her lifeline, pumping through her veins and pushing her heart to beat, while stopping her blood from escaping the vital organ.

Dragon blood was unpredictable, never affecting anyone the same way. But in all the books and archives about magic, nothing like this had ever happened in the past. Even in the magical community, being kept alive but not healing was unheard of. This rare magic was never meant to be used for purposes beyond the reasons it had been created for, and history had proven this theory. In addition to being fickle with the magical creatures who consumed it, dragon blood had no effects on non-magical beings. It could heal those containing magic, but only to an extent—fatal wounds were uncurable. And, other than dragons themselves, their blood could not heal an immortal.

Worried for the safety of Karramis and the babies, Alfina insisted Karramis be on bed rest. The middle-aged elf was hesitant to allow her out of the infirmary, fearing the magic keeping her alive would fade over time. But the magic never weakened, and the expectant mother was anxious, wanting to birth her children in the comfort of her home. Alfina reluctantly allowed her to leave but insisted she be monitored at all times.

As Karramis and Will waited for their children to make their grand entrance, they were met by an unexpected guest at their front door.

A short woman stood in the doorway, the dark circles under her eyes making her appear older. "I'm sorry to bother you, but my name is Marie Andralae."

Karramis rose from the couch, wobbling over to stand beside Will. "Yeah, I know you. You're a seer, right?"

"Yes," Marie said, holding back a yawn.

Will flashed them both a concerned scowl. "A seer?"

Marie nodded. "Yes. And I have to show you both something." She handed Karramis an old wrinkled parchment. "I was going to go to Zarrius, but I think this is something you two need to see, not him."

Karramis analyzed the aged piece of paper, confused by the two symbols etched onto it—both identical but drawn centuries apart.

"Flip it over," Marie whispered, her voice unsteady.

Karramis turned it over and read the words scribbled on the back out loud.

*Given to one and yet another,*
*a powerful creation bound together*
*Carried within a vessel born of fire,*
*conceived by love with a true desire*
*The oldest magic within the heir,*
*protect a power mighty and rare*
*Magic will flow within the veins,*
*for an arrival is all that remains*
*When the stars lie across the sky,*
*and distant clouds rumble and cry*
*Before the eve of the longest day,*
*and waves along the shore pull away*
*When wild orchids bloom across barren meadows,*

*and the half-moon peeks from the shadows*
*A power stronger than those before,*
*rest in the hands of fate no more*
*For all magic will fade,*
*awaiting the end of this destined trade*

"What is this?" Will asked as the pit of his stomach twisted.

"I think it's another verse to the prophecy," Marie said, her eyes staying on the parchment as thunder clapped in the distance.

Karramis studied the symbols. "Where'd you get this?"

"I don't know." Marie shrugged and shook her head. "I don't remember anything from the last few hours, and I have no idea where the paper came from or why that symbol and those words are written in my handwriting."

Karramis read the words again, her eyes stopping in the bottom corner on a set of barely legible letters drawn in ink. "What's M-D-C-C-X-L-V-I-I?"

"I don't know." Marie shrugged again, the distress on her face pulling tighter. "I—I didn't do that part. That's not my handwriting."

Karramis dropped the paper and grasped her stomach as fluid gushed down her leg. Backing away from the doorframe, Marie's face went pale, the color fading as the circles under her eyes grew darker.

"The prophecy was right—" Marie jumped as lightning flashed behind her. Grasping her chest, she announced, "They're coming."

~

*The present*

The hall was quiet as Rhiannon and James sat next to each other, their parents leaning into the table across from them as the others sat quietly listening.

Rhiannon rested her cheek against her palm, her eyes focused aimlessly on the table. She opened her mouth to talk but paused.

"What?" Karramis asked. "What were you about to say?"

"I'm . . . I'm not really sure where to begin." Rhiannon exhaled, leaning back into the chair. "I mean, I have a lot of questions."

"Yeah," James added. "Okay. So, first of all, how are you so sure the prophecy is about us? It didn't seem that obvious. At least, not to me."

Rhiannon nodded. "Right. Me either. Can someone please explain?"

"Yes," Karramis said. "It's quite simple. The first part is about me because I was born among the same fire that killed my mother. And I carried you inside my body, my vessel. And you two were conceived with love. A true love, driven by desire."

The twins scrunched their faces. "Eww."

Will laughed. "Hey, you two wouldn't exist without that love."

"Eww," the twins repeated, drawing out the word.

"Anyway," Karramis continued, "when I was pregnant with you, I was given the oldest power."

James leaned into the table. "The dragons' blood, right?"

"Yes. But the part that really made me know it was also about you two was the section about the arrival. 'When the stars lie across the sky, and distant clouds rumble and cry.' There was a storm off the coast that night, but the sky above the island was clear. 'Before the eve of the longest day, and waves along the shore pull away.' You were born on the day before the eve of the summer solstice—the longest day of the year. And there was a low tide that night. Finally, 'When wild orchids bloom across barren meadows, and the half-moon peeks from the shadows.' The morning after you were born, flowers bloomed throughout Shadow Forest, a forest which hadn't seen new life in centuries." She paused, meeting Rhiannon's thoughtful gaze. "And to answer the question bouncing around in your head, we aren't sure what the rest means exactly. Only that you both have some kind of powerful magic. We just don't know what."

Rhiannon lifted a brow. "How'd you know I was thinking that?"

"I could see it on your face. You've always analyzed everything, even as a kid. You were always an overthinker, to say the least."

"She still is," James said with a grin.

Rhiannon scoffed. "Would you get out of my head."

"Sorry, I can't help it, you tend to be a loud thinker. Plus, you always have the best questions."

"Speaking of that . . ." Rhiannon leaned into the table, mirroring her brother's relaxed posture. "Here's another one. Why did we have to leave as babies?"

"That was my doing," Will admitted. "After finding out there was another part of the prophecy, I panicked. I was worried once Merrick learnt there was another verse, he'd come after you. I had no way to protect you, and I knew there was no way to guarantee your safety until you both developed your powers. I'm the one who convinced your mum to run and hide until we were sure you'd be able to protect yourselves."

Karramis grasped Will's hand. "I didn't want to leave, but I knew he was right. You two were defenseless, and there was no way to protect you both at all times. So, we left. I was too weak from labor to use my own portal, so I traveled through one of the realm's and went to England, the closest thing I had to a second home. There was a safe house there, one I was very familiar with. I only knew about it because I had planned to run away and live there if your dad wasn't accepted here. I even stashed money there during the early part of our relationship, just in case. But I forgot all about it once your dad moved to Kiluemar, which actually worked out in my favor later on since I forgot to bring any money with me when we left."

Zarrius gulped, a strain pinching his throat. "We all thought you were dead, Karramis. For so many years. We thought you *all* were dead."

"My apologies," Will said with sadness in his voice. "It's just . . . if anyone knew the truth . . . I couldn't take the chance with Lucas."

Rhiannon peered at her father. "Not to be morbid, but how did you explain the lack of bodies? I mean, didn't you all want a funeral for us?"

Karramis smiled. "See, an overthinker."

"I told everyone I burnt your bodies," Will answered.

"What?" Rhiannon flinched in disgust. "Why would you do that?"

"I didn't really do it."

"Well, obviously, but why say that? Why not bury us?"

Zarrius tapped his fingers on the table. "We don't bury bodies on the island anymore."

"Why?" James asked.

"Because when we buried them, some of the creatures would dig them up and eat them, so we have to burn the bodies now."

Rhiannon wrinkled her nose. "Eww. Gross. They would eat them?"

"Yes," Will said. "Which worked in my favor at the time because they never questioned the fact there were no bodies."

James shifted in his chair, directing his attention to his mother. "Was Merrick really going to kill us as babies?"

"No. He would've had to wait until you had your powers."

"Why?"

"Well," Zarrius cut in, "because you can't take something that isn't there."

"What's that mean?" Rhiannon asked.

"Even when someone is born with magic—possessing it like witches and Guardians—it isn't really present. It's dormant, hidden deep inside the person. Magic will stay locked away until the person containing it is fully ready for it."

"Right," Karramis said as voices grew louder outside. "He wouldn't have killed you, but he might have killed us to get to you, so he could kidnap you and just wait until your powers arrived. Or maybe he would've just waited until you were older. We don't really know for sure."

Pavian took Liam, who was asleep in Raina's arms, and headed for the door. Raina followed as Kavana and Aidan trailed closely behind. As Pavian opened the door, the voices outside accompanied multiple footsteps shuffling down the path.

Rhiannon twisted her body sideways. "What's going on out there?"

"Let's go find out," James said, rushing enthusiastically from his chair.

Everyone stood at the top of the steps outside the hall as familiar faces appeared from the shadows, the others finally arriving to welcome them all home.

# Chapter 12

## Welcome Party

James and Rhiannon stayed on the steps as Karramis and Will made their way over to the approaching group with the rest of their family. A thin woman with short black hair and golden skin led the way, with a tall slender man with sandy-blond hair following closely behind. The feet of two others could be seen, but they hid behind the leaders of the group.

Pavian and Kavana eagerly strolled up to the woman as Karramis trailed behind, unable to determine who she was.

"I've missed you," the young woman said, a wide grin beaming across her oval face.

Kavana threw her arms around the woman, and Pavian leaned in for a side hug, making sure not to disturb Liam as he slept in his arms.

"I've missed you too," they both said to her.

Karramis studied the young woman as Kavana and Pavian embraced her, a rush of disbelief and happiness racing through her body. "Meadow?"

Pavian and Kavana backed away as Karramis and Meadow analyzed each other.

"Kare?" Meadow smiled. "Is it really you?"

Karramis rushed over and threw her arms around Meadow, refusing to let go of the teenage sister she had left behind who was now a grown woman.

Meadow Ward was the youngest child of Zarrius, twelve years younger than Karramis. Her mother, Randolyn Natomna, was a Water Witch and had moved to Kiluemar when she was in her early twenties with her younger sister, Aayrah. Wanting to be more than just a witch, Randolyn made herself useful on the island by being the first librarian the realm had. She organized all the books, scrolls, and archives scattered throughout the various locations on the island and placed them in an old abandoned building, giving Kiluemar its first official library.

"Where's Randolyn?" Karramis asked, finally releasing her sister.

"Oh, my mom wanted to come and see all of you, but I needed someone to watch the kids, so she offered to stay with them while I came to see you first. She figured I took priority."

"You have kids?"

"Yeah, two girls."

"How's that even possible?" Karramis grinned. "I mean, you're only thirteen, right?"

Meadow laughed. "Yeah, like fifteen, almost sixteen years ago."

"How old are they?" Kavana asked, sounding just as surprised by the news as Karramis.

"Well, Iris is six, and Ivy is five." Meadow scanned the group. "Wait, where are they, Karramis? Where are your little ones?"

Rhiannon grabbed James's hand as Karramis waved them over, uncomfortable with the number of unfamiliar eyes staring at her.

"Meadow, I'd like you to meet Rhiannon and James, your niece and nephew. Kids, this is your aunt, Meadow."

Meadow smiled and glanced up at them. "My goodness, I think *little* was the wrong word." She hugged them. "It's great to meet you both. Oh! And everyone . . ." She removed herself from the embrace and urged the man behind her over. "I'd like you to meet Tristen Cannington, my husband."

Tristen offered his hand, unsure where to direct it, and grinned, his shy smile pressing his cheeks into his noticeably deep green eyes. "Pleased to meet y'all fin'lly. I've heard some amazin' stories about y'all."

Pavian took Tristen's hand, shaking firmly and sizing him up. "Nice to meet you too." Standing face-to-face with him, Pavian raised his chin in an attempt to make himself taller. "So, where are you from, Tristen? That's a strange accent you have there. What are you? Magically, I mean."

"Pavian!" Meadow jerked her hands onto her hips. "Tristen and I have been married for almost six years now. I think we've passed the need for the third degree."

"Yeah, but *I* only met him ten seconds ago, and as your big brother, I deserve to interrogate—I mean, question—the man my baby sister married."

Tristen chuckled under his breath. "She was right 'bout ya." He patted Meadow's shoulder. "It's fine, sweetheart. I reckon he does this with all the new fellas enterin' the family."

Confirming Tristen's statement, Will and Aidan nodded aggressively. "Yeah."

"Even if he's known them for years," Aidan added.

"Right then," Tristen continued, "I'll just consider this an initiation to me officially bein' accepted into the family by *all* the men of the household. So, like she said, my name is Tristen Cannington. I was born and raised in the bayou of Louisiana. I have a hint of a Cajun accent with a bit of southern because, after I was adopted, I moved to Alabama. I've lived here in Kiluemar for about thirteen years now with my brother, Maverick—"

"How come I've never met you before?"

"I couldn't tell ya. I registered and ever'thin'. Do ya know all the residents of the island personally? Their names, and who they are?"

"Hmm." Pavian scowled. "Good point. Continue."

"I'm actually not the one with the magic, my brother is. And I know what you're fixin' to ask, but we aren't biological brothers. We were adopted by the same family. We lived with them until they died in a boatin' accident when we were teens. The event triggered Maverick's magic, and we decided to come here to get him some help controllin' it."

"How'd you find this place? What kind of magic does he have?"

"Pavian!" Meadow slapped her hands against her thighs. "He's not a criminal."

"I don't know that."

Tristen cleared his throat. "Are ya always this assertive?"

"Yes!" everyone declared.

"Okay then . . . Well, now I don't feel so attacked. Uhm, anyway, I didn't find this place. Maverick did. He's a Water Witch, just like Randolyn and Meadow. He heard rumors about this place and was determined to find it. He traveled all over, usin' his magic and hopin' someone would sense him. And sure enough, someone did and told us about the portals."

"Did he kill your parents?"

"Pavian!" Meadow yelled, stomping her foot.

Tristen flinched. "What? No!"

"Shh!" Pavian said, rubbing Liam's back as the little boy squirmed in his arms. "Would you all stop yelling?"

Meadow gently backhanded her brother across the arm. "Well, would you stop interrogating my husband?"

"Yeah, in a minute." Pavian turned to Tristen. "I was just curious. I mean, you said they died in a boating accident, and he *is* a Water Witch."

"No," Tristen repeated. "He wasn't even there when they died. Neither of us were. They were killed when vacationin' in Florida. His powers arrived after learnin' about their deaths."

Pavian glared at Tristen, searching for any telltale signs of dishonesty.

"Pavian." Meadow stepped between them. "Are you done?"

"Yeah, I think we're good."

"About damn time."

"Is it our turn yet?" a female voice asked from the back of the group.

Karramis beamed from ear to ear, recognizing the soft Hispanic voice as an old woman stepped closer.

Fayemeara, with her full head of gray hair pulled back in her usual French braid, hugged her. "Mija, te a extrañado mucho."

"I've missed you too," Karramis whispered, "so, *so* much." She winced as Fayemeara squeezed tighter. "Ow."

Fayemeara jerked back. "I'm so sorry, mija. Are you okay?"

"It's okay. I'm fine. It's nothing a little eucalyptus and lavender salve, cinnamon tea, and a good night's rest won't fix."

Observing the bruises along her face, Fayemeara asked, "Aye mija, who did this to you?"

"Someone who's not worth our time."

Fayemeara held Karramis's hands. "They'll get what's coming to them."

Karramis grinned over at Will. "I have no doubt about that."

"I can guarantee it, Miss Faye," Will said confidently.

Fayemeara tapped her palm against Will's bearded face. "Good."

"Okay, everyone, my turn," a soft-spoken, female Scottish voice said from behind Meadow as a red-headed woman stepped into the light.

"Nina!" Aidan said ecstatically, wrapping his arms around his sister.

Nina shrieked as he lifted her into the air. "I've missed you too, Aidan." She slapped his arm as he lowered her down. "I didn't think you'd be gone this long though!"

"My fault," Will said. "He was doing me a favor."

"All of us a favor actually," Kavana added, taking hold of Aidan's hand.

Nina smiled as her brother interlocked his fingers with Kavana's. "It's about damn time you two got back together."

Aidan gave Kavana a side grin, his bright emerald-green eyes beaming at her.

"Oh!" Karramis exclaimed. "Fayemeara. Nina. This is James and Rhiannon."

"Nice to meet you," Nina said, shaking their hands.

"Yes, it's very nice to meet you." Fayemeara cradled their faces, kissing both sets of cheeks. "Welcome home, my precious angels."

"Are you related to us?" Rhiannon asked tenderly.

"Not by blood—"

"No." Karramis placed her arm around Fayemeara. "Not by blood, but she's definitely family."

"Yes." Zarrius removed himself from the shadows. "Fayemeara is my honorary sister. We've known each other for a very long time."

"Awesome," James said. "I've always wanted a big family."

"Hey, wait a minute." Karramis stepped forward with a worried expression on her face. "Where are Tiffasa and Avery?"

"They're fine," Zarrius answered calmly. "Tiffasa is in Stoweward. She didn't want to take the chance and travel here with her boys."

"She has kids now too?" Karramis asked with both shock and sadness in her voice.

"Yeah," Pavian said, "two sons—"

"Three actually," Zarrius corrected. "She has three sons now."

"Wow." Karramis exhaled as she lowered her gaze. "I . . . I've missed so many things."

Will put his arms around her. "Yes, a lot has happened over the years." He kissed the side of her head. "But you have been given a second chance. And now you have plenty of time to catch up on everything you've missed."

"Right." Karramis leaned into him. "So, what about Avery?"

"According to Tiffasa," Zarrius said, "she left the day after the portals reopened."

"She left?"

"Yeah. Avery wanted to go back to Israel and see her family, to make sure they were okay and introduce them to Caleb."

"Caleb?"

"Caleb Kittleman?" Will asked.

"Yeah," Nina said. "Avery and Caleb married almost two years ago."

Karramis shifted her weight from one foot to the other, the mix of lingering pain and clashing emotions gnawing at her insides. "I think I need to sit down."

Everyone retreated into the hall, talking amongst themselves as Karramis rested in one of the chairs, overwhelmed by the events of the day. She loved being home again with her family and friends, but losing so much time and missing so many important events was hard for her to handle. She had lost not only eight years of her children's lives, but she had also missed out on over fifteen years of her family and friends' lives as well. She had cheated death, but she still felt robbed.

Karramis arched an eyebrow. "Guys? How are you all getting home tonight? Don't some of you still live in Stoweward? You can't travel this late. It's not safe."

"They're not going to, mija," Fayemeara said steadily, her voice reassuring as always.

"Yeah," Zarrius said, "I made sure everyone had accommodations here in the village for the night. Trust me, we have plenty of room here now."

"Excuse me." Rhiannon raised a hand. "Uh, quick question while we're on the subject. What exactly is outside the borders of this place?"

"Things that want to kill us," Meadow said candidly.

"Like what?" James asked.

Kavana snickered. "Where do we start? Hmm. Well, there are vampires, ogres, trolls, Merrick, werewolves—but that's only if they don't get to the highlands on time. Oh, and vampires, sirens—although you have to be near the water for them to get you. Uhm, let's see, what else? Oh right! Raamko, Merrick, and, oh yeah, did I mention vampires?"

Rhiannon gulped. "I'm assuming vampires and Merrick are the biggest threats?"

"You would assume right." Pavian rubbed Liam's back. "Vampires are bloodthirsty, and Merrick is worse. And I would think that, having been locked up for so long, they're probably starving."

James shifted in his chair. "What have they been eating all these years?"

"Anything they can sink their teeth into," Zarrius said somberly. "The realm has lost a lot of family members, friends, and creatures over the years."

Pavian narrowed his eyes at his father. "How many?"

"A lot. We aren't sure how many, but we've had hundreds go missing over the last eight years. Anyone who didn't leave before the portals were sealed has been forced to stay within the borders of the village or Stoweward. Venturing out at night is suicidal. Going out during the day is usually safe, but not always."

Rhiannon was absent from the conversation, churning up the same concern her mother worried about.

James jerked his head in her direction. "That's a good question."

Karramis observed the distress on her daughter's face. "What?"

Rhiannon sighed, hesitant to bring up a sore subject.

Karramis glared at her son. "James?"

He cleared his throat. "She wants to know about Lucas."

"What about him?" Will asked bitterly.

"She wants to know what's going to happen when he comes back. Won't he be able to sense us? Won't he be able to track us?"

"Not if you stay within the borders," Zarrius said confidently. "The spells around here protect us."

Rhiannon picked at her lip, her gaze focusing on nothing. "But he's . . . he's human."

"Yes, he is." Zarrius sat down across from her. "But he hasn't shown his face anywhere near here or Stoweward in years. Plus, everyone knows he works for Merrick, so no one would allow him past the threshold."

James drummed his fingers along the table. "But what about the cabin?" He peered over at his parents. "Is the cabin safe for us?"

Will shook his head. "No, it's not safe for us there, James. We never placed a protection spell around it, and after your mum left with you and your sister, I moved here to the village for a bit to stay off his radar."

"So, what do we do then?"

"Well, your mum and I decided that you two should remain with your aunt and uncle here for the time being."

"What?" the twins snapped, their voices echoing through the quiet hall.

Karramis closed her eyes, waiting for the ringing in her ears to fade. "It's just for a little while until I can get a protection spell around our home and the three of us can get our magic under control. We have to make sure you can protect yourselves with some kind of defensive magic. Your powers, and even mine, aren't reliable right now."

"But we want to stay with you," Rhiannon said as her voice cracked. "I mean, no offense to Aunt K."

"Oh, none taken. But I have to, uhm, interrupt here for a minute." Kavana placed her hands on the table and leaned in. "I . . . I just realized that I don't have a place to live. Before I left, I told Dad to pack up all my stuff, and I planned to find my own place when I got back. I mean, it was kind of embarrassing to still be living at home."

Nina bounced her bright green eyes between Kavana and Aidan. "You actually do have a place to live—both of you—if you want it."

"Where?" Kavana and Aidan asked.

"Here in the village. Together."

Aidan's brows gathered. "What'd you mean?"

"Well, when I found out this mornin' you had returned, with Kavana and the others, I figured you both made up, so I asked Zarrius if you could have one of the empty homes here since there are so many. I knew you'd want to be closer to her—not knowin' she moved out. Zarrius thought it was a great idea. Plus, I kinda like livin' alone. So, there's a place for you . . ." Nina grinned at Kavana. "And you if you two want to live together. Sorry if I'm oversteppin'. I just think—"

Aidan raised a hand, cutting her off as he smiled at Kavana. "What do you think? Wanna live together?"

Kavana's lips curled upward, her voice shaking with surprise. "Really?"

"Yeah. Want to take it slower this time and just move in together?"

Kavana leaned in to kiss him but was interrupted as Pavian's chair slid across the floor.

"Sorry to cut off this lovely show of emotion here," Pavian said, heading over to the door, "but it's getting late, and I need to get this little guy to bed." He stopped and waited for Raina. "And we have some . . . catching up to do." He winked at her. "So, I'll follow you. Where do you live now?"

"Here. I moved to the village during my pregnancy. Your dad wanted me close by to make sure I was taken care of."

Pavian faced his father. "Thank you, sir, for taking care of them while I was gone."

"You're welcome, Son. Take a few days to enjoy being home, but I expect you back in the guard soon."

"Yes, sir."

James glared at his uncle. "When did you become so formal and stiff?"

"Hush." Pavian strode away, pausing when James didn't follow. "Aren't you coming?"

"Yeah, but can I talk to Rhiannon and my parents first? Say goodbye?"

"Goodbye?" Zarrius asked. "There's no reason to say goodbye to Rhiannon. Raina lives not far from the place I gave to Aidan and Kavana."

"Oh! That's good, I don't want to be separated from her again anytime soon."

"Understandable," Aidan said. "Well, we'll wait outside. Go say goodbye to yer parents." As James jogged away, he called out, "Hey, James?"

James stopped and turned. "Yeah?"

"You don't have to worry about them. They'll be okay."

"Thanks, Aidan."

The winter air was cool but comfortable and blew quietly through the village. Only a small sliver of the moon lay across the starry sky, darkness fast approaching. As the new moon crept closer, the days leading up to the full moon lingered like a stalker hiding among the shadows.

James waited for the others to fade out of sight before addressing his parents. "Why do you two have to leave?"

"Yeah, if it's not safe for us," Rhiannon said anxiously, "then it's not safe for you either."

Karramis placed her hands on their shoulders. "We'll be fine. Nothing is going to happen to us."

"But how do you know?" Rhiannon grabbed her hand. "We just got you two back. I—I don't want to lose you again."

"You won't," Will reassured her. "If your mum and I feel it's unsafe, we will come right back."

"Promise?"

"Yes, we promise."

"Okay, I'm going to hold you to that."

"Yeah, me too," James added.

Karramis and Will hugged the twins and waited as they left with their aunt and uncle.

Will let out a long exhale, grabbing hold of Karramis's hand. "So, what's the plan?"

"Is Callie nearby?"

"Yeah. She's probably over at the stables with the other horses."

Karramis twisted on her heels, moving down the path toward the stables. "Good."

"Hey, wait a minute." Will trailed behind her. "Are you going to tell me the plan? What are we going to do when Lucas and the others come through?"

"We're going to make sure they don't go looking for the kids. They are not ready to deal with any of this yet."

"And how are we going to do that?"

"Bait them."

Will ran in front of her, forcing her to stop. "What does that mean?"

"We're going to use ourselves as bait to make sure Lucas and those other idiots focus their attention on us, at least for right now."

"And how do you suppose we do that?"

"Lucas is hell-bent on getting what he wants, and he won't stop until he does. He wants me. And by getting away—and doing it in a scheming and unjust way—I most definitely pissed him off. He has no self-control and a one-track mind. He's going to want to find me, and I'm counting on it."

"Why? What's your plan?"

The full moon was coming, and there was no way to slow it down or stop it. However, Karramis did not want to hinder the event. Instead, she welcomed it. Her fear was no longer controlling her, but rather her determination to fight back. Having made a promise to herself after she woke up in France with another chance at life, Karramis vowed that if she survived the night and escaped, she was going to stop the threat trying to take her children. No matter what she had to do, she was not going to let her children die.

Lucas was coming, and Merrick would not be far behind, but for now, the twins were safe. The magic around Caerwyn Village would protect them, and with Lucas sensing Karramis and Will at the cabin, he would focus his attention on them at first.

Merrick wanted the twins, but only when they had the full extent of their powers. Karramis trusted the prophecy enough to know they were powerful, but until they could master their abilities, Merrick would not want them. At least, she hoped. As babies, he could have taken them and raised them not to be afraid of him, but as teens, he would have one hell of a time keeping them obedient. Plus, some of their magic was present, and they had been able to defend themselves before, something she had witnessed for herself.

The plan now was to hold them off and distract them with the fact Karramis and Will—two people who also possessed powers Merrick wanted—were back.

# *Chapter 13*

## Rising to the Occasion

The stable doors creaked open as dawn inched closer, erasing the dark hues of the night. A crisp air blew through the deserted streets of Caerwyn Village and swayed the dew-kissed blades of grass around like the waves of the ocean. Quietness. Calm. The residents lay asleep, hidden within their dreams and unaware of the deceptive deeds unfolding in the silence of daybreak.

James ushered Rhiannon through the partially open doors and hurried in behind her.

"I can't believe I let you talk me into this," Rhiannon said, unlatching one of the stall doors as the horses in the stables rose from their slumber.

James mounted the familiar black stallion he had ridden before. "Oh, come on, Sis. Live a little."

"That's just it, James . . ." Rhiannon adjusted her dress, positioning herself atop Cinnamon, the mare she had claimed for herself. "I want to live, and this plan is going to get us killed, either literally or figuratively. I don't know who I'm more afraid of—whatever the heck is outside the village, or Aunt K and Uncle Pavian. Not to mention our parents."

"You're just afraid of getting in trouble."

"Exactly. Why aren't you?"

"Because we've been held up for over two weeks now with nothing to do. I mean, come on, they don't even have internet here. We're bored, worried, anxious. I just . . . I just want to go home."

"I want to go home too, but they all think we aren't ready. It's not safe for us out there." She sighed. "And personally, I haven't been bored. I actually find the library quite interesting."

"Yeah, okay." He rolled his eyes. "Whatever. Don't forget the restricted section, Miss Know-It-All. That's where all the good stuff is hidden, right?"

Rhiannon flashed him an approving smile.

"What?" James clicked his tongue and nudged his horse toward the door. "Don't look so surprised. I've seen the movies before." He pulled on the reins, bringing Shadow to a halt at the front of the stables. "Listen . . ." He peeked outside before directing his attention to Rhiannon. "I can't spend tonight worrying about Mom and Dad or wondering if we will ever see them again. I just can't. I spent a good portion of my life wanting a family. And now . . . now that I have you and both our parents back, I'm not going to sit around being useless and defenseless. We've protected ourselves in the past, and I truly believe, if the circumstance arrives, we can do it again. I mean, the prophecy did predict us, right? And magic supposedly created us, right? Shouldn't that give you some hope that we can do this?"

Rhiannon drew in a long inhale. "Fine. I won't argue with you about this anymore."

"Good. I'm glad."

"But I will say this. This is a *stupid* idea."

James nodded, exiting the stables. "Probably."

They made their way under the stone archway and beyond the meadow in between the village and Dryad Forest. The sun rose along the horizon, ascending behind the trees of Kitra Forest in front of them. The air was still, and the meadow lay quiet, the sounds of Mother Nature not yet awake.

Laughter raced across the open field as the twins bonded, discussing secrets, interests, fears, and everything in between. This was the first time they had truly been alone since returning to the island, given the freedom to talk openly with each other without prying eyes or listening ears. Being monitored during all waking hours, they enjoyed their independence once again, a simple thing neither had been given after arriving back in Kiluemar. Solitude was a familiar aspect in their lives before but was not something either truly wanted. Although they valued living without limitations all those years with their aunt and uncle, they adored having their other half back in their lives. It was, however, the unrelenting watchful eye following them around which grew annoying and tiresome to the twins.

"Do you think we'll make it before they realize we're gone?" Rhiannon asked.

"Oh, yeah, definitely. I doubt they'll actually come looking for us at all."

"How can you be so sure?"

"Well, I left a note with Uncle Pavian saying that I went with you to the library to meet up with Randolyn—I mean Yaya. Man, it's so weird having grandparents. Why do we have to call her that again?"

"She said Iris started calling her that a long time ago, and it just stuck. Anyway, you were saying?"

"Oh, right. So, I wrote that we were going to do some research with Yaya. And the note I gave you to leave for Aunt K pretty much said the same thing, so if they think we're with another adult and in the safety of the village, I doubt they'll question it."

"But what if they do come looking for us once we don't return or they run into Yaya?"

"Well, the sun goes down early this time of year, so if they do figure it out and go to the library, I left them another note telling them we went to the cabin. I doubt they'd try to bring us back at night."

"I hope you're right. This whole thing is giving me a stomachache."

"It's fine. We'll be fine."

"Yeah, you say that now," Rhiannon mumbled under her breath.

Rhiannon hated disobeying orders even if she did not agree with them. But she never wanted to disappoint her brother, let alone leave him to his own devices. James had a knack for getting himself into trouble, and Rhiannon considered him her responsibility even though she was technically the younger one of the two. She was not comfortable with the plan playing out, but deep inside she was happy to be going home to her mother and father. As they headed into the tree line of the forest not far from the cabin, her body tingled, a rush of excitement prickling her nerves. Even though she was sure consequences would soon follow their arrival home, and the fear of tonight pulled at her insides, Rhiannon was pleased with her decision to come along. The adrenaline of being a rebel boiled inside, making her warm and exhilarated.

"Interesting feeling, huh?" James said with a giggle, sensing his own emotions rising in his sister.

"It . . . it's different. Does it feel like this every time you do something you're not supposed to?"

"No. Only when I'm doing it for the right reasons."

"What makes this right?"

"Because we're going home. And not just to be a family again, but to protect them. Their fate should not be dependent on our destiny. The full moon tonight will bring darkness, so let us be the light to scare it away."

"When did you get so philosophical?"

"I think you're rubbing off on me."

~

The horses snorted as they came to a stop outside the cabin. James and Rhiannon waited, searching for the courage to dismount and knock on the door.

"Ready?" James asked, swinging his leg behind him.

"As ready as I'll ever be, I guess." Rhiannon grabbed hold of James's raised hand and slid off Cinnamon. "No turning back now, huh?"

"Nope."

Stepping onto the landing of the porch, the twins experienced a twinge along their skin and a warmth flowing through their veins.

"What was that?" they said, both stumbling to inspect the area behind them.

Footsteps rushed closer on the other side of the entrance. The door swung open, and Karramis and Will lingered, frozen in disbelief.

"Surprise!" the twins said flamboyantly, their arms extending outward.

"What . . ." Karramis fixated on her children, moving through the threshold and entering their outstretched arms. "What are you two doing here? You're not supposed to be here."

Rhiannon spotted Will's short hair and five-o'clock shadow. "Hey, you clean up nicely, Dad."

"Thanks, but don't change the subject. What are you doing here?" Will pushed past the others, stopping at the railing and letting out a piercing whistle. "It's too dangerous."

"What's he doing?" James asked as Callie landed on the other side of Cinnamon and Shadow. "Whoa! How'd she get here so fast?"

"Winged horses are exceptionally quick," Rhiannon said, "but they can't travel like that when people are on them."

"Why?"

"Physics."

"Right." James nodded, unaware of what she meant.

Will ran his hand along Callie's neck, whispering inaudible words before the winged horse took off, galloping in the direction the twins had arrived from as Cinnamon and Shadow followed closely behind her.

"Where are they going?" Rhiannon stepped down the stairs, the blood within her body growing warm and tingling along her flushed skin.

"Callie's taking them back to the village," Will answered, meeting her along the steps.

"Why?"

"Because it's not safe for them out here, especially tonight."

Will returned to the porch, but Rhiannon hesitated to follow him as her hand led the way.

James glared at her, his raised eyebrows creasing his forehead. "What the heck are you doing?"

"There's something weird right here."

"It's the spell," Karramis said. "You can feel it?"

"Yeah."

James placed his hand over the top of the step. "What kind of spell? Are we not supposed to be able to feel it?"

Karramis walked through the invisible wall, turning around and entering again. "Most people don't, but I can see how a few might be able to. Some people are more sensitive to magic. And it's a boundary spell."

"Is this the same kind of spell that was around our home when we were little?"

"No. That was a protection spell."

Rhiannon rubbed her arms, lessening the strange sensation beneath her skin. "What's the difference?"

"A protection spell is for magic. Boundary spells are for people."

James walked through it again. "Are those the spells that are around the village and Stoweward?"

Karramis nodded. "Yes."

"But how come we can't feel those ones?"

"Because it's stronger magic. Some of my powers are still too weak, so it's not as strong as it could be. Or maybe it's because this one is linked to my and your dad's blood, and maybe your own magic can sense it through our natural connection."

Will opened the front door. "I think we should go inside. Since you're here, we might as well prepare you for what might happen tonight. But don't think you two are off the hook for going against our wishes to stay in the village. You two were mad to come out here alone, especially without any training on how to protect yourselves."

Everyone entered, and the twins hung their heads in dismay at their parents' disappointment.

"Listen, this was all my doing," James said. "I'm the one who convinced Rhiannon to come along. I'm the one who wouldn't accept being away from you two any longer. I didn't want to hide anymore. I didn't want you two hurt because of me. I won't lose you again."

Karramis and Will sat next to each other, unable to find the words to express the revelation of their son's declaration.

Rhiannon stood next to James, the top of her head reaching his chin. "It's true, he did convince me to come along, but I stand by my decision. We won't let you two do this alone. I know we aren't prepared by any means, and we may never be to the extent the prophecy needs us to be, but we won't know if you don't let us try. Magic is all about control and focus, right?"

Her parents nodded.

"Well, then give us the chance to tap into our innate abilities. Let the events and emotions of tonight push our magic to the surface. *All* our magic."

"Yeah, what she said," James added. "We won't know everything we can do if we don't force it out. I'm sorry for disobeying you, but I'm not sorry I'm standing here right now. This is where I'm meant to be. With you."

Rhiannon casually placed her hands on her hips. "I second that."

"Fine, then let's do this." Karramis stood up. "First, you need a crash course in how magic works and what might happen tonight." She paced and pinched her lower lip. "Now, I can guarantee Lucas will be here tonight, but what I can't be too sure of is his plan. He has two different sides, and I'm not positive which one we will get tonight."

"I am," Will declared, drumming his fingers along his leg. "Once he sees me, he'll rain hell upon us. And if Leif is with him, which I have no doubt he will be, we're in for a rough night."

"Why?" James asked. "Who's Leif?"

"Leif's a vampire, and he's one of the bad ones. He's the devil constantly whispering in Lucas's ear. Lucas is very much all mouth and no trousers, but with Leif around they tend to feed off each other. They're both bloody mental, if you ask me. But Leif is definitely not someone you want to mess with. He's always eager to start a fight."

"So, with that being said, I think it's time I teach you the basics of controlling your magic." Karramis headed outside, the others following behind her. "It's not something that comes naturally. Well, I mean, your powers are natural—you were born with them—but controlling them is another thing. Trust me, I should know."

Will waited on the steps, taking notes of the conversation between his wife and children.

"Now, all magic requires mental and physical strength, but physical strength is not about brute force. You don't need actual muscle to master your abilities. It's more about controlling your power mentally without allowing exhaustion to take over the body. The mind is powerful but surrenders to the limitations of the vessel."

Rhiannon stepped from the stairs. "So, is all magic mental?"

"All magic? No. Magical abilities? Yes. And there are two guaranteed ways to summon one's powers."

"How?" the twins asked.

"Physical pain and emotions. Both trigger a magical response. Now, sometimes it might be delayed—speaking from personal experience here—but it generates a magical response nevertheless. A defense mechanism."

Rhiannon raised a hand. "So, I don't need to be strong physically to control my powers?"

"No. Mastering physical strength when it comes to magical abilities is all about mind over matter, fighting against the body's innate desire to quit. Magic is part of you. It's programmed into you like the ability to breathe. There is an instinctive nature inside of you that dominates your abilities. All you have to do is trust yourself and your instincts."

The four of them remained outside, discussing different ways to master their abilities. Even though no one was sure of all the powers the twins possessed or the extent of their magic, there was one thing Karramis and Will were sure of, James and Rhiannon were not the type to back down.

# Chapter 14

## Lesser Evil

Karramis lingered outside as the full moon lowered on the horizon. Trapped in her mind, she reflected on the events from a month ago and pondered the possible outcomes of tonight. She was not nervous about Lucas's return, nor was she scared. Instead, she was angry, enraged by the incident at Château Rouge. She had allowed Lucas too much power, and not just in France. Not only had he wiggled his way into her mind, making her live a life in a constant state of dread, but she had yielded to him. Karramis had accepted defeat, granting him the ability to lay a hand on her and nearly killing her in the process. Twice. But there would not be a third time. Once a friend she trusted, a person she cared about, Lucas was no longer the man she had grown up with, the man she thought she knew. He was different—controlled by an unnatural temper, hatred unlike anything she had ever seen before in a human, jealousy, and resentment. Molded into someone she did not recognize, he was a product of pure evil. The love for the man she had once called her best friend was still deep below the surface, but a loathing burned inside, compelling her own rage to boil.

"Anything?" Will asked, leaning against the railing as he and the twins joined Karramis on the porch.

"I'm not sure. Some people came through, but I couldn't pinpoint their magic."

Rhiannon closed the door. "How do you know people came through the portals?"

"I can sense them. Guardians are aware of everyone who travels to the realm. It allows us to keep the island safe, kind of like an alarm system."

"So, you know who comes through at all times?"

"We don't know the person or creature, only their magic. And we only sense them when they travel from the non-magical realm. We can't monitor those traveling between the different portals in Kiluemar or those leaving. It's a good thing too, or else that would get super annoying."

"Annoying?" James asked, sitting down on the porch and leaning against the wall.

"Yeah." Karramis joined him. "All Guardians hear a sound when anything comes through. Again, like a security alarm. And it allows us to focus on what type of magic is coming through or if they have no magic at all."

"So, you don't know if it was Lucas and the others who came through?"

"No, and I'm not sure why. I think my magic is still wonky. Some of them have been harder for me to control since I . . . I came back to life."

Will pushed himself away from the railing. "Maybe they won't come tonight."

Lucas emerged from the side of the cabin with Camille closely behind. "Sorry to burst your bubble, mate." He strolled casually before stopping a few feet from the stairs and smiling at Karramis. "Hello, love."

Karramis and James rose to their feet as Will bolted from the porch.

"Will!" Karramis called, being pulled back by the twins as she tried to follow behind him.

Will flung his fist across Lucas's face. "Son of a bitch!"

Lucas lifted his hand to his face, letting out a heckling laugh. "My, someone must be a bit jealous."

Advancing over to Lucas, Will stopped inches from his face. "Mark my words, Lucas, I'm going to kill you one day."

"Ha! I'd love to see ya try. You're an exceptionally loud thinker, mate."

"I got a hit in this time, didn't I?"

"Yeah, because I let ya. I mean, it's only fittin' with what happened between me and your wife."

Will clenched his fist, but Lucas backed away with a grin.

"Will!" Karramis snapped. "He's not worth it."

Memories of Lucas flooded the twins as they remembered their first encounter with him. The years had been good to him, only showing a few signs of aging along his chiseled face and brown hair. However, despite still being confident and handsome, he now had a more pronounced evil radiating from him, making him unpleasant and unattractive.

As Will stepped back onto the porch, Karramis asked sternly, "Where're the others, Lucas?"

"Whateva' do ya mean, love?"

"I know more came with you."

"Not to mention," Will added, "you're missing your shadow. Where is that bloody bastard anyway? I know he can't be too far behind you."

Lucas cracked his neck as he met Will's gaze. "It's a shame you're still alive. A bit disappointin' actually."

"Likewise."

Lucas flashed a snarky grin at the twins. "Hello again. You two have grown so much since the last time I saw ya. You're lookin' more like your parents these days." His eyes stopped on James. "That's unfortunate for ya, mate."

"Oh, I beg to differ," Camille announced flirtatiously, her nasally tone deep as her voluptuous chest pointed at Will.

The blonde swayed her hips closer, her short dress clinging to her body. Her sultry beauty and accentuating curves intrigued James as he kept his eyes locked in on her. But despite her physical appearance, there was an ugliness to her, something making James uneasy. A strange sensation bubbled in the pit of his stomach, his instincts finding her innocent and beautiful persona untrusting. There was an evil inside her.

Camille kept her eyes on Will, finding him even more attractive than the man she lusted after. "It seems Karramis has a type." She tilted her head over to Lucas. "Excusez-moi, mon amour." She pointed at Karramis. "May I ask her a question?"

"Go ahead."

"*Merci*," Camille said, overemphasizing her French accent as she faced Karramis. "How did you get these two to fall in love with you, chère? I mean, you even have deliciously handsome Leif's attention. Although, I think he would rather kill you than bed you, which I am totally fine with. But still, what's your secret?" She gazed dreamily at Lucas and Will. "Look at them." She turned back to Karramis. "And look at you. You are so . . . How do you say it? Uhm . . . *ordinaire*. Plain. Nothing special."

Karramis ignored her. "Where are they, Lucas? I know you're not alone, so your element of surprise is gone."

"You're right, love. I can't get anythin' by ya, can I? Well, if ya must know, Haydrin is . . . unavailable at the moment. He was a bit homicidal comin' through. And Gastell has never been good company, so I let him head back to whereva' home is for him until we need him again."

"And Leif? I know he's—" Karramis's eyes widened, her composed tone unstable. "Wait! He's a werewolf, isn't he?"

The large brooding man with glasses and long dark hair from the manor, the one absent on the night of the full moon when she awoke at Château Rouge, and the one they called Haydrin, was a werewolf.

Lucas stood tall with a smug grin on his face. "Ding, ding! Ya finally figured it out, love. Good for you."

Karramis rushed down the stairs.

Reaching out and failing to stop her, Will called, "Karramis!"

"You let a werewolf run wild?" Karramis shoved Lucas. "Are you fuckin' crazy?"

Panic filled Rhiannon's stomach, the tightness squeezing her gut as her heart raced. "There's a werewolf on the loose out here?"

"What do we do?" James asked, his adrenaline taking over as Will grabbed a crossbow from the rafters.

Raising the bow, Will aimed through the darkness. "Don't die."

James flinched. "Well, duh! Anything else?"

"Yeah, no matter what, stay on the porch."

Will kept his eyes narrowed, focusing on the shadows beyond the lights of the porch. The moonlight sparkled off the tops of the trees as darkness swallowed the rest of the forest. The air was still, and a moment of quietness engulfed them, anticipation crawling up everyone's spine.

Lucas broke the silence, rapidly sucking his tongue against his teeth as he leaned into Karramis and whispered, "Ya shoulda stayed on the porch."

A rush of wind swept across Karramis's skin, her thick waves swirling through the air as her body jerked back into someone's chest, a set of muscular arms pinning hers against her sides.

"Mom!" the twins yelled, racing over to the stairs as Will threw out an arm to stop them.

Aiming the crossbow at Leif, Will slid his finger next to the trigger as he steadied his breath, releasing the fear and hopelessness taking over his body. The sights fixed on the vampire's back, the metal arrow with a wooden shaft directly on target with his heart.

"I wouldn't do that if I were you, Will," Lucas said slowly as he peered over Leif's shoulder.

The hungry vampire rotated around, holding Karramis tightly against his body as he spoke softly. "Drop it." He pulled her hair and exposed her neck. "Or I'll kill her."

Rhiannon drew herself away from the action unfolding, studying the man she remembered from years ago and taking James with her.

Leif's voice was a mellow tone filled with a unique accent—Texan mixed with a hint of Southern, but with a calm European twinge hidden behind it—something neither of them had ever heard before. Although the twins did not remember this distinctive trait, they did recall how he had looked all those years ago. Leif had not changed in eight years, his physical and emotional responses still burned in their minds. The ageless creature was delighted by the chaos taking place, reveling in the horror with each passing moment as he held their mother hostage. But through it all, the twins observed their mother's composed nature, unfazed by the dangers surrounding her.

Will lowered the crossbow as Lucas stalked over to Karramis. Examining her face, Lucas signaled for Leif to let her go as he brushed his fingers along the scar on her cheek and traced it up her temple.

Karramis jerked her head away. "Your handiwork."

"Sorry about that, love. You were tryna escape, and ya just needed to be put in your place." He lowered his voice. "But ya forgave me in the end, right?"

Will clenched his teeth, his defined jawline even more prominent. His knuckles turned white as he aimed the tip of the arrow at Lucas's back.

"It seems Will is a bit jealous of us." Lucas rotated around, flashing a conniving grin. "My, how the tables have turned." Twisting back, he whispered to Karramis, "Does he know about us? About the kiss we shared? The passion between us? It was so raw and real. Absolutely amazin', don't ya think?"

Karramis's eyes beamed with hatred. "I don't keep secrets from him, you sick bastard. You're delusional, you know that? There was never anything between us, and there *never* will be. I only kissed you to distract you so I could get away, and it worked. You were trying to kill me."

"Now, don't be so dramatic, love. You were in good hands. No pun intended. And if I remember correctly, ya seemed to enjoy that kiss." Lucas smirked at Will. "Sorry, mate."

Karramis scoffed. "It won't work, Lucas. I told him everything. And everyone here, except for you, knows that I took no pleasure in *anything* relating to you, so you can take your disgusting fantasy and shove it."

Lucas tightened his gaze before smacking Karramis across the face. The sting sliced into her recently healed injuries like tiny papercuts. Leif loosened his grip and zoomed over to Will with lightning speed. Being forced back with a sudden jerk, Will pulled the trigger as he dropped the crossbow, the arrow narrowly missing Lucas as it shot into the trees. Karramis fell against the ground at the same time as the crossbow. Fighting against the vampire's undeniable strength, Will grunted as his arms were pinned behind his back. Leif's hunger raged and drove the veins along his face to the surface, his blue eyes turning black.

Karramis laughed as she rubbed her face, peering up at Lucas from the ground. "A smack? That's all you got this time? It seems you're getting soft, Lucas. Not something a man wants to hear."

"Lucas," Leif said with strain in his voice, the saliva building in his mouth. "Don't let her start with you. That's how she got away the last time." His lips parted and revealed his fangs. "Listen, bitch, if you don't stop your mind games, so help me, I *will* kill him."

Camille clapped her hands. "Oh, oui! Finally, after all these years, I get to see some blood spilled. You would think living with a vampire I would've seen it by now, but Leif has some amazing self-control. I was, however, hoping it would be"—she pointed at Karramis—"her, but he'll do." She leaned her head against Will's shoulder. "Such a shame, though. He's quite a catch."

"You're sick," Rhiannon said, her voice riddled with terror after spotting Leif's monstrous appearance. "You have some serious problems."

"Oh, chère, the only *problème* I have is how your mother could catch the attention of two men, and I am stuck fighting for the attention of just one." She puckered her lips at Lucas. "I mean, look at me. I'm far more attractive than she is."

A snickering scoff erupted from James. "Far more annoying is more like it. Plus, aren't you a little young for him? I think you crave a daddy more than a lover."

"Enough!" Leif yelled. "If this bitch and these brats don't knock it off, Lucas, I'm going to kill him. I'm hungry, bored, and this shit is getting old. Either wrap this up or let me have one of them."

A growl echoed from the trees as heavy footfalls exploded in the clearing. An oversized humanoid gray wolf appeared under the glow of the fading moonlight.

"Shit!" Leif released Will and hurried Lucas and Camille away from the others. "It's Haydrin!"

Standing on his hind legs, the werewolf, with bulging muscles, a hairy body, and sharp teeth howled into the sky with its large clawed hands outstretched.

Seconds passed like minutes as Rhiannon and James witnessed their parents in danger. Their instincts to help took over, and they rushed from the porch but halted a few feet from the steps as fear replaced their heroic advancement. Panting uncontrollably, Rhiannon's pulse raced, thumping along her neck and in her ears. Tightness pulled at her stomach and continued up her torso, catching in her throat as she swallowed. Her fear intensified, filling James with even more despair as his emotions flooded between his own body and mind, washing over him and his sister. They trembled as the overwhelming panic of two surged through their muscles, an uncontrollable ripple flowing within the depths of their bodies. Every moment dragged on as the future of their parents played out in slow motion in front of them.

Snarling, Haydrin charged at Lucas and the others on all fours. Leif ushered Lucas and Camille away from the charging beast, but the werewolf closed in. Karramis hurried to her feet, raising a hand and tossing the beast into the air. Will sprinted to Karramis, but the werewolf was back on his feet, now charging after him as blood and drool fell from his sharp teeth. Running toward the twins, Will rushed them over to the cabin.

Karramis raised a hand again to stop the werewolf from attacking her family but was yanked back by Leif.

"You're coming with us!"

"Let's go!" Lucas demanded, grasping Karramis's face and kissing her. "Thanks for savin' us, love. See, I knew ya cared."

Karramis pulled away in disgust. "Don't flatter yourself, you sadistic bastard." She winced as Leif grasped tighter around her wrists. "I'm a Guardian, it's in my nature to protect people."

The twins' legs were heavy, burning with each stride as they ran from the beast. Fighting through the pain, they sprinted as their hearts battered against their ribs and their accelerated breathing burned along their throats. James and Will raced up the stairs and crashed into the wall. A piercing scream ricocheted throughout the clearing as the werewolf bit down on Rhiannon's leg and dragged her away from the cabin.

"Rhiannon!" James and Will yelled as they chased after her.

Haydrin's wide mouth clamped down, his teeth burrowing into her ankle and calf. Her flesh ripped open, blood gushing from the deep wound.

Spotting the vicious animal attacking her daughter, Karramis struggled to get away. "Rhiannon!"

The ground rumbled and the wind howled as James grabbed hold of his sister's arm, the elements of earth and air rippling outward from them. Everyone standing stumbled as the rattling intensified. Karramis threw her head back and rammed it into Leif's chest, the two surprising events releasing his grip. She twisted around and threw Leif, Lucas, and Camille through the air as she sprinted away.

The earth beneath the twins and werewolf shook harder as gusts crashed into the beast's massive body, tumbling him onto his side as he held tight to Rhiannon's leg. A deafening cry wailed from Rhiannon as she gave in to the pain, her body going limp.

"Fight him!" James yelled as Will jumped on the werewolf, trying to strangle it. "Fight back!"

Rhiannon focused on his words, battling the urge to surrender as the werewolf unclenched his jaw and rose to his hind legs. Haydrin dug his claws into Will's back, blood rising from the tattered shirt as Will was tossed through the air.

"Dad!" James exclaimed as he pulled Rhiannon away from the towering beast, his sister screaming as their father lay facedown on the ground, struggling to return to his feet.

The wind settled and the ground stopped shaking as an invisible force erupted from the twins, a shock wave of energy so powerful it sent the snarling werewolf hundreds of feet backward, throwing him hard against the trees.

Karramis picked up speed as the earth stopped moving beneath her, but Leif tackled her to the ground. Flipping her over, he straddled her and jammed his knees against her arms, the force almost crushing her bones. He placed his hands around her neck, his eyes solid black as his sharp fangs aimed for the veins pulsating wildly along her neck.

Leif placed his mouth against her ear. "An eye for an eye."

His teeth pierced her skin, blood oozing from his mouth and along her neck as he released his strangling grip. She arched her back and screamed, the sharp pain searing through her body as his fangs dug deeper.

Rhiannon's body shuddered, matching the intensity of the earthquake present only moments ago. Her eyes glazed over, spotting the mangled flesh pulling from her gruesome injury. Twisting sideways, she vomited, the fear and disgust from the grisly sight escaping her body. James grabbed her arm as she wiped her mouth, pulling her to her feet. They hurried over to their father, James helping Rhiannon as she limped along.

Sitting up, Will winced as a breeze swept over the bloody claw marks along his back. He rubbed his neck and tried to focus as the children shuffled closer. Blood gushed from Rhiannon's leg, and the pain faded from Will as his adrenaline took over.

"Rhiannon?" Will removed his bloody shirt and quickly wrapped it around her leg. "We've got to stop the bleeding."

"I-I'm okay," she said unconvincingly, peering down at her father's injured back as he tended to her leg.

"No, you're not." He glanced up at James. "We've got to get her onto the porch."

Lifting Rhiannon into his arms, Will struggled to stand up straight as the pain forced out a muffled groan.

"Dad?" James rushed behind his father. "Are you okay?"

"It's not that bad"—he grunted—"just a tad uncomfortable." Will lowered Rhiannon onto the porch. "Rhiannon? Can you hear me?"

His voice disappeared through the shadows of Rhiannon's mind as he whispered, his words calling out and fading like echoes through a canyon. The pain was gone, buried beneath the cavernous voids within her soul. She stared at the blood seeping from the shirt around her leg, her eyes lost in the darkness with no feeling or emotions.

"Rhiannon." Will observed the color draining from her face and the emptiness in her eyes. "I think she's in shock." He hurried to remove his belt and fastened it above her knee. "We need to slow the bleeding and keep her awake."

*"Rhiannon."* James held her hand as his inner voice entered her mind. *"Listen to my voice."*

Karramis bucked beneath Leif, his teeth digging deeper into her neck with each lurch. She fought through the pain as he sucked more blood from her body.

She lifted her hips and grunted. "I've had about enough of you!"

Forcing Leif to one side, Karramis loosened his crushing weight and freed one of her arms. She concentrated and flicked her wrist. A loud crack rang out as Leif's head jerked sideways, and he collapsed on top of her.

Karramis groaned under his dead body as she rolled and pushed him away. "Get off me!"

Lucas panted as he came to a stop next to them. "That wasn't a good idea. He's gonna be even more pissed when he wakes up."

Karramis returned to her feet, refusing to acknowledge him as she headed over to her family.

"Hey!" Lucas snatched her arm. "Where'd ya think you're goin'?"

Haydrin rose to his hind legs, shaking himself as Rhiannon's blood flew from his snout and mouth. He howled as he charged on all fours over to the cabin, determined to finish the meal he had started. Jumping from the ground, he crashed into the boundary spell and tumbled down the steps. He attacked again, fighting against the invisible force stopping him. Snarling, he pushed against it, his claws scratching against nothing.

A growl rang out, and Rhiannon jolted back to reality, her fear shifting into an instinctive defense mode. Warmth filled her hand as flames rose from her palm, a fire rising from beneath her skin. She stared in disbelief as the fire grew, trailing up her fingers and engulfing her whole hand.

"Holy shit!" James exclaimed, his eyes widening as his jaw hung open. "Where'd you learn to do that?"

"I have no idea!" Rhiannon extended her arm, putting space between herself and the fire raging in her hand. "What do I do with it?"

"Throw it!" Will yelled as Haydrin's claws sliced through the barrier. "He's breaking through!"

Rhiannon threw her arm out, her palm facing the werewolf, but the flames stayed against her hand. "It's not working!"

"Try again!"

"Let me help!" James clasped her wrist and pulled her arm back. "Now!"

They both flung their arms forward, and the fire in her hand exploded outward, shooting into the werewolf. The flames seared across his body and singed his pewter fur. Haydrin rolled aggressively along the ground and set the grass on fire as he smothered the flames along his body. The burned animal whimpered and rose to his feet as smoke billowed from him. Limping back into the forest, he disappeared into the darkness.

Karramis jerked herself from Lucas's grip. "Get your damn hand off me!"

He reached out again to grab her, but she rammed a fist into his face, and he fell to the ground.

"You will never touch me again," she said firmly as she towered over him.

Spotting the flames dancing across the grass, Karramis ran to the cabin and stopped on the steps. She drew out her arms and concentrated on the fire, and the flames rose higher and stretched out, creating a wall between the two groups.

"Rhiannon!" Karramis exclaimed, kneeling on the porch with one hand still facing the fire. "Are you okay?"

"I'm okay, Mom. It barely hurts anymore."

"How's that even possible?"

Rhiannon shrugged.

Dumbfounded by the lack of concern from the others, Karramis frowned at Will.

Mimicking Rhiannon's carefree expression, Will drew up his shoulders. "Our children are tough, that's for sure. And pretty damn extraordinary. I can't wait to see what they can do with the full extent of their powers. Speaking of that, when did you learn how to control your fire magic?"

Karramis tossed a quick glance at the fire wall she was manipulating. "I told you I've been practicing. It's not perfect, but it's getting better."

"Yeah, I'd say so."

Karramis observed Will's bare back as they stood up. "Oh my gosh! Are you okay? We need to clean that up before it gets infected."

"I'll be all right, darling. I'm fine. It's looks worse than it really is." He spotted her injury. "I reckon you're the one we need to worry about, though."

"What do you mean?"

Will pointed to her neck. "How much blood did he take?"

She relaxed her hand a bit, and the fire wall lowered slightly. "Not enough to worry about it."

James helped Rhiannon to her feet. "I think all three of you need to get inside and get cleaned up."

Keeping a watchful eye on the others across the fiery field, Rhiannon asked, "What about them?"

As Lucas and Camille sulked away, Leif hollered over the raging fire, "Don't worry little girl, I'll be back!" He locked eyes with Karramis. "I'm not done with you. You'll get what you deserve, witch! Just wait until Merrick finds out you're back!"

"I wouldn't worry about them tonight," Karramis said with a calm voice.

The four watched the sullen group as they disappeared into the trees. They were certain Lucas and the others would be back, but now they no longer feared the lesser evils but rather who they were returning to. A war was coming. Merrick was hours away from finding out they were back, and the battle between good and evil would commence. A chain reaction would soon occur, setting off a series of events leading everyone down a path to an unknown future.

# *Chapter 15*

## Twofold

*Centuries ago*

The Age of Magic originated back in the time of ancient Mesopotamia, the period when magic evolved and fully embraced its ability to connect to a human life. Stories of people enhancing the farmlands, mastering fire, controlling the waters of the Tigris and Euphrates, protecting villages from troublesome winds, and siphoning powers from the moon to enrich the livelihood of the people had traveled for miles and through many generations. Hieroglyphs found all over the world and clay slabs with Mycenaean script depicted numerous accounts of magic-related tales throughout history. Findings of potion bottles, ritual writings, spell books, and artifacts proved magic had been around for thousands of years. However, one of the most widely described legends was not of witches, magic itself, or even the creatures commonly talked about in fairytales, but rather of a monster with razor-sharp teeth, eyes as black as night, and unnaturally cold and pale skin. Vampires.

Myths and folklore were riddled with tales of these bloodthirsty creatures. Many legends were etched with these ravenous beasts, the vicious acts they performed to maintain immortality, and the lust to quench their thirst. But absent from these stories was the truth—the facts behind their existence, the reality of living as a monster, and the never-ending guilt cursed upon some of them.

Many believed the birth of vampirism had originated in Europe during the Middle Ages, but the truth dates back over four thousand years. During a time when magic was new among the human race, a very powerful witch in ancient Egypt used dark magic and necromancy to resurrect her mortal husband, sacrificing five for the sake of one. But dark magic came with a price, either in the form of a curse or with deadly consequences, and this time it came with both.

When the witch's husband rose from his restful slumber, he was dead but alive. Blood flowed through his veins, the dark fluid moving like molasses. A heart rested in his chest, a rhythmic beat still present but slow. But everything else inside him was dead, even the love for his wife.

He thirsted for more blood, for the sacrificial ritual required a constant source of life. The hunger burned inside him, and he craved the essence flowing through his wife's veins. Her smell was intoxicating to the ravenous monster, her blood calling him like a moth to a flame. Every inch of him yearned for her, desired her warmth against his cold body, and begged for one little taste. The hunger consumed him, and he sank his teeth into her, giving in to the lust raging inside. Every drop of blood was drained from her body as the witch met her fate. Her death was her punishment for the evil she had unleashed onto the world. But the creature, and the lives of all vampires, would also suffer at the hands of this curse. Plagued with five weaknesses for the five souls that had given birth to vampirism, the new species could die, a loophole in their immortal existence.

Vampirism was not a choice given to the very first of its kind, but many throughout history opted for the chance to be immortal. Being reborn with the ability to heal, to live out life without aging, and having unnatural strength, speed, and heightened senses made being a vampire ideal to many. But it came with a price. Driven by a powerful and uncontrollable hunger, most vampires were murderous monsters, taking life without remorse or any emotional repercussions.

The ritual was never meant to be what it became, but the dark magic within the vampire flowed through the newly created creature, making the curse more powerful with each life it took. A life taken was a life given, for each mortal strengthened the effects of the curse. Over time, the magic grew. With each intentional venomous slaughter, even more vampires were reborn, granting the creatures the power to tap into their instinctive nature to live as the dominate species. And so, like an unstoppable plague, vampirism traveled throughout the world.

~

Cillian Merrick Elldon Devlin was uncertain of the path he was given, troubled by the idea of living forever with an unquenchable thirst, but he was left with no other choice as he woke up covered in his own blood.

Adele was a beautiful woman with long auburn hair and the fairest skin Cillian had ever seen. As a childless widower creeping closer to middle age, Cillian, a handsome Irishman, found the young Adele captivating. Wondering how a woman with breathtaking beauty—and who was nearly fifteen years younger than he was—could be interested in a disheartened, lonely man made him question her intentions, and he was right.

Adele's attraction was keen on the man with a wide devilish grin and eyes so enchanting she often found herself lost in them. Cillian was sophisticated, charismatic, and a gentleman, a rare treat for the well-traveled and experienced woman. She yearned for him, desiring not only his blood but an immortal mate.

Over the centuries, the idea of being a vampire had become less popular as the transition into these creatures was an unbearable transformation. Unlike the original vampire, the change associated with the curse was horrific and excruciating, lasting days and causing non-stop pain until death finally ended the suffering. Every vein burned as the blood boiled. All the nerves in the body ruptured, firing a piercing blow of a thousand hot-iron razors slicing beneath the skin. The muscles shriveled, pulling away and ripping from the skeleton as the bones shattered. The throat burned, incinerating as if swallowing acid. The stomach seethed, retching bile from the depths of the lining of the digestive tract. The eyes glazed over, and the body convulsed as the curse took over, poisoning the blood with its incurable toxins. A pain like no other, surviving the torture of becoming a vampire was nothing compared to the thirst after being reborn. And the cravings were worse for Cillian.

Like the first vampire, Cillian had not chosen to be a bloodthirsty creature. His hunger and desire for blood drove him into a frenzy, and he ravaged the village he called home, murdering everyone, including Adele. Attempting to remove her gluttonous mate off the body of a young boy—children being off-limits to the female vampire—Adele was desperate to help tame his urges. But Cillian fought against her as he continued to drain the boy of blood, devouring every last drop from the gaping holes in his neck. Adele pulled harder, but her strength was no match for the fully charged beast. In an uncontrollable rage, Cillian attacked her, his anger for what she had done to him driving him to rip her heart from her chest.

Reverting to his civilized self, Cillian witnessed the damage he had inflicted. The village was covered in blood as dead bodies lay about, some intact and others barely recognizable as people. He could not believe his actions, nor could he remember the events after waking up as a vampire. But his activities did not disturb him, and neither did the death of Adele. He experienced nothing upon witnessing her mutilated body—no sadness, no anger, no regret, nothing. He was detached from his humanity, something most vampires still possessed after their thirst subsided. Cillian, however, was different. He was barbaric, merciless, and always hungry, never being able to satisfy his bloodlust. Purely evil, he was truly the monster described in the stories throughout history.

~

Cillian left his human life behind and fully embraced the monstrosity he had become, existing within the world as Merrick, the cutthroat vampire from Ireland. He spent his immortal life fleeing various parts of the world, escaping countless attempts at stopping him, which only left him wiping out entire towns and villages.

Determined to find a more suitable place to live out the remainder of his life, Merrick left Europe after almost one-hundred-and-thirty years of running. But the decision to leave would be one he would soon regret.

Struggling aboard a ship headed for Central America, the hungry vampire fought against the urge to murder all the crewmen. He grew weak on the long journey, falling into a conscious sleep as his veins dried up. He waited for death to take him as his heart reduced to an even slower unsteady rhythm. The thirst burned in his throat, the pain slicing as the dryness made every swallow unbearable. Merrick was certain he was dying, but he refused to take the life of a single soul aboard the ship. Once he tasted blood and refueled his strength, he would not be able to stop. And with everyone dead, he would be lost at sea, unable to steer a ship by himself, especially when the sun was out.

After months of travel, the ship landed in Central America, and Merrick disappeared. Hiding from the dense population of the port village, he headed inland. Desperation set in as his thirst intensified, wringing his neck and rubbing like sandpaper inside his throat. He could no longer take the torturous pain, so he listened, his heightened hearing searching for any poor soul wandering the area.

Two men tiptoed nearby as they hunted the area for food in the early dawn hour. Merrick focused on their steady heartbeats, each thump pumping blood through their bodies. A sweet smell filled his nose and made his mouth water. His cold skin tingled as his rigid muscle swelled, his own blood radiating through his veins. His body straightened, warmth rising along his spine. His heavy legs moved forward as he hunted the two men, catching them off guard and breaking their necks before draining their lifeless bodies. Rising from their slaughtered corpses, Merrick wiped his bloody face as his body returned to its powerful state.

Twigs snapped behind him as pain shot through his torso, half a dozen arrows piercing his body and narrowly missing his heart. His black eyes returned to their normal light blue as they flickered with fear. The veins around his face faded and revealed his pale skin. His sharp teeth retracted, making the injured vampire appear innocent and no longer a danger. But the locals knew better than to believe the vulnerability lying before them.

Merrick had wandered into the midst of a magical tribe and had murdered the two sons of the leader and the grandsons of the shaman. Distraught by the deaths of the chief's children, the tribe demanded vengeance, but death was too easy for the coldhearted beast. The people wanted pain and just punishment. They sought to torture the monster, giving him an endless life of misery for his bloodlust and inhumanity, so Merrick was cursed again. This time his own blood was used in the ritual, being drained from his body by vampire bats as the shaman controlled them. The pain was excruciating as every drop was sucked from his body, his heart shriveling within his chest. But before his heart stopped, the shaman slit the throat of each bat, placing the open wound against Merrick's mouth. The vampire consumed another curse, one bound to the mixed blood within the sacrificial animals. It surged through him, his cries ringing out as it killed him. Bringing to life a new immortal creature, the second curse resurrected a rare and demonic being unlike any other.

Merrick awoke even more dead yet still alive. His heart no longer beat, but the blood within his veins flowed, the black sludge oozing even slower. The curse raged through him and seeped into his muscles and bones, the dark magic becoming one with his body. It was no longer just a craving for blood controlling him, but rather a real hunger. A hunger ripping at his insides as he craved not only blood, but flesh. However, the ability to eat came with a painful penalty, a transformation linked to his only way of feeding. Merrick could only satisfy his hunger by becoming the true creature of his curse—an enormous, humanoid, demonic bat. His shift into a monster of hellish proportions and ghastly features was torturous, tiresome, and gruesome as he experienced the pain of the same agonizing death of the second curse each time he transformed.

He yearned for the needs and pleasures controlling his body and suffered the consequences of his actions every time, dealing with the pain of both becoming the monster and returning to his usual self. The beast inside him managed his desires and needs, while the humanity still present influenced his emotions. Although he was this creature, he enjoyed it, accepting the pain for pleasure, fear for control, needs for power, and the wants for manipulation. He was invincible. Unstoppable. A force to be reckoned with. He was Merrick, the demonic being who would stop at nothing to have the world cower at his feet and fear his very existence. But first, he would need even more power, more magic to fully become a true immortal. Magic itself could not stop him if he had enough power to control his transformation and the abilities of other magical creatures. All he needed now was a plan and the patience to see it through.

# Chapter 16

## Inside the Castle Walls

Daybreak approached, erasing the shadows along the eastern side of the island as sunlight crept inland. The air was cold and still, and a menacing silence lay across the mesa. With the darkness fading, the area was illuminated, bringing to life the somber beauty of the forbidden side of Kiluemar.

The dead trees of Shadow Forest stood tall, stretching their twisted and blackened branches up to the sky as if worshiping the sun. The ground within the forest lay barren and dry, all signs of life gone from the desolate wooded meadow. Nestled along the northern side of the forest next to the base of Maevis Mountains was Casteya Castle. Once the central residence of the less ethical and more devious creatures of the realm, the fortress now lay in partial ruins, falling victim to abandonment and inadequate care. The malevolent creatures who had not left Kiluemar had deserted the castle and retreated to the caves or woods on this side of the island. Taking their chances with surviving in the wild, the creatures hid, disappearing from the dangers of being Merrick's next meal. But many remained in the castle walls, submitting to Merrick and proving their loyalty to the powerful creature. Hopeful Merrick would show them mercy and grant them sanctuary, those choosing to stay were his obedient servants, surrendering all their morals and integrity to the monster and his demands.

Lucas, Camille, and Leif passed under two large iron gates, stopping at the overgrown castle grounds as daylight stalked behind them. The area was empty and unusually quiet. Years away had resulted in major changes to their once beautiful home as the odor of rotting flesh and decaying corpses filled the air. Blood stained the grass and dirt as they made their way closer to the second castle within the stone walls. Pushing the large wooden door open, they hurried to close it behind them, leaving the horrid smell outside. The walls were lit with flickering flames as candles lined the hallways leading to the east wing, the section of the castle dominated by Merrick and his followers. The rest of the cold, dreary citadel lay uninhabited and showed years of neglect.

Camille clutched Lucas's arm as they made their way down the hall. "I don't know about this, mon amour. This place is not how you described it."

Lucas shook his head in annoyance and slid his arm from her hands, ushering her over to Leif.

"It seems they decided to redecorate," Leif said, avoiding Camille's advancement toward him. "Don't worry so much,

Cami." He followed Lucas, turning the corner and continuing down another hallway lit up by the sunlight coming from the windows. "I'm sure Merrick will find you quite useful."

"That wasn't very reassuring." Camille stared out the enormous rectangular panes as she trailed behind. "This place is huge, no?"

Leif traced the walls within the shadows. "Casteya Castle is massive, consisting of two separate structures. The first castle was not sufficient after more creatures moved to this side of the island, so the second one—the one we're in now—was built about a hundred years after the first one. Most of the sections are add-ons. Merrick himself added the tall tower to the right out there."

"How do you know all this?"

"I was here when it happened."

"How long have you lived here?" Camille asked as she observed the cobweb-filled crooks along the arched stone ceiling.

"I was one of the original inhabitants of the island."

"So, you're very old, no?"

"You can say that."

"You look good for your age. And you are much more attentive than"—she glared at Lucas—"*some* people."

Lucas stopped at a large door at the end of the hall and directed his stern gaze at Leif. "Finished?"

"Whoa, someone's in a rather unpleasant mood. More than usual, I might add."

Lucas scoffed under his breath. "Piss off."

"Wow," Leif said with a snicker, "what's got your knickers in a twist? Has it been a while? A bit backed up there, Lucas? Or is it the fact Karramis got away . . . yet again?"

"Watch it, mate."

Leif took a step and leaned closer. "Or what?"

Camille stepped between them and brushed her fingers along Lucas's chest. "Now, mon amour, this—"

"Cami!" Lucas snatched her wrist. "It's neva', I repeat neva' gonna happen between us. I have zero feelin's or even the slightest bit of attraction to ya. None."

Camille jerked her hand away as her face turned red. "Va te faire enculer, connard!" She shoved Lucas. "Fine! You're not worth my effort. I'm done! I'm finished with you."

"Good. About fuckin' time."

Scowling, she crossed her arms. "Your loss, you worthless swine."

Leif gently nudged Camille aside, placing himself in front of Lucas. "Don't worry, Cami, it's not you. You see, Lucas here is obsessed with someone he can't have and who will *never* love him back, and it makes him crazy. You've had the displeasure of meeting the witch." He inched closer, narrowing his eyes down at Lucas. "You'll never have her. She doesn't want you. When will you get it through your head? You mean nothing to her. And when the time comes, I'm going to take pleasure in watching Merrick kill her so this fixation ends." Backing away, he paused. "Oh, and by the way, I hope I get one more sample of her before he does because she tastes mind-numbingly delicious, unlike—"

Lucas rammed his fist into the vampire's face.

Leif crashed against the wall but swooped to his feet.

Rushing at Lucas, he declared in a calm voice, "You're lucky."

"And why's that?" Lucas asked with a condescending tone.

"Because if you were anyone else, you'd be dead by now."

The door flung open, and a hairy beast on two legs stood towering over them, huffing loudly through its snout. With his brown fur, bull head, and body of a man, Lucas and Leif recognized the beast as Theseus, the minotaur. A pet to the Celestial Witch, Tressa, Theseus was not only her companion but also her bodyguard, protecting her from the unpredictable nature of Merrick.

A soft Indian voice called from behind the minotaur, "Theseus, who is it?"

"Hey, Tressa," Leif said lively, entering the room. "It's me. Did you miss me?"

A beautiful Indian woman with full lips and long, wavy black hair rose from a chair in the center of the room. She pecked Leif's cheeks and bowed her head as he kissed her hand.

"Well, it's about damn time." Tressa spotted Lucas's angered expression. "Whoa, what's got him vexed?"

"Don't mind him, he's having a temper tantrum." Leif's voice became childish as he pouted. "He had his wittle toy stolen from him, and he wants it back."

Tressa observed the hostility between the two but decided their quarrel was not worth her time. "Where are the others?" She moved her deep brown eyes over to the petite blonde standing in the doorframe. "And who's this?"

"Oh," Leif announced blankly, "this is Cami."

"Bonjour, madame." She curtsied. "Camille De la Rue Beaumont."

Tressa cringed, the young woman's overzealous and nasally voice buzzing in her ears. "Pleasure." She walked over to Lucas. "And the others?"

"Gastell returned to the woods soon afta' we got back. And Haydrin . . . well, I'm not sure where he is."

Tressa was calm as she circled the others. "And why's that?"

"We haven't seen him since last night. He got into a scuffle with some people and ran off."

She halted, perfectly statuesque as her black leather dress lay against her voluptuous figure. "Scuffle?"

"Yes," Leif said, "it seems Lucas insisted he take a detour to see Karramis last—"

"What?" Tressa asked with composure, a hint of excitement in her voice. "Karramis is alive?"

"Yes." Lucas glared at Leif with disapproval. "She's alive, just like I suspected. And so are her children."

Tressa smiled as a chuckle rose from her throat. "Delightful news."

"So, where's Merrick?" Leif moved over to the arched windows along the outside wall and peered up from the shadows. "In the tower?"

"Yes." Tressa sighed. "He spends most of his time up there these days."

"Feeding?"

"Yes. But mostly hiding out, groveling and being a huge pain in my ass."

Lucas glanced out at the tower. "Hidin' out?"

"Yes. The food supply has been scarce around here the last few years, so he hides up there to manage his hunger and bloodlust. He hasn't been the best of company lately."

"Hunger?" Camille gulped. "Bloodlust?"

"Oh, you poor thing," Tressa said, placing her hand over her cleavage as another chuckle erupted from her. "They didn't tell you about Merrick? Well, this'll be fun." She strolled over to Camille and tucked her bleached-blond hair behind the young girl's ears. "You're in for a real treat. I hope you're tougher than you look."

Camille's widen gaze zoomed between Leif and Lucas. "I thought you said he was a vampire." Blue eyes stopped on Leif. "He's like you, no? Does he not have control like you do?"

"He is," Leif admitted, staring at her with a blank expression on his face. "He *is* a vampire . . . sort of. And he does have control. Most of the time."

A shadow flew past the window and sent the room into a moment of darkness.

Camille ducked, avoiding the ghostly black figure. "*Merde! Ca c'était quoi?*"

"Fuckin' hell, Cami!" Lucas said, irritated. "Will you please speak fuckin' English?"

Helping Camille upright, Leif muttered under his breath, "Christ, you'd think after all that time in France, he would've learned some damn French."

Camille searched out the window. "What was that thing?"

Tressa sat regal and poised as she crossed her legs with Theseus standing behind her. "Master's home." The declaration was intoned with anticipation and mischief.

A man cried out somewhere in the castle, his painful shouts bouncing off the stony interior. Tension built as everyone's eyes fixated on the end of the long hall outside the door. Footsteps slapped against the floor as a man appeared, his bare feet moving swiftly down the corridor. The black robe wrapped around his lean body made his alabaster skin seem translucent, even more so with deep crimson painted across the lower half of his face as it trailed down his neck. Stopping, the man sniffed, sensing the presence of others within his chambers, along with a smell he did not recognize.

Merrick swooped into the room and stopped inches from Camille. The rush of air chilled her to the core, sending a wave of fear racing through her body as the man's sudden appearance startled her. She shrieked and stumbled back, stopping against the stone wall. Merrick advanced closer, leaning over and drawing in a long inhale. Wrinkling her nose in disgust as she stared at the blood on his face, Camille held her breath and pressed herself harder against the wall.

"You smell . . ." Merrick closed his eyes and licked his lips before sniffing again and moaning. "Delectable."

"Merci," Camille said nervously, angling her face away from him. "Enchanté, monsieur. Je suis Camille De la—"

Merrick grasped her neck, slamming her head against the cold stones. He snarled and placed his nose against her skin, taking in another long inhale and licking her neck. Closing his eyes again, he fell into a trance, lost as the young woman's blood pumped through her jugular against his fingers. Her body went limp beneath his hand as Camille's knees weakened, his grasp constricting as gagging whimpers escaped from her mouth.

Lucas placed his hand on Merrick's shoulder. "She's with us."

Merrick released her, and she fell to the floor. Drawing herself into the corner, Camille coughed and gasped for air as she rubbed her neck, the remnants of blood spreading across her fingers.

Rotating on his heels, Merrick smacked his lips and disappeared behind a decorative screen. He tossed his robe over the partition as he reached for the damp towel Tressa was holding. The room was quiet, the silence unnerving to the audience awaiting his return.

Tressa crossed her arms as she swayed over to Leif and Lucas, the tight material of her black dress clinging to her curvy hips. Resting her chin against her lifted hand, she whispered,

"You two really shouldn't have brought her here. I know you guys have been away for some time now, but you couldn't have forgotten his ways that easily."

Lucas matched her tone. "He agreed neva' to harm us."

"Aye," Merrick announced, stepping from behind the partition fully dressed and clean. "And I am a man of my word. However, I have made no such agreement with her."

Despite his recent actions, Merrick's subtle Irish accent and smooth tone made Camille relax as the man meandered across the room. His stoic and calm presence was hypnotizing. Not to mention, he was undeniably handsome. With beautiful pale blue eyes and a casual disposition, Merrick exuded a unique charm, one she found comforting and arousing. He reminded her of Leif, dangerous and intriguing. Sensual and charismatic but every bit threatening.

"But I can help you," Camille confessed as she rose to her feet, lowering her hand from her neck. "I have magic. I'm an Echo."

Tressa inhaled with a gleam in her eyes. "An Echo? Really?"

Merrick paused his perusal of the young woman, angling his attention over at Tressa. "And what exactly is an Echo?"

"They're supposed to be able to share powers with other magical beings. I thought they were a myth though."

Merrick held his hand out to Camille. "What is your name again?"

"Camille De la Rue Beaumont," she answered, hesitating as she placed her hand into his, "but you may call me Cami."

"Well, it's a pleasure to meet you, mademoiselle. Je suis Cillian Merrick Elldon Devlin, but you may *only* address me as Merrick." He kissed her hand, lingering as he enjoyed the sweet-smelling blood racing through her veins. Tightening his grip, he stood up straight, refusing to release her. "Now Camille, prove yourself. Prove you're worthy of my time and allegiance. Tell me, what sort of magic lingers deep inside me?" He squeezed harder as he cocked his head, a sly grin twisting the corners of his mouth upward. "Do it." The command was unyielding. "Use your powers on me."

Camille opened her mouth as a silent cry fell from her lips, the crushing grasp cutting off circulation to her fingers. Trying to focus, she fought through the discomfort and concentrated on her ability. Living with the others for all those years had made mastering her powers easy. Leif's curse was powerful, and Camille was able to sense what it was like to be a vampire. Leif's true nature was terrifying, but it was also exciting, making her feel alive with unlimited possibilities. Lucas, on the other hand, rarely allowed her to practice on him. But when he did, his ability was hard for her to control. Magic was not an easy thing to master and having to consciously command it to work was mentally draining. Lucas's powers were not constant, and there was not a simple on-and-off switch. He had to concentrate, clearing his own mind before allowing the thoughts of others into his. Manipulation to his own mind was key to truly mastering his Telematra powers.

The magic inside Merrick was mind-blowing as Camille sensed a massive amount of power flowing within him. The dominate curses raged but there was something more, much more. A strange presence burrowed deep within the depths of him, a mix of unusual and displaced power, ones she could not pinpoint. There was a combination of magic coursing through him, a blend of power so strong it frightened her, but it was not his. Only the curses belonged within the soul before her, and only the curses Camille could invoke.

The smell of everyone's blood in the room wafted past her nose with each breath, the difference in their scent making them even more unique. Heartbeats pounded in her ears as sweat trailed down her forehead. A yearning warmed her skin, a sensual and energizing hunger unlike anything she had ever experienced before. Her attention pulled to Lucas, her pelvis tingling as her insides grew warmer. Breathing heavily, she listened as his beating heart made her body quiver, his veins raging with an intoxicating elixir—a tonic filled with life, pleasure, and exhilarating decadence. She could taste his mouthwatering blood as she licked her lips, the thirst exploding in her throat.

Camille jerked her hand from Merrick's crushing grip. Panting, she pulled herself away from the fantasy she was lost in, fanning herself and wiping the sweat from her forehead.

"That was rather stimulating," Leif said, his own desires awakened.

"No kiddin'," Lucas admitted as he cleared his throat and stared at Camille, baffled by what he just witnessed. "What exactly did she sense?"

"I don't know, but I would very much like to retreat to my room right about now."

"Why? Are ya tired?"

"Nope."

"I believe you," Merrick said, flashing Camille an exceptionally wide grin.

Camille was disgusted with herself. The pleasure she had just experienced at the expense of devouring a living soul made her stomach turn. She had not only admitted her keen admiration for Lucas, but she had also wanted to taste him—kill him—all the while enjoying every moment of it. Merrick was not just a monster, but he was a revolting beast who drew sensual pleasure from his killings.

Tressa rolled her eyes. "Enough. Can we please move on?" She sat down and crossed her legs. "Lucas, tell Merrick the good news."

Intrigued, Merrick faced Lucas. "You have good news?"

"I do." Lucas pulled back his shoulders. "I was right about Karramis. And her children. They didn't die all those years ago, like we were led to believe. It was all a lie."

"A guise?" Merrick asked, tilting his head in thought. "To conceal 'em from me, I reckon." Not a question. "You are positive the children are alive?" The inquiry directed at Lucas. "You can confirm this?"

"Yes," Tressa said, her face beaming with excitement. "And so is Karramis. Now we can finally take her powers. And with all four elemental powers, that kind of joined magic will be unstoppable."

"Don't forget about Will," Leif said with a sidelong glance at Lucas. "You still want his powers too, right?"

Tressa smiled. "Will is alive too?"

"Yeah, he is," Lucas admitted with resentment in his voice. "Why are ya so surprised by that? Was he supposed to be dead or somethin'?"

"Aye." Merrick ran his fingers over his stubbled chin. "We have been searchin' fer him fer a while now. No one has seen him in years. We just assumed he was dead."

"It's a shame he isn't. That bloke has been a constant pain in my ass." Lucas lowered his voice and directed his attention at Merrick. "What's this about killin' Karramis? That wasn't part of the deal. Ya promised me I could have her."

"Have her?" Leif asked with an irritated groan and a roll of his eyes. "Jävlar helvete, Lucas. This shit again? Really? Why do you have this obsession with her? She's a nuisance! A nobody. Nothing. She's a meaningless witch. She's done nothing but hurt you and manipulate you. When are you going to get it through your thick head that she's not fucking worth it? She's a lying, scheming bitch who can't keep her damn mouth shut. She doesn't want you, Lucas. And she sure as hell doesn't love you. And she's *never* going to."

"Fuck you! Mind your own fuckin' business!" Lucas shoved him. "This doesn't concern you!"

Leif whooshed over to Lucas, stopping inches from his face and growling down at him.

"Leif," Merrick said calmly as he signaled him over.

Merrick and Leif retreated away from the group as both spoke in a different dialect to one another.

Camille leaned over to Lucas, ignoring the rage streaming across his face. "What language are they speaking? They are not the same, no?"

Filling the silence, Tressa tapped her fingers against her folded arms and answered, "No, they aren't. Merrick's speaking . . ." She trailed off, listening to their conversation. "He's speaking German, and Leif is speaking Russian."

"Russian?" Camille asked, her brows pulling together as she scrunched her face. "But I thought Leif was from Scandinavia."

Lucas shook his head and rolled his eyes, letting out an exasperated sigh. "Scandinavia isn't a country, Cami. Leif is from Sweden, but he can speak ova' a dozen different languages."

"Then why do they not just speak in the same language?"

Tressa sighed loudly. "Because, you silly girl, they don't want anyone to know what the hell they're talking about."

"Leif," Merrick said as he returned to the others, "you and Mademoiselle Beaumont are free to go. You two are done here."

Camille did not argue. "Merci, monsieur." Grasping Leif's arm, she urged him over to the door. "Au revoir."

Closing the door behind them, Tressa leaned against it. "Okay, look, I know you care about Karramis, Lucas, and I'm sorry about this, but she has to die. She's—"

"I no longer deem the Fire Witch to be beneficial to me or my plans, Tressa," Merrick announced firmly. "Her magic is insignificant in comparison to her children's abilities."

Tressa gasped, the unexpected shock forcing her head to jerk back. "What? Since when? Why didn't you tell—"

"Because I do not owe ya an explanation. Nor do I believe it is essential to communicate my every decision before the move is played."

"But Merrick, she's only going to get in the way. Not to mention—"

"No." His voice was calm but his formidable expression pierced through her. "Karramis is not your concern. She is no threat to me, nor I to her. She is obsolete and irrelevant. Her children on the other hand . . . I want those children, and I want 'em now. I have been waitin' far too long to have 'em slip through my fingers again. Their powers are what I've been waitin' fer. *They* are who the prophecy is truly about, not her. And I will not let 'em get away again."

"But Merrick—"

He slapped her, causing her to twist sideways and fall to the ground. Theseus let out a roar as he charged after Merrick, but the confident man did not flinch as he growled and braced for a fight.

"Theseus!" Tressa yelled as she rubbed her throbbing face. "Stop!"

The minotaur halted as a low growl escaped with a heavy snort. Retreating away with his eyes on Merrick, Theseus headed over to Tressa and helped her up.

Merrick made his way over to them and stopped in front of the minotaur. "Stand aside."

Theseus stood tall, refusing to move.

"Move now, on your own free will, or I will gladly do it for you."

"It's fine, Theseus," Tressa said, placing her hand on the minotaur's arm.

Merrick ran his finger over the small bloody cut along her cheekbone. "You and your beast are no match fer me, witch." He licked his finger. "Remember, you are only alive because you have been of use to me. But that can easily be reevaluated. No one, I repeat, no one is goin' to stop me from gettin' what I want. Got that? *I* am in charge, and I will do as I please. I want those children, Tressa. Not Karramis. And I want Will . . . And I *will* have 'em. But no one, and I mean no one, is goin' after Karramis."

Lucas narrowed his eyes. "But what about—"

"Oh. You're still here?" Merrick waved him away. "You may go now."

"But—"

"Dismissed, Mr. Fraye."

Opening the door, Lucas cleared his mind, his head pounding as he concentrated on the voids within the depths of Merrick's subconscious.

"You're wastin' your time, Telematra," Merrick declared, amused. "Ya know your silly powers don't work on me."

Lucas walked through the threshold, grabbing hold of the handle.

"Oh, and Lucas," Merrick said, "ya might want to remember this fer future reference. Ya really shouldn't go meddlin' around where you aren't welcome, or overspeppin' your position 'cause it might just get someone killed one of these days."

Lucas exited the room and closed the door behind him.

Tressa returned to her chair, holding a piece of cloth against her injured face. Merrick had never hit her before, and she was grateful he had kept his anger under control all these years because his powerful blow was painful. Reeling from the throbbing ache, Tressa was concerned by his actions. Merrick was a persistent man, and she was afraid his patience was fading. After centuries, the powers he desired were within his grasp, but his fortitude to withstand waiting any longer was proving to be a challenge. Tressa needed to keep his yearnings at bay, and not just his hunger. She was his conscience, reminding him of his ultimate goal, but she was not sure how much longer she could hold him back before he made his final move. However, he needed to remain patient, or else the plan would fail, sending years of hard work and carefully thought-out decisions out the window. Now, more than ever, patience was a virtue, a trait no longer apparent in the man before her.

# Chapter 17

## Overcoming Obstacles

Rhiannon rested her cheek on an open book, her gentle snoring filling a quiet room in the corner of the library. Candles lit up the stone nook as the flames disappeared among melting wax. Inside the fireplace across the room, coals glowed with fading embers, the heat fighting against the cold air blanketing the dusty books, old documents, and girl sleeping on the desk.

"Rhiannon?" a soft voice whispered.

Rhiannon twitched in her chair. Her snoring stopped, but her head remained planted against an old, tattered book.

A hand grasped her shoulder. "Rhiannon?"

Springing upright, she flung her arms across the table and threw items from the desk onto the floor. "Holy Gorgons from Tartarus!" Spotting a familiar face, she relaxed. "Jesus, Ryan, you scared the crap out of me!"

Ryan pinched his lips together, and his brows drew inward as he held back a laugh. "What?"

"What, what?" Rhiannon knelt on the floor. "What's so funny?"

"Holy Gorgons from Tartarus? What does that even mean?"

Rhiannon giggled. "I have no idea. It just kinda came out."

Joining her on the floor, Ryan shuffled papers into a pile and stacked the remaining books before placing them on the table. "Don't you ever go home? This is the third time this week."

Rhiannon spotted the streetlights beaming outside through the large cathedral windows. "What time is it?"

"Four."

"Ugh! Aunt K is going to be livid if she wakes up again and I'm not home."

"Well, I reckon we'd better get you home then."

Ryan Hillvec was a regular around the library, aiding Randolyn with various chores and duties. Despite being present more often than not, he had only met Rhiannon a few weeks ago. A regular herself, Rhiannon spent most of her time in the library in the evenings, enjoying the escape from reality.

Rhiannon and Ryan blew out the candles and headed for the entrance. Passing the fireplace, she spotted a spontaneous fire now raging.

"Wait," Rhiannon said, stopping and allowing the heat to warm her chilled body. "Why are you here so early?"

"Looking for you."

"Are you stalking me?" she asked sarcastically.

Ryan grinned. "No. I was up early and figured I'd check on you. I've only known you a short time, but you seem to make a habit out of sleeping here."

"Yeah, I do, huh?" Rhiannon made her way to the door again, smoke billowing from the abruptly extinguished embers. "I don't do it on purpose, but I just can't seem to sleep."

"Why?" Ryan closed the door behind him. "Is it the werewolf thing again?"

Still reeling from the attack at the cabin, Rhiannon had opted to stay in the village with Kavana and Aidan, the safest place for her in her opinion. The scars left on her leg after the attack were minimal, nearly unnoticeable after her ability to heal erased all permanent damage. But the mental wound was harder to repair. Her dreams controlled her life, the nightmares forcing her to relive the attack over and over again.

"Most nights it is," Rhiannon said, "but no, not that. It's something else. Something that I feel deep inside . . . There's just something not right going on around here."

The months following the attack at the cabin had been quiet. Peace returned to the realm, a long-forgotten luxury of living on the magical island. With the portals open, the residents of Kiluemar were at ease again, knowing they could leave at any time. Even the nighttime slayings stopped as many creatures returned to the non-magical realm to feed. No longer trapped in a perpetual nightmare, the inhabitants roamed the island again, traveling freely between the different portals, no longer afraid of what lay beyond the protection of Caerwyn Village and

Stoweward. Even Merrick had not been seen after the return of Lucas and the others. But while many welcomed this calm and serene way of life, the quietness was not accepted by all.

"Well, what do you think it is?" Ryan asked.

"I think he's playing games with us."

"Merrick?"

"Yeah. Like some strategic plan—A mind game of psychological warfare. I don't trust it. I mean, considering everything I've learned about Merrick these past few months, and everything I witnessed from Lucas, not to mention his friends, I don't feel they would give up so easily. Everyone thinks I'm reading too much into it and I should just accept the peace and calm while it lasts, but I don't know. Something is just off."

"Well, I believe you."

Rhiannon was relieved. "You do?"

"Yeah. I mean, why not? There hasn't been peace around here in a long time, so why question your theory? Plus, you *are* the almighty magic the prophecy predicted, right?"

"I guess so."

"You guess so? You haven't decrypted it yet? That's surprising. I mean, you spend so much time researching, but you never thought to decipher the prophecy?"

"I don't think there's much to decipher. But maybe your right, maybe I should take another look at it. I'll start doing that in the morning."

"No." Ryan hurried in front of her, making her stop. "You need a break."

"A break?" Rhiannon said skeptically as she frowned.

"Yes. I'm taking you around the island. You've been here months already and you still haven't seen anything outside this village except the area between here and your parents' place." Ryan grabbed her hand as she shook her head and backed away in protest. "Yes. We'll be fine. I promise. I mean, we both have magic, so—"

"I wouldn't rely on mine."

Ryan ignored her. "And things *have* been quiet lately. Plus, we'd be going during the day. What's the worst that could happen?"

"Don't say that! Great, you just jinxed us. Now I'm really not going."

Ryan laughed as he continued down the dirt path. "I didn't realize you were so superstitious."

"I'm not. I'm just . . . cautious."

"You know, you should try to live a little. Maybe it will do you some good. Help clear your mind. You're not going to be any good at saving the world if you're tired and unbalanced. You're too tense. It's okay to not be the one with all the answers."

Rhiannon smiled. "You sound like James."

Ryan reminded Rhiannon of her brother in many ways. The dashing nineteen-year-old carried himself like James, self-confident and never taking himself too seriously. Both shared deep brown eyes, brunette hair, and warm ivory skin, but it was Ryan's bashful smile that separated him from her brother, for James was never shy about anything. And his English accent was even more comforting. Ryan was not only her friend, a companion to fill the void of missing her family, but he reminded her of two important men in her life.

Rhiannon lowered her voice as she reached the door of her temporary home. "Fine. I'll go with you. What time?"

Ryan matched her tone. "Ten. And why are we whispering?"

"I don't want to wake my aunt or—"

The door swung open, and Aidan stood on the other side of the threshold.

"Aidan," Rhiannon finished.

"Fall asleep at the library again, lass?"

"Yeah. Sorry."

"No worries, but ye're lucky it was me openin' this door and not yer aunt."

"Yeah, I know." Rhiannon twisted to Ryan. "I'm going to take your advice and get some rest. So, can we meet at noon instead?"

"Sure. I'll meet you at the north entrance at noon then."

"North entrance?"

"Yeah. You didn't think we were going to walk the whole island, did you?"

"Oh. Good point."

"I thought so," Ryan said with a smug grin.

"You're such a smartass, you know that?"

"So I've been told."

Rhiannon rolled her eyes, but cracked a half smile as she entered the house. "Goodnight, Ryan." She turned to Aidan. "Hey, thanks again for not telling Aunt K about all this. I'll do better. I promise."

"Ye're welcome. Now, go get some sleep."

Ryan disappeared down the street as Aidan closed the door.

Rhiannon strolled under the stone archway and crossed her arms as chills blanketed her body, her apprehension overpowering the smoldering sun beaming down from a cloudless sky. Her long, flowy dress blew in the hot summer breeze as she made her way over to the garden. A large herd of deer caught her attention in the distance as they wandered throughout Muse Meadow and alongside an even larger herd of wild horses.

Ryan sat in the grass among a lush field of blooming foliage as Rhiannon approached him.

"Are there always that many of them?" Rhiannon asked, the grass rustling as she came to a stop.

Ryan followed her gaze into the meadow. "The deer or horses?"

"Both."

"Yeah. There are thousands of horses and deer here. And rabbits, wolves, elk, birds—"

"How'd they get here?"

"The same way everyone else did, but most of the ones nowadays have a magical influence behind their creation. That's why we have so many. When the portals closed, we had to be self-sufficient, so magic helped create a lot of our food."

"You ate the horses and wolves too?"

"Yeah, if food was scarce, but that didn't happen too often, so those were mostly for the other creatures."

"Right. Oh, by the way, sorry I'm late."

Glancing down at his watch, Ryan said with confusion in his voice, "It's only a quarter past noon."

"Yeah, so I'm fifteen minutes late then."

"You're definitely a tenacious one."

Rhiannon snickered. "Hey, that's what my dad calls my mom."

"Is your mum just as stubborn as you are?"

"Yes, but I like to think of us as . . . spirted and determined."

"Whatever you say." Ryan giggled quietly as he stood up. "So, where would you like to go first?"

"I'm not sure. How about you take me to some of your favorite places?"

"All right then, that's easy enough."

They headed into the trees along the northwestern corner of the village as a mix of oak and elm towered above them. After a short trek, they stopped at a whirlpool swirling a few inches from the ground, the watery portal transparent, almost invisible.

Ryan raised his arm with his palm facing up. "You'll have to hold my hand."

"Why?"

"To make sure we end up at the same place. You aren't familiar with everywhere, so you might end up in some random place, either on the island or back in the real world."

"Oh. Okay." She clasped her hand around his. "How many portals are there anyway?"

"Hmm. I've never really thought about it before. Well, I know there are five in the non-magical realm . . . and I think there are maybe a dozen here, give or take. I haven't been through all of them, so I'm not really sure of the exact number."

"And people can just travel freely between them?"

"Only around the island and to the outside. The doorways into Kiluemar are closed until the full moon. Didn't you learn all this from your parents or aunt?"

"No. Other than reading about a lot of this stuff, I haven't really asked anyone any questions lately."

"Why?" Ryan sensed she did not want to answer. "Well, if you ever have any questions, feel free to ask away. I tend to get bored sometimes when helping at the library, so I've been known to pick up a book or two. Plus, living here my whole life also helps." He pulled her forward and paused. "Ready?"

Rhiannon fixated on the portal, squeezing Ryan's hand and nodding unconvincingly.

"Relax," Ryan said with a comforting tone, gently mimicking her tight grasp. "You're acting like I'm escorting you to your death or something. You'll be fine. I won't let anything happen to you." He ushered her into the portal. "I promise."

Rhiannon landed on a soft surface, a warmth squishing between her toes as her sandals pressed deeper into the sand. Amazed by the sight before her, she scanned the breathtaking bay as the gentle waves blanketed the off-white coastline. A cool breeze blew off the water and gave Rhiannon some relief from the uncomfortably dry heat she dealt with back by the village. Smiling, she drew in a long inhale as a unique blend of saltwater, musk, and jasmine swirled around her. She closed her eyes as a calmness took over, relaxing her racing heart and bringing ease to her anxious nerves.

"Never been to a beach before?" Ryan asked.

"No. Never. Where are we exactly?"

"Cavern Beach." Ryan pointed at the bay. "And that's Half Moon Harbor. This is my favorite place on the island."

Rhiannon tucked her dress behind her and sat down. "I can see why." Removing her sandals, she dug her toes into the sand, giggling as the shoreline covered her feet. "This place is so magical."

"You should see it during a full moon."

"Why? What happens then?"

"The mermaids and Water Dragons come together and dance."

"Dance?" Rhiannon brushed her fingers through the sand. "Mermaids and dragons can dance?"

"They're not really dancing, but it seems like it. The magic in the waters around the island and the powers of the moon illuminate the mermaids' tails, and these vibrant, beautiful colors light up the water. Many years ago, when going out at night wasn't so dangerous, the mermaids put on these shows for the people of the island, and one night the Water Dragons joined in. They manipulated the water and made it appear as if it was dancing. It was absolutely magical. A pure work of art."

Rhiannon stared at him as his eyes showed him escaping deeper into a joyous memory.

He sighed. "I haven't seen it in years, but I hear the mermaids and dragons still do it every full moon. It's a tradition they refuse to abandon."

"What are those?" Rhiannon asked, directing her attention over to the openings along the cliffs in front of them.

"Those are the caverns that give this beach its name. They go a few miles in and end at an underground river." Ryan faced behind them. "And those back there are Ember Cliffs. Below there is a grotto and more caves. The grotto is quite massive, and the only way to get there is either through the water or under the land bridge. Or from the opening along the cliff itself, but I wouldn't recommend that because it's a long way down. I'll have to show it to you one day."

"Why not now?"

"Because we have other places to see first."

Rhiannon slipped her sandals on and brushed the sand off her dress. "Okay. Where to next then?"

Heading back over to the portal, Ryan said cheerfully, "You get to decide this time."

"But I don't—"

"I'll give you the names of two other locations I love on the island, and you can decide where we go next."

She smiled and the light freckles under her eyes faded against her rosy skin tone. "Great idea."

"Thanks. Okay, so my other two favorite places are Guardian Lake and Valley of the Giants."

Rhiannon grabbed Ryan's hand and yanked him forward, both disappearing into the portal and stepping onto a stony surface.

Ryan narrowed his eyes and shifted his head in all directions.

Copying his frantic search, Rhiannon asked with concern in her voice. "What's wrong?"

"This isn't right." He hurried north along the rocky plateau. "Something's wrong."

"Ryan," she called after him, "what do you mean? What happened?"

"Where were you thinking when we went through?"

"Valley of the Giants. Why?"

Ryan bolted and the pebbles along the rocky, dirt-covered ground clanked beneath his shoes.

"Ryan!" Rhiannon chased after him. "What's wrong?"

Stopping at the edge of a cliff, Ryan hunched over, his breath flowing rapidly from his mouth. Rhiannon halted behind him, the burn in her chest aching with each deep inhale.

"*That's* Valley of the Giants." Ryan pointed into the canyon below them. "We should've landed down there. Not up here."

Below rested a lush valley with a steady river painted against a bright green landscape. A waterfall echoed calm whispers as it fell from a mountainous backdrop, the gentle waters running through the center of the valley and exiting into a beautiful lagoon. Nothing else could be heard beyond the sounds of Mother Nature, the water element dominating this part of the island.

Confused by his reaction, Rhiannon asked, "So . . . what does that mean?"

"I'm not sure, but I've never heard of the portals shifting before, at least not inside the realm."

"Well, I'm sure there's a perfectly good explanation." Rhiannon paused, searching for a subject to ease his mind. "So, where are the giants?"

Accepting the distraction, he answered, "They live beyond the waterfall in the caves. They don't usually come out, but when they do, it's pretty spectacular. They're definitely a unique and magnificent species."

"Have you seen *all* of them?"

"No. And how did you know—Oh right, I'm guessing you found the book on them?"

"Yeah. I think I've read almost every book about magical creatures at least twice now." She headed back over to the portal, her voice getting louder as she moved away from him. "Since we can't get down there, let's go see Guardian Lake instead. Come on, we've got lots to see still."

Ryan jogged after her with a smile on his face. "So, you're having a good time then, and this *was* a good idea? I mean, I was right by getting you out of that stuffy library?" He paused and waited for her to answer. "Admit it, I was right, right?"

"Don't gloat, Ryan. It doesn't suit you well."

"Ha! You just don't want to admit you're wrong. Fine, fine. I won't rub it in, but still, you're having a good time, right?"

"Yes," Rhiannon admitted with a sigh. "Yes, I'm having a good time." She smiled and playfully nudged him. "Thanks, Ryan."

"No problem."

"I just wish James was here. He'd love seeing all of this."

"When was the last time you saw him?"

"A week ago, for our birthday."

"What?" Ryan exclaimed. "I missed your birthday?"

"Don't worry about it. It's fine. We had a small get-together. It was nothing fancy."

"No, I will not forget about it. It was your birthday. Your sixteenth birthday, mind you. The big sweet sixteen, the pinnacle age for all girls. I must sing to you."

"No, that's quite all—"

"Happy birthday to you," Ryan sang dramatically, his off-key voice booming across the mesa. "Happy birthday to you. Happy birthday—"

"Ryan!" Rhiannon interrupted as she smacked his arm, her cheeks bright red.

"Ow!" He rubbed his bicep. "What?"

"Stop it!" His charisma was hard to ignore, and she grinned. "You're embarrassing yourself."

"Fine, but you have to at least let me make it up to you with a gift."

"Not necessary. And by the way, what does 'pinnacle age for all girls' even mean?"

"No clue," Ryan admitted, chuckling as he shrugged. "But it sounded good, right?"

She flashed him a smile, matching his soft laughter. "If you say so."

Ryan stopped next to the portal, his expression now serious. "Hey, before we go, may I ask you something? Something that might be a little personal."

"Uhm, okay. Yeah. I—I guess."

"Why don't you train with James? I mean, you talk about not having powerful enough magic to protect yourself and being afraid all the time, so why not focus all your attention on getting better at that so you *can* protect yourself instead of spending so much time in the library?"

She sighed.

"Sorry, I was just curious."

"No, it's fine. And it's a valid question. But the truth is, I did. I did practice. For weeks I tried to control my powers, but I couldn't do it. Communicating with the dragons is the only thing that comes naturally to me. I'm not like James, you know. My mental strength to physically control my magic lacks precision. And I don't get it, honestly. I mean, I've always been a fast learner, but I guess it was always more about being book smart and not much of anything else. So, I stopped training. I just figured if all I could contribute to this whole thing was my brain, then I was going to give it my all—Learn any and everything there is to know about this place, magic, and the creatures."

Ryan placed his hands on her upper arms and gently squeezed. "Rhiannon, you do realize it takes months, even years to master just one ability, and you have many. You've got to give it time. It's not going to happen overnight or as fast as you want it to. I'm sure James has difficulties with controlling his magic, he just works harder instead of dwelling on it."

"Yeah . . . that does sound like him."

"See! There you go. You just need to give yourself time. And I really think you need to face your fears. You can't master your magic if you don't get your emotions under control. Like my dad always says, 'learn to rule your emotions, don't let your emotions rule you.' And I've always lived by those words."

"And how do you suppose I do that? It's not like I can go fighting a werewolf right now. Not to mention, that would be a completely stupid idea."

"No, that's not what I mean."

"Well, what *do* you mean then?"

"Learn about them. Step into their shoes and understand them and their perspective. Educate yourself on them as people rather than monsters. Learn about the curse they are plagued with. Dig deeper into their history and not just what you've read about them."

Rhiannon placed her hand on her hip. "Again, how do you suppose I do that?"

"I have an idea . . . But I have to know if you trust me first."

Rhiannon pulled her brows together and puckered her mouth to one side. "I trust you enough to come out here with you. Isn't that enough? And why? What are you planning?"

"First, we have to deviate from the plan and go somewhere else." He paused, his alluring gaze staring over at her. "And . . ."

"And what?"

"And go somewhere so I can tell you something."

Rhiannon cocked her head and asked suspiciously, "And that would be?"

Reaching out his hand, he smiled. "Well, you've got to come with me to find out."

"Fine." She slapped her hand into his. "Lead the way."

Rhiannon peered up at the sky as they stepped into a valley. Her stomach tightened with anxiety, nervousness setting in as the sun lowered closer to the horizon. But despite the knot twisting in her guts, she welcomed the cooler temperatures again as they trekked north within the shadows of a grassy gorge. A dense forest waited for them at the opening to the north, the lush canopies and closely arranged trunks creating a wall of nature.

"Where are we?"

"Lucien Valley." Ryan pointed at the trees in front of them. "And that there is Full Moon Forest. That's where we're going."

Rhiannon halted. "Why are we going *there*?"

"Come on, we have to hurry if we want to get there and back before dark."

Full Moon Forest was even more compact as they reached the tree line. Making their way farther into the woods, the area opened, the pink and orange sky beaming through the channel-like gaps along the canopies.

Lifting a low-hanging branch, Ryan asked, "So, what do you know about werewolves?"

Rhiannon ducked under it. "That they were cursed a long time ago by some witch. And despite what is told in modern fantasy and even folklore, a bite doesn't turn one into a werewolf. Something I was relieved to read about, by the way."

"Yeah, I bet. Anything else?"

"A few tidbits, but nothing major. There actually isn't much about them in the library."

"I've noticed that myself, but what is in there is correct. Werewolf bites do not create new werewolves. They are born from a bloodline cursed by a witch. A Celestial Witch, to be exact. It was a punishment."

"Punishment for what?"

"Infidelity."

"Really? That seems kinda harsh. I mean, to curse a single person is one thing, but to curse a whole bloodline? It seems a little extreme. But hey, you know what they say, hell hath no fury like a woman scorned."

"More like hell hath no fury like a *man* scorned."

"Seriously?" Rhiannon asked, intrigued.

"Yeah. The original story dates back to the Roman Empire era, but the location has changed over the centuries. The story goes that a Celestial Witch found out his wife was having an affair, so on the next full moon he performed a spell to punish her. It's been said he didn't mean to actually curse her, though. He only wanted to make her feel the same rage and pain he did. But his spell backfired because he used the blood of her lover."

"Wait, how'd the witch get the lover's blood?"

Ryan stared at her with wide eyes and a raised brow. "How do you think?"

Rhiannon's jaw dropped. "He killed him?"

"Yep. The husband wanted her to suffer, so not only did he murder her lover, but he also made her drink his blood. And when his wife consumed it, the blood and dark magic went into her unborn child. The *lover's* child. And the curse was magnified because of the connective link between the child and the biological father. Their joined blood was cursed, affecting their future bloodline, and thus werewolves were born."

"So, every descendent from that same bloodline is cursed to be a werewolf?"

"Yeah. But it's not from birth. Well, not really."

"What do you mean?"

"No one knows why, but many think it had something to do with the ritual the witch performed. Something he did or said in the spell."

"What?"

"The curse only surfaces after one loses their virginity. Once a member of the line, uhm, *mates* with someone, anyone, then the curse takes effect on the next full moon."

"Wow! That *is* harsh."

"Yeah, no kidding."

Rhiannon went silent. She planted her feet against the ground and drove her hands to her hips. Her head leaned sideways as her eyes stared at nothing.

"What is it?" Ryan asked. "What's churning in that head of yours?"

"So, first off, how did the pregnant woman turn into a werewolf? Didn't that kill her baby?"

"According to the story, the woman never actually turned into a werewolf herself, but her child did when it was older."

"The child got the whole curse instead?"

"It would seem so. But to answer your other question, when a woman is pregnant, she doesn't transform. The curse flows between the mother and child, but the magic is somehow severed until the child is born, then the mother goes back to being a werewolf every full moon."

"Right. Okay, so . . . so, uhm, how do you know all of this? I mean, you seem pretty well informed about this . . . And you brought me to the forest where werewolves hide out during the full moon." She glanced up at the sky before starting to pace, panic rising in her voice. "And close to dark, I might add. But it's not a full moon, so I'm not sure what's going on."

Ryan moved in front of her wavering march. "Rhiannon."

She jumped, halting and backing away from him.

"Rhiannon, I'm not going to hurt you. You're still perfectly safe with me. Just calm down, please. I only brought you here to tell you the story and to show you that there is nothing to be afraid of up here." He pointed back to the dense tree line. "Did you notice the cluster of trees back there?"

"Yeah," she answered, drawing out the word.

"And did you notice how they're covered in bright green moss with full and beautiful branches?" He strolled over to a tree not far from them. "And how these here are stripped of most their bark, how they have no moss, and the branches, although full, lack the same beauty?"

"Yeah, actually. The ones back there looked similar to the ones in my astral projection."

"You see, the trees back there are dryads. They line the forest leading into Lucien Valley to stop the werewolves from getting through. The highlands are where the werewolves go during the full moon to make sure they don't hurt anyone. Haydrin is the only exception to all the other werewolves on the island. None of those who are cursed with this want to hurt anyone. It's just something they can't control. But they do whatever they can to keep everyone on the island safe."

Rhiannon crossed her arms and moved closer to him. "Again, how do you know all of this, Ryan?"

"Because . . . because I'm a werewolf."

Dropping her arms, she gasped, the shock halting her ability to breathe for a moment. "What? But you. . . you told me you were a Celestial Witch."

"I am. I didn't lie about that."

"But you lied about this!" Rhiannon paced away from him.

"I didn't . . ." Ryan rushed over to her and grasped her shoulders, staring into her distant deep blue eyes. "Rhiannon, please listen. I didn't lie. I just . . . I just kept the truth from you."

"Oh no you're not!" She jerked out of his grasp. "You're not getting out of this on a technicality. It was a lie, Ryan, and you know it! I can see it in your eyes."

"Fine. Yes, I lied. But I didn't want to tell you because I knew you'd act like this. When I first met you, you were so scared, and I didn't want to make it worse. I didn't want you to be afraid of me just because I'm something I can't control. And when we became friends, it only got harder for me—"

"Harder for *you*?" Rhiannon asked, dumbfounded. "Seriously, Ryan? I've been living in fear for months. I can't sleep. I barely eat. I—"

"Rhiannon."

Her voice grew louder. "I don't even see my family that much because I'm terrified of leaving the village. How selfish could you possibly be?"

"Rhiannon."

"And this is hard on *you*?"

"Rhiannon!"

"What?" she screamed, her voice driving the birds from the trees.

Ryan jerked her around.

Rhiannon's mouth dropped as her eyes widened, spotting a controlled stream of fire and water circling around each other. Steam billowed from the elements as droplets of water crashed into the flames, the swirling phenomenon rising higher as she focused on it. She traced her eyes down the dancing elements and observed the fire raging as it floated in mid-air, mixing with the water trailing upward from the damp soil. Both staying in place, the elements did not stray, trapped within a controlled embrace.

Keeping her eyes focused on the strange event, she asked, "What . . . what the hell is going on?"

Smiling, Ryan announced proudly, "I think you figured out how to control your magic."

"What?" she said with a breathy exhale and a confused expression on her face.

"Yeah, you're the one doing this."

"I—I don't get—*How* am I doing this?"

"What were you feeling before? I mean, when you were summoning this. What emotions were—are—you feeling?"

"Uhm . . . afraid."

"Afraid?" Ryan narrowed his eyes, his tone deep with sarcasm. "You were afraid whilst you were yelling at me?"

The elements continued to flow in a controlled stream as Rhiannon lowered her voice, the softness coupled with confidence. "Yeah, but it was different. The fear was there, but it wasn't controlling me. Instead, I was the one controlling it somehow. Turning it into something else."

"Then that's how you tap into your powers. You have to turn your fear, the thing blocking your magic, against itself. You have to rule your emotions—"

The trees swayed as a figure zoomed by overhead and brushed against the tops of the canopies, sending leaves floating to the ground. Rhiannon turned her eyes upward, and the elements disappeared, the water sucking back into the ground as the flames extinguished.

Ryan cowered. "What the bloody hell was that?"

"It's Raeth," Rhiannon said, running back toward the clearing by Lucien Valley.

"Hey!" He ran after her. "Who the heck is Raeth?"

Rhiannon panted as she came to a stop outside the forest. She smiled, continuing over to the Earth Dragon waiting for her a few feet away. Ryan slid to a stop as he exited the forest, turning around and hurrying back into the trees as another Earth Dragon landed next to the other.

"Uhm, Rhiannon," Ryan said, immediately pausing as the dragons turned their heads in his direction.

Rhiannon stood between Oakley and Raeth, stroking them as they kept their eyes on Ryan. "Relax." She waved him over. "They're not going to hurt you."

Ryan slinked out of the forest with his arms raised as if surrendering. "Are you sure?"

Rhiannon rolled her eyes. "Yes, I'm sure. Don't you trust me?"

"Touché." Cautiously, he continued forward. "Uhm, did you call them?"

"Not on purpose. But they said they could hear me. They sensed my fear when I was afraid earlier."

"From this far away?"

"Yeah, that's what they said. I guess my Drolnogard powers are stronger than I thought. Not even my dad can do it from this far away—Only a couple of miles, give or take."

Ryan paused a few feet away, monitoring the green-and-brown creatures. "Do they bite?"

"Only when provoked. But Oakley and Raeth are pretty friendly. I think you're safe."

The dragons huffed and snarled as Ryan stumbled away from them, panic rising from his stomach and across his colorless ivory face.

"Relax," Rhiannon said, laughing. "They're only messing with you."

Glancing up at the darkening sky, Ryan said, "I think we should go."

"I agree, but we should just take the dragons instead since they're here."

"Like ride them?"

"Yeah."

"Really? But aren't you afraid of heights?"

"Yes, but I trust the dragons not to drop me. And they usually fly closer to the ground with me, or I just close my eyes. Being able to communicate with them helps my fear." She climbed onto Raeth. "So, what do you think? Feeling adventurous?"

"I've always wanted to ride a dragon."

"Well, here's your chance."

"Uh, can I ride with you?"

Rhiannon laughed. "Why, are you scared?"

"Hell yeah, I'm scared! These things are huge. And that one there"—he tilted his head to Oakley—"looks like he wants to eat me."

"He's not going to eat you." Rhiannon reached out a hand. "Now, get on."

He mounted the dragon and held on to Rhiannon. "So, what now?"

"With what?"

"With us? Our friendship? With you and your magic?"

Raeth walked into the valley as Oakley followed behind.

"Like my mom would say, one day at a time."

"Meaning?"

"You're right, I did act irrationally with both your secret and my fears. I would like to know more about you and this curse. And I don't want to be afraid anymore."

"I'd be happy to tell you everything about me, especially what makes me different than the other werewolves. I promise I'll tell you everything. No more secrets. And I can help you with your fears, help you train and fight against the emotions controlling you. And I'm sure your brother will too. You just have to tell him what you're feeling. You need to stop avoiding him."

Raeth stretched out his wings and took flight, and Oakley trailed behind, both gliding through the dim sky and closer to the glow of Caerwyn Village.

Rhiannon pressed her legs into the dragon and held tighter as Ryan clung to her waist. She closed her eyes and thought about James.

Ryan was right. James was the one person who understood her fears more than anyone else, but she had never thought to discuss them with him. She was embarrassed by her emotions and self-conscious about her inability to control and render them into something useful. James had never shown an inkling of fear nor a moment of weakness—at least, not one she could recall. He was a true fighter, a warrior against his emotions. James was surely the more powerful one out of the two of them, and not just with his mental strength, but with his physical and magical force as well.

# Chapter 18

## Mastering Magic

The hilt was weightless in James's hand as he held tight to the grip, swinging the sword through the air. Two weapons collided, the loud thuds flowing across the field outside Stoweward, matching the echoes of heavy grunts. Pavian swung his weapon and the blade connected with the opposing sword, sliding down and stopping against the guard. He pushed harder into his adversary, inching closer to victory as James's knees buckled. Kicking out his leg, James rammed his foot into his uncle, forcing him back as they both stumbled to the ground. James rolled to his feet and fought against the weakness in his knees, rushing over and kicking Pavian's sword away. He placed the tip of his blade against his opponent's chest.

"Not bad," Pavian said as he reached up a hand.

"Not bad?" James lowered the sword to his side and yanked Pavian to his feet. "Not bad? That was awesome! I totally just kicked your—"

"Don't get too cocky, James. Arrogance might just get you killed one day."

"Come on, Uncle Pavian. Admit it. That was pretty great."

Pavian rolled his eyes before smiling. "Fine. Yes, that was some pretty impressive fighting."

"I knew it! So, when do I get to fight with a real sword?" James lifted his weapon, running his fingers across the wooden blade and blunt tip. "This won't be very effective against my enemies."

"No, not against some of them, but it's better than getting maimed during practice." Pavian picked up his wooden sword off the ground. "And this training isn't really for your enemies."

James flung a quiver filled with arrows over his shoulder and grabbed a bow hiding among the grass. "Then why have we been training for months with these things?"

Pavian playfully patted his nephew's back. "To help you fight against your enemies, of course."

James shook his head as Pavian wandered away in the direction of town. "Wait! What?" He jogged behind him, catching up before asking, "What does that even mean?"

"Your weapons training hasn't been to use against your enemies. Although, it wouldn't hurt to be extra prepared when it comes to some of the creatures around here. No, it's been for teaching. Teaching you patience, to trust your instincts, how to read your opponent, test your reflexes, and how to respond quickly in chaotic situations."

"Right, that makes sense. But when are we going to go back to practicing my magic? I still haven't gotten any of it under control."

"Yes, you have," Pavian said encouragingly, pointing to James's bow. "Why do you think you are so good with that thing?"

James's recurve bow, handcrafted specifically for him by Quinian the weaponsmith, was his favorite line of defense. After months of training, he was a master archer, but it was not simply his ability to hit a target that made him a prodigy in the art of archery—it was his magic which lent him a helping hand.

James glanced down at the weapon. "I don't understand."

"You spent the first few months so focused on controlling *all* your magic at once that you got frustrated. You never took the time to just manage one ability first. You were so determined to *be* the best, that you let it *get* the best of you. You have more abilities than any other person I have ever worked with before, so trying to get you to concentrate on one was proving to be a bit of a challenge. So, I decided to take your mind off of it. At least, that's what you thought I was doing."

James halted. "Okay . . . So . . . What?" He caught up to Pavian. "You mean, we've been practicing my magic this whole time?"

"Yep. We can only focus on a single ability at a time when trying to master them. Elemental powers are the easier ones to control because the elements are bendable. One simply manipulates whichever element they have control over. But your air magic is different. I witnessed that the first day we were back in Kiluemar. You don't just manipulate it or control it, but you can create it as well. Summon it to you like your mom can with fire. All I needed to do was get you to focus on creating and controlling your own air, thus manipulating where the arrow would land. You thought you were just getting better at shooting, but the truth is, you were controlling the air and moving the arrow where you wanted it to go."

"Huh! That's sneaky."

"Yes, but effective."

"So, I'm not that great with a bow and arrow then? Well, that sucks."

"No, you *are* that good. You only recently learned how to manipulate the arrow to go where you wanted it to, so every other time, that was all you. It's just, now, you never miss."

James and Pavian walked under two massive wooden posts as a sign displaying the town name hung overhead. A fence made of logs surrounded Stoweward, extending out for acres as the entrance rested perfectly in the center. Gravel lined the wide streets and led to various buildings made of red brick, wooden slats, or rounded logs. Reminiscent of a quiet old West town combined with a serene mountain retreat, the town gave off a unique rustic vibe. Laughter and voices echoed from each house as every window and door lay open, a silent plea for some relief from the smoldering heat. Children played, giggling and running as quiet footsteps and the counting of numbers traveled through the streets. Dryness filled the air, the heat forcing the moisture from the trees and cracking the parched ground. The smell of dirt blew with the hot wind, the warmth burning against the two men's skin.

James wiped the sweat dripping down his forehead. "Man, is it always this hot here in the summer?"

Pavian fanned his shirt as he forced saliva down his dry throat. "No, it has never been this hot here before. Kiluemar has always been comfortable all year round. This is very unusual."

"Kiluemar has climate control?"

"The island has always been the ideal place to live, with almost every type of environment possible. So, yes, the weather has been manipulated. The magic of the island has allowed the barrier to fight against the natural elements outside the border. The weather here has always been perfect, never being too hot during the day or too cold at night. The wind coming off the ocean can sometimes make it cooler, but it's never gotten below freezing down here, though we sometimes get snow in the mountains."

A shadow fell across the path in front of them, circling around overhead like a vulture waiting for its dinner. James squinted as he searched for the creature, but the sun forced his eyes closed.

James blinked erratically, attempting to remove the spots from his vision. "What was that?"

Pavian lifted his eyes to the sky, the sun blinding him as well. "Probably just a bird. Or it could've been Viktor. He's been patrolling more lately."

"Viktor?"

"Yeah. The gargoyle."

James paused both his stride and the flickering of his eyelids. "Did you just say gargoyle?"

"Yeah."

"I've lived here for six months now and you never thought to mention there are gargoyles here?"

Pavian laughed. "Oh, James, there are so many creatures here, you might as well either get used to learning these things or just realize this place is always going to have something surprising about it."

"Good point."

They made their way farther into the center of town.

"Okay," James said, "so this Viktor fella, he's a gargoyle? Like a real-life stone statue?"

"Yes and no. He can turn into a stone statue, but when he's awake, he has flesh and bones. He was once only stone, but a coven of witches brought him and others to life. Viktor is the only one in Kiluemar. As far as we know, the others still live in the non-magical world, protecting good magic."

"Oh, that's kinda cool actually. So, they're good creatures then?"

"Yes. Gargoyles protect against dark magic and evil spirits. They're the guardians of light magic."

"Light magic? There's such a thing as black and white magic then?"

"No. Magic is neither black nor white. It is simply magic. It's the intent behind it that makes it good or evil. All magic starts off as pure and good, but when used for the wrong reasons, it becomes dark magic."

"What makes something wrong in the eyes of magic?"

"The intention behind it. Magic will always do what is necessary to survive, but certain things are deemed immoral or unnatural, and it breaks the balance. Curses, sacrifices, blood rituals, and murder all result in personal gain at the expense of others. And it's all linked to dark magic."

Turning the corner, James and Pavian spotted Raina outside with Liam, fanning herself and holding a glass of ice water against her forehead as the young boy splashed in a large bucket of water.

James slowed down, hoping to get a few more questions answered before arriving home. "What happens to those who use dark magic for personal reasons? I mean, it's our intention to kill Merrick, so isn't that dark magic?"

"Anyone who uses dark magic eventually gets what's coming to them. This type of magic always comes with a consequence. And yes, we intend to kill Merrick, but only in self-defense. He plans on killing you, Rhiannon, and anyone else who gets in his way or has magic he wants. He's already killed so many, and who knows how many more will die before this is all over. But self-defense is not murder. Magic created you and your sister to stop him. We simply have to figure out how you're supposed to do it without getting yourselves killed in the process."

"I agree. So, shouldn't we start focusing on some of my other magic? I have some control of my air powers, so why not focus on some of my other abilities?"

"Like what?"

"Well, we know Rhiannon has fire and water magic, but one of us has earth powers too. That was pretty obvious the night at the manor when we were kids and when we were attacked at the cabin. But aren't I also supposed to have Guardian magic? Why hasn't that showed up yet? And my Drolnogard powers have gotten much better, but they're nowhere near as powerful as Rhiannon's. Also, we still need to revisit my ability to astral project."

"What about astral projecting?" Raina asked, swallowing a gulp of water.

Pavian's and Raina's home was nestled in the center of town. Trees, grass, and natural flowerbeds separated them from the closest neighbors next to them, and a gravel road divided them from the empty house across the street. A covered porch sat at the front of the red brick building, and a stone fireplace rose along the side. The single-story home was perfect for the small family and their welcomed guest.

Liam stopped splashing and ran over. "Daddy!"

Pavian lifted him, his soaked clothes making him heavier than usual. "Oh, goodness! You look like you're having a good time."

"Liam, sweetie," Raina said, "you're getting your daddy all wet."

"Oh, it's fine." Pavian pressed Liam into his body, giving him a squeeze. "It's refreshing."

Raina pulled an ice cube from her glass. "Why is it so hot?" She rubbed it on the back of her neck. "It's been hot the past few years, but this is ridiculous."

Pavian lowered Liam to the ground. "Go cool off some more and then come give me another big hug."

Liam raced over to the bucket and continued splashing in the water.

Pavian frowned and leaned his elbows onto his thighs as he sat down beside Raina.

"What's wrong?" James asked his uncle.

"I was right."

A newly soaked Liam ran over, but James swooped him up. "Nope! It's my turn for some hugs."

Playfully rocking back and forth, James squeezed tightly as the wetness from his cousin's clothes cooled his body.

Raina smiled at Liam and James before turning to face Pavian. "Right about what?"

"The barrier is weakening. That's why the weather is all weird and the portals keep shifting and disappearing, and possibly why James was able to astral project."

"What the heck do you mean the portals are disappearing?" She shifted her eyes to James. "You can astral project?"

Pavian tossed her an apologetic grimace. "Did I forget to mention that?"

"Yes!" She gently slapped his leg. "I could've been helping him this whole time with that, you know."

"I wasn't trying to keep—I honestly forgot he was able to do it. With everything else going on with him, it just escaped my mind."

"Escaped your mind? Yeah, right. Nothing ever escapes your mind. Anyway, so what is this about the portals not working?"

"They're still working, they just . . . aren't staying put. They're moving around and some are even gone altogether."

"What does that mean? Will it affect our ability to travel around the island?"

"It might," Pavian said with uncertainty in his voice. "The magic here is fading."

"Why?" James placed Liam on his feet. "Is it Merrick?"

Footsteps shuffled as a door closed behind the small grouping of trees next to the house.

"It has to be," Pavian said positively, ignoring the noises next door. "He's finally stolen enough magic from the island that it's starting to affect the realm."

"How is he stealing it from the island though? I thought he could only steal powers from other creatures."

"Yes, but he's stealing the magic that is supposed to be recycled back into the island, the magic to keep the realm and the barrier functioning properly. The ritual to give Kiluemar its power was centered around magic having to return to the island. But if Merrick is taking that magic—"

"Then the island no longer has a continuing flow of magic to keep itself alive."

"Right."

Raina tapped Pavian's leg as a woman with tight black curls and tanned skin moved closer to the house. "Tiffasa's coming over."

"Hey, everyone," Tiffasa said, her bubbly personality beaming across her face. "I heard Liam playin' out here, and I figured I'd bring you the herbs I promised you to help with your stomach issues."

Born in New York but raised in Kiluemar, Tiffasa Hernandez was a Puerto Rican to the core, a pure mix of sass and grace. She was kindhearted and caring, acting as everyone's best friend or mother. The true definition of a Latina woman, she treated everyone like a member of her family—with love, honesty, compassion, and a bit of feistiness.

"Stomach issues?" James asked curiously.

Tiffasa handed Raina a satchel of herbs. "Yeah, for her morning sick . . ." She trailed off, witnessing the apprehension across Raina's face. "Oh, crap. Whoops. My bad."

Pavian and James twisted to Raina.

"Surprise," Raina said timidly, her eyes beaming at Pavian.

The shock faded from Pavian's face and he grinned. "You . . . You're pregnant?"

Raina nodded, a dimple rising along her cheek as he hugged her.

"Congratulations!" James said excitedly. "Marriage *and* a new baby. Man, you two move fast. No! Wait!" His voice became flustered. "That's not what I mean. Not that you don't deserve to move fast—I mean, it's not fast—It's just, you waited years, so you deserve—"

Pavian nudged his nephew's arm. "James!"

"Yeah?"

"You're rambling like your sister."

"I am?" James chuckled under his breath before meeting his uncle's friendly gaze. "Man, I really miss her."

"When are you going to see her again?"

"I'm not sure." His attention pulled to Tiffasa's dark hair and beautiful olive-green eyes. "Wait a second. I have a question."

"What's up?" Tiffasa asked with a giggle at his perplexed expression.

"Weren't you a redhead with blue eyes when I first met you a few months ago and then very blond last week?"

A quick snicker escaped with Tiffasa's exhale. "Yeah, but this is my natural hair and eyes. I'm an Illusionist."

"Illusionist?"

"Yeah," Pavian said. "She can make you see whatever she wants you to. Some days she's a redhead, others she's blond. She even made herself taller once. She's really good at her abilities."

"Thanks, Pavian. Hey, I gotta go. I promised my boys I'd take them to the beach today. This heat is horrible." Tiffasa waved as she walked away. "Let me know how those herbs work out for you, Raina."

"Will do. Thanks, Tiff."

"Another question," James said as Tiffasa met her boys on her front steps. "I noticed a lot of families—like Tiffasa's and Meadow's—live here in Stoweward, but do they have to? Is this the family area or something?"

"No," Pavian answered, shaking his head. "The residents here on this side of the island can choose wherever they want to live. Now, all the werewolves live here with their families because it's closer to the highlands, but Stoweward has always been more of the family-oriented neighborhood. That's why we moved back here. Plus, the village is so outdated and not really up to par on the amenities when it comes to certain things."

"Speaking of Caerwyn Village, why does Aidan live there? Didn't he used to live here? I mean, Nina lives here, so I would think he'd want to live next to his sister. I know I sure do."

Pavian faced Raina, his eyes expressing a deep thought. "Actually, why haven't we seen Nina since we've been back other than that one time? It's been months. We used to see her all the time."

"Aidan has been here a lot to see her, but even he has a difficult time finding a moment in her spare time. When Aidan left, it was really hard on Nina. She was depressed and lonely, so she decided to keep herself busy. Not only is she a teacher at the school, but she's a nurse with me down at the infirmary. She and I help the elves with whatever they need, and we learn along the way. She's even learning how to be a surgeon."

"Hang on a second," James interjected firmly with a stern expression. "Are you telling me there's a school here?"

Raina and Pavian nodded.

"So wait, does that mean I have to go back to school?"

Pavian choked on his spit as he held back a laugh. "No." He coughed, clearing his throat. "No. School here only lasts until the age of about thirteen or fourteen, sometimes longer depending on the student. Here, we teach the basics, like language arts, math, history, science, reading, that kind of stuff. Then, once the kids get their powers, they either train with me or someone with their shared ability. Anyone wanting a more normal life and better knowledge of magic will usually attend a special school in the non-magical world. But the students at MUSE now only come from a magical bloodline. No actual powers yet."

"What does MUSE stand for?"

"To us, the name stands for Magic, Understanding, Strength, and Education. And they teach all about magic and how it works, the realm, other creatures and how to understand them and their ways, curses, how to build mental and physical strength to master your abilities, and regular education, like what we teach here. But the non-magical people think it's just a school for gifted and advanced children."

James snickered. "So, is it in upstate New York and run by a bald guy? Or is it a castle in the countryside with owls who deliver the mail?"

Pavian jerked his head back in confusion and narrowed his gaze. "No. It's run by muses, and it's in Canada. Why would you think that?"

"Never mind," James said, giggling. "So, if that's what it means to us, what does it mean to the non-mutants and Mug—I mean, non-magical people?"

"My Unique Skills and Excellence."

"Sounds stuffy."

A shadow traveled across the ground, and James glanced up as a bird disappeared, shaking the branches and rustling the leaves among the lush trees.

James closed his eyes and tilted his head, turning his ear upward. "What the heck is that?"

Pavian glanced around. "What's what?"

"I don't hear anything," Raina added, "except Liam."

"A voice," James answered as he opened his eyes. "I can hear a voice."

Pavian and Raina listened, the subtle sounds of Mother Nature and laughter filling their ears.

James pulled his brows inward, concentrating on the muffled sounds echoing in his head. The voice was soft and pleasant, but it was distant, broadcasting from what seemed like miles away. Lowering his eyelids, he turned his head, his mental focus drawing closer to the source of the voice in his mind. His eyes popped open in surprise, words failing to emerge from his open mouth.

"Is it Rhiannon?" Pavian asked, concerned. "Is she in danger?"

James shook his head, closing his mouth and swallowing. "No. It's . . . it's someone else."

Raina stood next to Pavian. "Who?"

"I'm pretty sure it's the bird in the tree."

"A bird?" Raina asked, frowning over at Pavian. "Oh! Maybe it's your Messenger. Like Edrick."

Pavian and James flinched back with surprise.

"What's an Edrick?" James asked as the voice in his head faded.

Pavian's eyes were wide and his voice was soft. "How do you know about Edrick? I've never talked about him before."

"Okay," James interrupted, "so I gather Edrick is your—"

"Yes, he's my Messenger."

"Right. That's what I figured. So, what about him?"

"Edrick was my Messenger before I left, but I haven't seen him since I've been back." He directed his attention back at Raina. "How do you know about him?"

"Him." Raina pointed over at Liam as he poured a cup of water from the bucket over his head. "A week after I found out I was pregnant with Liam, Edrick showed up outside my bedroom window. He followed me around and watched over me, protecting me. I couldn't hear him, but I knew he was there because of the baby. I don't know how I knew, I just did. And about a year after Liam was born, Edrick showed up again when we were outside, and I could tell they were communicating with each other. I eventually learned he was yours from Liam. But he . . .”

“He what?” Pavian asked.

“He stopped showing up. I haven’t seen him in over a year. I’m not sure what happened to him.”

Liam strolled up and grabbed his mother’s hand. “He died, Mommy.”

Raina crouched down and stared into her son’s innocent brown eyes. “Why didn’t you say something, sweetie?”

“I didn’t want you to be sad, Mommy. I knew Edrick reminded you of Daddy, and I didn’t want you to cry again.”

“Oh, honey.” Raina pulled Liam into her chest and wrapped her arms around him. “But what about you? You should’ve told me so I could’ve been there for you. He was your friend.”

“But I wasn’t sad . . . because he said he’d be back.”

Raina yanked herself from the embrace, her terrified expression beaming at Pavian. “What does he mean by that?”

Pavian grinned, cupping the side of his son’s face. “That’s right, Edrick will be back one day.”

“Hold up!” James interrupted. “Are you saying there are zombie birds flying around? Or . . . or is there going to be some weird spirit Messenger thing talking to you from the great beyond?”

“No,” Pavian said, laughing. “No . . .”

"Uh, what's so funny?" Raina asked, her petrified face matching James's. "I'd also like to know the answer to his question. I mean, I know we live on a magical island, but I don't think I'm cut out for zombie or ghost birds. I really don't want to be part of that horror story."

"No." Pavian waved his hand, trying to catch his breath. "No. It's nothing like that." He exhaled, pulling himself together. "Sorry, but that was funny. No, we don't have zombies or ghosts here, especially not as birds. No. Messengers are magical, but they aren't immortal. They are regular birds, just with magical abilities linking one of them to one of us. They still have to die, though. But the essence—the spirit—of our Messenger goes into a magical offspring of theirs. And eventually, a new Messenger is born. Each Guardian's Messenger will continue to be reborn until that Guardian dies. But until then, only the body of the bird perishes, growing old and dying. We all just have to wait for a new bird to be born and old enough to come find us again. I mean, Edrick came to me when I was five, and an average raven only lives about ten years. Did you really think they live forever?"

"No, I just thought . . ." Raina paused. "I just assumed—I'm not really sure what I thought, honestly. I never really thought about it. I kind of just assumed since they were magical, and Hermes has been around for as long as I can remember, that they just lived as long as their Guardian."

"Yeah," James added, "she's right. What would make her think differently? They're magical, right? So, why not think they live forever? We aren't mind readers, Uncle Pavian." He chuckled. "Well, I kinda am, but that's beside the point."

Pavian pulled his shoulders back, his eyes widening as the corners of his mouth turned upward.

"Hey, I know that look," James said. "You're planning something. What is it?"

"How far are you able to communicate with Rhiannon telepathically?"

"I'm not sure. Why?"

"Do you think you could help him astral project?" Pavian asked Raina.

"Yeah. I think so. He's been able to do it before, so helping him tap into it shouldn't be too hard. We can probably do a simple jump within a week, maybe a few days if he's strong enough. Why?"

"Let's aim for sooner."

"Why?" James and Raina asked, both annoyed.

Pavian rubbed the short beard along his chin. "I think it's about time we start training these two together. If James is sensing his Messenger, then I'm sure Rhiannon is too. If not, she will be soon, which means their Guardian magic has arrived or is about to."

James waited for him to continue. "And . . . so what does that mean?"

"The full moon is in two days, and I want to test out yours and Rhiannon's Guardian magic, but I would also like to combine those abilities with astral projection to see if you can mentally teleport yourself to each portal as people and creatures come through."

"Why?"

"Because we can't teleport anymore."

"What?" Raina snapped. "And you're just telling me this now!"

"I didn't want to worry you."

"How long has this been going on?"

"Kavana and I noticed right after we got back, but my father said he and Meadow haven't been able to in almost two years. Guardian magic is really off right now."

James folded his arms. "What does this have to do with me and astral projection?"

"When you projected yourself before, it was because you were connecting yourself to something—your magic, this world. And then when you did it again, you were pulling yourself in because of Rhiannon. So, I'm hoping if your Guardian powers are showing up, at least some of them, then maybe we can get you to focus hard enough to astral project yourself to each portal."

"And why do I need to do that?"

"To see where they all are and how many are left. Your grandfather and I have searched, but we can't seem to find more than a few. And if we can get Rhiannon there, we can not only help her control her new abilities but maybe get both of you to find all the portals before the window closes."

"But why do we need the outside portals open? Why can't we just try anytime with the ones inside the barrier?"

"Because Guardians can sense each person as they come through, their powers, and how many. So, if you have something to focus on, it will allow your powers to work faster. You don't really have much experience with the portals, so asking you to just sense them and project yourself there isn't going to work."

"Yeah, okay, that makes more sense. So, what do you need me to do?"

"I need you to try and communicate with your sister and tell her to meet us at the cabin tomorrow afternoon. We don't have much time to get over there and get as much training in as possible."

James sighed. "Man, I wish we had telephones here. That would make things so much easier. Okay, I'll try, but what if it doesn't work?"

"Then we'll have to do it the old-fashioned way and leave early in the morning on the horses and head to the village, then head over to your parents' house."

"Uhm, hello?" Raina waved her hand at them and pointed to herself. "I have a better idea."

Raina was an Astral Traveler and a master at her abilities, having perfected her talents years ago. Astral projection was a parlor trick to her, a low-level power she could use without difficulty. She not only would be able to convey the message to Rhiannon, but she could also get word to Karramis and Will of their arrival, making sure they were ready for the number of guests soon arriving at their doorstep. After years of repressing her abilities to stay off Merrick's radar, Raina would finally get to use her powers again, a gift she had once feared but now cherished.

# Chapter 19

## Silent Truth

*Decades ago*

Raina had spent the first four years of her life in an orphanage in Bulgaria. Abandoned by her mother after visions plagued the young woman during her pregnancy, the newborn had been left on the doorsteps of the orphanage with nothing but a note stating the baby's birthday and first name. Unaware her unborn daughter was gifted with magic, Raina's mother feared she was carrying a demon child and left her problem for someone else to handle. The only one in her lineage to possess this rare power, Raina's dormant abilities flowed through her veins, coursing wildly into her unsuspecting mother's body and creating astral projections, not dreams.

When Raina was four, she was moved from her home country to Romania after the orphanage was forced to close. The frail girl hid in the shadows of her new home, a makeshift orphanage run on low funds and insufficient staff. In an attempt to alleviate the overflow of children surviving in these overcrowded conditions, missionaries from around the world came and helped find the children new homes. Raina was one of these lucky children, being taken under the care of a young man.

Edmond Richards was an American but had lived in France for many years. A lover of art and the French culture, he moved there as a teenager, following his dream of traveling the world and helping people. Adopted himself, Edmond wanted to give other children an opportunity to live a life like his own—with love, care, compassion, and understanding. Gifted with a magical ability, Edmond was determined to rescue those who had been abandoned simply because they were different.

After finding out many of the orphanages in Romania, Bulgaria, and Russia were in need, Edmond jumped at the opportunity to help. Joining a group of missionaries, he boarded a bus and traveled to Romania from France, living for months in various locations and learning as much of the culture and language as he could. Already fluent in English and French, he was determined to master other languages. After months of traveling and moving between countries, he came across a very special little girl. Raina was the first one like him, one blessed with the gift of magic, but he was unsure of her abilities. Although she was too young for her powers to surface, Edmond moved forward with his plan to adopt her.

Once in France, Raina was taught how to speak, read, and write. Only being able to converse with simple words and phrases in Bulgarian and Romanian, the four-year-old girl was given an education and proper attention. Edmond focused on aiding Raina with learning English and French, all the while helping her continue to learn both her native languages, so she would always remember her culture and where she had come from. He also taught her about his ability, magic, and how someday she would also have a power.

When Raina was ten, they left France for Russia, living there for a year before finally returning to his home state in America. But tragedy struck soon after Raina's sixteenth birthday—her father died.

Now alone, Raina was determined to find a doorway to the magical land Edmond had often talked about, a place he had learned about years ago throughout his travels. He had discussed moving to the magical realm and settling down so he and Raina could live without the fear of what powers she would one day possess and the possibility of being hunted for a magic she might not be able to control.

Just before her seventeenth birthday, Raina discovered Kiluemar by accident. The pain of being alone, the sadness of missing her father, and the disappointment of not being able to find any proof of the magical realm took over, and she fell into a state of depression. Surrendering into the deep dark valleys of her mind, she was yanked to a place of warmth, peace, and salvation. Her mind had faded into the depths of her consciousness, summoning the dormant magic hiding within her soul. With each tear, her astral body grew stronger, a physical form stepping from the grassy plains just outside of Stoweward and disappearing, reappearing again a few feet from the nearest portal to her in the non-magical world.

By the next full moon, Raina was in Kiluemar, celebrating Christmas with the locals.

~

*The present*

The sun breached the top of Maevis Mountains, the morning sky painted with bright shades of orange and yellow. The air was warm and dry, but it was not yet unbearable. Thick gray clouds trailed across the sky in the distance, rumbling with thunder and stopping short of the barrier walls as lightning traveled across the skies of Kiluemar.

Insisting Raina and Liam stay behind in Stoweward, Pavian headed out with James. Their horses trotted down the trail heading to Caerwyn Village before disappearing into Kitra Forest. Even though they were only going to practice the twins' magic, Pavian could not guarantee Lucas or anyone else would not show up and cause problems. With the twins out in the open, away from the magical protection around the town and village, anything could happen, and he would not put his wife, son, and unborn child in jeopardy. Everyone going to the cabin had combat training, a defensive power, or both, but Raina lacked any skills when it came to fighting. However, her powers had helped with conveying a message to Rhiannon, as well as

Karramis and Will. Soon, the family would be back together again, practicing and preparing for whatever dangers would eventually arrive.

~

Karramis waited outside, holding a cup of coffee as she scanned the forest walls. She hated being away from her children, but she understood why they had chosen to stay with their aunt and uncle. Not only were they having to deal with the truth of their existence, but the twins also had to manage a new life in an unpredictable world. The attack on the cabin had proven their home was not safe for them, but Karramis refused to let Lucas, or even Merrick, drive her away from a place she loved. The cabin was her haven, the one location where, despite the night a few months ago, she was safe. This was her home. She had lived too long away from here, and she would not let anyone scare her away again. But her children were different.

The trauma Rhiannon had suffered was more than a physical wound—it was a mental ailment too. Karramis related to her daughter in more ways than one, for she was all too familiar with the dangers of allowing her mind to control her and surrendering herself to the fears taking over her body. Rhiannon was like her in many ways, and that terrified Karramis. If her daughter did not overcome the emotions manipulating her every move and decision, she would end up seriously injured again, or worse.

James, however, was more like Will, accepting a challenge and facing it head-on. He was never afraid to do what was necessary to stay alive or fight for something. Although Will had once been a pacifist, the years apart from his family had turned him into a man filled with an innate instinct of fight over flight. Refusing to be the weak link of the family, Will would stop at nothing to save them. Having trained for years with the elves, he was determined to fight for Karramis and the twins, or if nothing else, fight beside them.

The afternoon sun beamed down as the stifling air remained still, a haze dancing across the open field and creating the illusion of peering through a wall of water.

Will stepped outside, carrying a sheathed short sword and dagger and leaning them against the pillar.

"What're you doing?" Karramis asked before taking a drink.

"Getting ready." He removed the crossbow from the rafters and placed it next to the other weapons. "I'm prepared this time."

"I can see that." She kept her eyes on him as he lifted a hatch door blending into the porch. "Where'd that come from? Has that been here the whole time?"

Will pulled two other swords from the hidden access.

Her brows pinched together. "And what about those?"

"The door? Yes. I added it about five years ago. The weapons? No. Quinian brought me these right after the attack." He removed three daggers in various sizes and extra arrows for the crossbow. "Just in case."

"In case what? What exactly are you expecting to happen? We're only going to be practicing their Guardian magic."

"I don't know, but I'm not taking any chances. It's a full moon again, and with the kids outside the protective barriers, Lucas can sense them. I know we've been lucky the past few times they were here, but I have a bad feeling about all this. Something just isn't right. It's been way too quiet."

"I agree." Karramis stood up and held his face before giving him a kiss. "But these won't help us against Leif, and especially not against Merrick."

"No, but they will with Lucas and that bloody werewolf that hurt Rhiannon." He kissed her. "I won't allow them to hurt you or our kids again."

Pounding footfalls billowed from the trees, growing louder as Pavian and James came into sight. The horses trotted forward and came to a stop at the base of the stairs.

"Hey!" James jumped from Shadow and embraced his parents. "Is Rhiannon here yet?"

Pavian stepped onto the porch. "Is Kavana coming with her?"

"No, Rhiannon isn't here yet," Karramis said, giving her brother a side hug. "And I'm not sure about Kavana."

With a mix of surprise and worry in his voice, James asked, "Rhiannon's coming by herself?"

"Rhiannon will be all right," Will said surely. "You needn't worry about her. She'll be here soon. Let's get inside and out of this utterly ridiculous heat."

"Oh, thank goodness." James followed his father. "Please tell me you have air conditioning."

"Unfortunately, no. We've never needed it before. But we do have ice-cold water and fans."

"Well, that's better than nothing."

~

Temperatures inside were not any better. The ice in the water melted quickly, and the fan blew the suffocating dry air around the room. Over an hour passed and everyone waited for Rhiannon to arrive, refusing to move as sweat trailed down their faces.

James sprawled out on the floor with his eyes closed, visualizing himself floating across the surface of a lake. "If I astral project myself somewhere cooler, will my physical body feel the difference?"

"Yes," Pavian said, rubbing a damp cloth along the back of his neck. "But you haven't mastered that ability yet."

"Damn. I really need Raina to help me with that power, and soon. Speaking of that, why can't I do it anymore? I was able to control it without any major issues before."

"I have no clue."

Karramis gulped down the last of her water. "I don't think it's a matter of you can't, I think it's more about not being able to tap into that power right now. Trying to master one is hard enough, let alone multiple ones. I mean, look at me, I still have issues with my fire powers."

"How's that going by the way?" Pavian asked.

"Eh, it's getting better. I can control and manipulate it really well now, but trying to conjure it is harder. I can do it, but it usually only happens when I'm not meaning to. It's like my fire magic is controlling me and not the other way around."

"Well, your mother was the only one on record in Kiluemar to ever be able to do what you do—"

"Except for Rhiannon," James added.

"Yes, except for Rhiannon, so I can't even begin to help teach you how to master it, let alone summon it."

Karramis sighed. "I know. I just wish I could figure it out because it's the one thing that will help fight against Leif."

James aimed his eyes over at the others. "Vampires don't like fire?"

"No," the three adults answered.

Karramis continued, "Vampires have five weaknesses—all side effects of the curse. They were placed upon the species as a way to end their immortality, and fire is one of them."

James sat up. "Like a punishment?"

"Yes. The legend states that the five individuals killed by the witch were murdered differently, based on a spell found in an ancient necromancy script. Once the blood of those killed was consumed, the dark magic linked to those lives taken would resurrect as a single entity, being reborn into the one who drank the essence, which was the witch's husband. But each method of slaying resulted in a corresponding weakness."

"How'd she kill them?"

"She trapped one in a sarcophagus with venomous snakes and scorpions, and another was stabbed in the heart with a wooden stake before having it cut out. One was decapitated, another was burned alive, and the other was left out in the scorching sun to thirst to death."

"Eww, gross. That witch had some serious issues. Okay, but what about garlic? Holy water? Silver? Are any of those weaknesses?"

"No," Will said, fanning his shirt. "Garlic and holy water have no effect on them. And silver is a myth. In fact, no magical creature has a weakness to silver, not even werewolves."

"So, we can kill a vampire by cutting off their head, a wooden stake to the heart—"

"Or removing it altogether," Will added.

"Right. And . . . venom from a snake or scorpion?"

"No," his father answered. "The venomous murder only affects what they can't consume. Vampires are unable to drink animal blood, it's poisonous to them. They can live off it for a while, but they will suffer endless pain and eventually die without the life of a human keeping them alive and immortal."

"And what about the sun? Do they burst into flames or something?"

"No," Karramis stated with a shake of her head. "The sun does burn them, but it does it very slowly. Mostly, it weakens them, halting their enhanced abilities, like their speed, strength, healing—things like that. If out too long in the sun, they will grow very thirsty at a rapid speed and eventually burn and thirst to death. But this is a slow, painful process. Most vampires throughout history have never died this way, it's nothing like you see in modern representations."

"Right, and then there's fire," James clarified.

"Yes. That's the reason I'm so determined to get my powers under control. Leif will stop at nothing to get back at me for all the crap I've done to him, so my only defense is to be more powerful than he is."

A boom echoed outside as the ground rumbled and rattled the glasses of water in the room.

"Holy crap," James said as he kept his eyes on the tiny waves rippling outward inside the glass. "Is a dinosaur about to burst through the ceiling now?"

Karramis and Pavian frowned at him. "What?"

Will laughed. "I love that movie."

"What?" Karramis and Pavian repeated, even more perplexed.

"Never mind," James said with a smile as he rushed out the front door.

Rhiannon's inner thighs burned as she relaxed her body and released her tight hold on the Fire Dragon, Ignara. The massive creature lowered her red and charcoal body down, folding her wings back and pressing her knuckles against the grassy field. Rhiannon's stomach tingled as she slid along the dragon's rough, uneven scales and down the neck, her heeled sandals landing hard against the ground.

Straightening her dress and tucking her wind-blown hair behind her ears, Rhiannon whispered, "Wow, what a rush." She smiled, patting Ignara's red undercarriage. *"Next time can we please not go so high?"*

Ignara nodded as a huff of steam erupted from her nostrils.

James jogged over as the dragon took flight. "Not a fan of heights still?"

"Not really. I can handle a few hundred feet, but—Hey, stop reading my mind."

"Sorry." James wrapped his arms around her. "You just make it too easy. Plus, your emotional response is hard to ignore."

"Oh. Sorry. But that was insane. I mean, even though I was scared—and I am extremely happy to be back on the ground— that was exhilarating. It was totally different than riding Raeth or Oakley. It was like I was flying. Well, I *was* flying. I just mean that—"

"I know what you mean." James laughed. "Anyway, why are you so late?"

"I'm not that late. Am I?"

"You were supposed to be here over an hour ago. It's not like you to be late."

"I guess I didn't realize. I must've lost track of time. Sorry. I overslept and couldn't seem to connect with any of the dragons other than Phosmeratae and Ignara. But I was *not* going to ride Phosmeratae. I'm barely getting the hang of riding Raeth and

Oakley without having to close my eyes. But it's fine. Ignara was closer, so she came and got me, and I've been on her once before, so . . ."

*Oops.* Rhiannon's pulse quickened and her heart thumped hard against her chest. Her palms were sweaty, but it was not from the heat. She lowered her eyes, unable to meet her brother's gaze. *Shut up, Rhiannon. Control yourself. Breathe. He's going to sense it. Shh! Stop thinking! He's going to hear you.*

James raised an eyebrow and grinned at her. "Too late."

Rhiannon stomped her foot. "Dang it, James!"

Whispering, James asked with a stern voice, "What did you do? When did you ride Ignara before? Why didn't you tell me about it?"

Waving at her parents on the porch, she exclaimed, "Mom! Dad!"

"Rhiannon!" James called under his breath. "Get back here."

"No!" she said, matching his tone and sticking out her tongue.

James groaned and followed her, his voice ringing in her head. *"Dammit, Rhiannon! What the hell did you do?"*

*"Nothing,"* she responded internally as she kept a steady pace and scowled back at him. *"At least nothing you wouldn't have done yourself. Don't worry about it. Just be quiet."*

Karramis tilted her head, curiosity and suspicion looming in her gut as her children silently interacted with each other.

Will folded his arms, observing his wife's uneasy expression. "What's going on?"

"Nothing," Rhiannon said, stepping onto the porch. "Nothing—It's nothing."

James stopped at the base of the stairs and leaned against the railing. "She's hiding something."

Rhiannon jerked her head over to her brother. "James!" She huffed, giving him the evil eye. "Traitor."

"What's going on?" Pavian asked as he exited the open door and stopped next to Will.

Matching his father's serious stance, James interlocked his arms over his chest. "Rhiannon is hiding something from us."

Rhiannon gritted her teeth and mentally scolded him. *Would you hush?"*

"Rhiannon," Karramis said softly, "what aren't you telling us?"

Rhiannon shifted side to side and wiped away the sweat glistening across her forehead. Dropping her hand, she slapped her leg and stood up straight, a heavy exhale releasing from her flaring nostrils.

"Fine." She groaned. "I went to the forbidden side of the island a couple weeks ago."

"What?" the other four snapped, taking a step closer to her.

"Are you crazy?" Karramis asked with both concern and disappointment clinging to her words. "What were you thinking?"

"Why?" Pavian added. "It's not like you to be so careless."

"Yeah . . ." James snickered "That's kinda more my thing." He abruptly stopped as the three adults glared at him. "Sorry, I'll shut up now."

"But I was very careful," Rhiannon assured them.

Will pushed his brows together. "Why though?"

"I was curious why things are so quiet and why Merrick and the others are MIA. I didn't—and still don't—trust it. And I needed to see why. Something is just . . ."

"Off," Will finished for her.

"Yes. Something just isn't right about all of this. And . . . and it keeps me up at night, so I had to see for myself."

James wiped the sweat from his brow. "Well, did you find anything?"

"No, not really. And that's the weird thing. The entire castle is pretty much abandoned. I mean, I saw some of the creatures roaming around outside the cave and in the forest, but the castle itself was almost empty."

Unconvinced, James drew himself into her thoughts, but her inner voice was muted. "What aren't you telling us?"

Rhiannon rolled her eyes. "You know, James, you'd think after all the stupid things you've done, you'd learn to be quiet sometimes." She paced. "Fine! There was something—Well, rather *someone* there. A few actually, in the castle that is. I only saw them because it was too dark out—"

"You went at night?" Karramis exclaimed in a panic. "Seriously? What the hell were you thinking?"

"I was thinking that the only way I was going to see anything and not get caught was if they couldn't see me, so I took Ignara during a new moon so we were less likely to be seen. And it worked, no one saw me. I was perfectly safe. I mean, I had a freakin' Fire Dragon with me, who's going to challenge me?"

"Merrick," the three adults answered.

"Yeah, but he's not even here."

"How can you be so sure?" Pavian asked. "Maybe he's just laying low or hiding out in his tower. He's done it before, so why not do it again?"

"Because he's not. I'm sure of it."

James sat on the stairs. "How do you know?"

"Because the only ones there were some lady and—"

"Lady?" Pavian asked suspiciously.

"Yeah. Average height, tan, curvy, dark hair, and very pretty, I might add."

"That would be Tressa. She's his . . ."

James leaned back against the step. "Sidekick?"

"I guess you could say that," Pavian admitted. "Who else was there?"

"Some tall guy with blond hair. Similar to Leif but less attractive and more muscular. And I'm pretty sure he was a vampire as well because he was very pasty."

Karramis leaned against the pillar on the porch. "Sounds like Niko."

"Most likely." Pavian scratched his chin. "Anyone else?"

"Yeah. There was another *thing*, which I'm positive was a minotaur."

"That would be Tressa's bodyguard, Theseus."

"Theseus?" Rhiannon let out a belly laugh. "Seriously? The minotaur is named Theseus?"

James glanced up at her from the stairs. "What about it?"

"Oh, come on!" Rhiannon examined everyone's confused expressions. "Theseus? You know, the name of the man who slayed the *minotaur* in mythology?" She waited for them to respond. "The freakin' minotaur is named after the very man who killed—Oh, never mind."

Will joined James on the steps. "So, you only saw them? No one else?"

"No," Rhiannon answered, annoyed by her family's lack of irony. "When I got to the castle, all the lights were out except in a single set of windows, so I looked inside. Only those three were there, no one else was around. I even lingered a bit to see if anyone else would show up, but no one did. I left after the tall one kept glaring over at the window. I was expecting Lucas or someone else to show up—sense me or something—but nope. Nothing happened. It was completely quiet and a bit unsettling actually."

Karramis faced Pavian. "Maybe they took advantage of the portals being open and left to feed, taking the others with them. It's possible, right?"

"Yeah, it's possible, but why now? Why leave now when James and Rhiannon are finally back? And why stay gone for so long? Something's just not adding up. It's all very strange, even for Kiluemar."

"I agree," Rhiannon said, "and that's why we need to focus on our Guardian magic. We can see if he returns because whatever that lady was talking about with the others, her body language made her seem uneasy or scared."

Pavian's eyes widened. "Oh shit."

"What?" Karramis asked as James and Will returned to their feet.

"Why didn't I see this before?"

"What?" Karramis repeated, the anxiety building in her voice. "What's wrong?"

"I should've put this all together myself. I knew I shouldn't have trusted this."

Karramis grabbed his arm. "Pavian, would you please tell us what the heck is going on?"

"Merrick hasn't been laying low, I think maybe he just hasn't been here the whole time."

Rhiannon raised an eyebrow. "Yeah, that's what I just said."

"And I believe you. But I think the portals inside might not be the only ones not working right. The damn doorways outside must not be either."

James asked nervously, "So, he's been stuck out there this whole time?"

"Maybe. And if he has, when he finally comes back through, he's going to be pissed."

"But what if he wasn't stuck out there?" James walked up next to his sister. "What if the portals are still working right?"

Searching for an answer in their faces, Pavian asked, "Then where the hell has he been this whole time?"

# Chapter 20

## The Evil Within

Leif and Camille made their way down the long hall as Tressa closed the door behind them, leaving the three others to converse amongst themselves in private. The sun beamed through the windows and warmed the cold stones of the dreary corridor. Footsteps resonated, the remaining silence amplifying the uniformed pace. Avoiding the illuminating rays, Leif tucked into the shadows, the thin obscurity fading with each passing moment.

Camille mimicked Leif's hurried stride but chose the light over the shadows. "If Merrick is like you, then why is he able to be out in the sunlight?"

"Merrick isn't just a vampire like me, he's much more than that. His demonic state allows him to be out in the sun for short periods of time, but when he's in human form, it weakens him like the rest of us."

Camille gave a single nod as her mind wandered, curiosity pinching her eyebrows together.

"What?" Leif asked, observing her contemplative expression.

"What were you and Merrick talking about?"

"Karramis," he answered flatly.

"What about her?"

Leif tentatively held back an answer. "Well, it seems Merrick doesn't want Karramis. He stopped caring about her way before we were even locked out of Kiluemar. Other than her blood, there's nothing of use to him. There *is* something unique about her blood that entices him. It's not like anyone else's we've ever come across. And after tasting it myself, I can confirm that it's definitely different, and in a *very* good way. But her magic means nothing to him. Lucas has been lying to us all these years to protect her. Merrick only cares about her kids."

"He's just going to kill her then, no? But I thought he promised Lucas—"

"Merrick only promised Lucas he could have her, and Merrick will stick to his word. But they never agreed she had to be alive."

"Ah, je vois." Camille paused, keeping her gaze on the floor. "What else did you talk about?"

"Nothing," he declared, a hint of deceit in his voice, "just catching up."

~

"Get up, Cami," a deep voice demanded.

Camille blinked through the darkness as she yawned. "Lucas?"

"Do I look like Lucas?" the familiar voice asked, annoyed.

"How would I know? I can't see anything."

"Well, do I sound like him?"

"Haydrin?"

"Yes," Haydrin declared, slapping the side of her bare leg. "Now come on, get up. Let's go."

"Go?" Camille threw off the covers. "Go where?"

Haydrin grabbed her upper arm and dragged her into the dimly lit hallway. "Merrick wants to see you."

Spotting fresh blisters along his arm as they entered the hall, she drew in a breath through her teeth. "Ouch. Does that hurt?" She jerked herself out of his grasp as he ignored her. "Let me go! I'm perfectly capable of following you without getting lost."

Camille stepped onto the overgrown grass, and the dry blades tickled her feet. She stumbled over various objects along the clusters of cold, parched dirt, mumbling French profanities quietly to herself. Everything was still as the quietness and freezing winter air chilled her to the bone, her oversized shirt barely covering her upper thighs. The clouds parted and lit their path as the waning moon mounted high among the stars. A pungent odor filled the area as they trudged closer to the tower— a sickly-sweet, metallic scent mixed with rotten eggs, dead fish, and soured meat. She gagged, her stomach constricting as acidy bile traveled up her throat. She covered her mouth and nose, inhaling under her hand as she swallowed her vomit.

A large stone structure lay not far from the edge of the east wing, nestled along the corner of the exterior castle wall. Towering hundreds of feet above the ground, a single arched window at the top of the tower lit up with flickering lights. The stone frame lacked glass or bars, completely open to the outside world. Along the large irregularly shaped limestone walls rested dead vines, strangling the rounded watchtower as they crept upward and reached past the window.

Inside, Haydrin and Camille made their way up the stairs, the unstable steps creaking beneath them as they curved along the walls. Camille's legs grew tired as she hiked upward, the strain squeezing her thighs and calves.

Camille shivered, the air growing colder with each step. "You know, you could've allowed me to get dressed and put on some shoes first." She rubbed her arms, her voice falling to a whisper. "Or at least be good company."

A foul stench of musty old meat, a festering wound, and copper swimming in a vat of warm honey traveled down the stairs, the unusual and harsh odor pulling Camille's senses into disarray. The sweetness faded as a warm breeze blew across her exposed skin, the heat strengthening the rancid smells. Her stomach churned as her gag reflexes drove her chest into heavy spasms. She covered her mouth and pinched her nose, the vomit-inducing odor now lingering in her sinuses.

Haydrin entered the room at the top of the stairs, the large circular area lined with candles set aflame along the limestone walls. A firepit sat in the center of the tower, the warmth swirling with the cold draft of the poorly ventilated room. A large arched window opened to the outside as the starry sky rested beyond the stones. Camille held her breath as she stopped next to Haydrin, peering at the dark red splatters scattered across the smooth stone floor. Her muscles tensed, her rigid body frozen as her broadened gaze fixated on the blood.

"Pardon the manky disarray up here," Merrick said, emerging from the shadows wearing a black robe, "I was a wee overzealous with my meal."

"Doesn't bother me," Camille said as she shrugged her shoulders. "However, the smell is a bit . . ."

"Strong," Haydrin finished.

"Oui. Yes, it's very potent."

Merrick ran his fingers over Camille's body, tracing them along her lower back as he circled around her. He closed his eyes and drew in a long, deep inhale. Brushing his hand over the goose bumps on her arm, he moaned under his breath as Camille shuddered, his cold embrace like ice against her already frigid skin.

"C'mere, mademoiselle," Merrick insisted, escorting her farther into the room. "Come closer to the fire, you're freezin'."

She lifted her eyebrow flirtatiously. "Merci, monsieur."

Returning to Haydrin, Merrick whispered, "You may go now, Mr. Tevlak. But go wake Tressa and Lucas first. Inform 'em I wish to see 'em at this hour."

Haydrin rotated on his heels, crashing into Leif as the vampire zoomed up the stairs.

"Oops! Hey, my apologies . . ." Leif noted the clusters of burns along Haydrin's face and arms.

"Brutal, right?" Merrick asked quietly. "But it is impolite to gawk, Leif. Dismissed, Haydrin."

The brooding man gave a single nod and headed down the stairs, his footsteps descending away from the others.

"Where's he going?" Leif asked, smirking as he caught sight of Camille warming herself by the fire.

"To summon Tressa and Lucas. I demand their attendance."

Leif spoke in Norwegian as he lifted his chin in Camille's direction.

Merrick nodded with a malevolent grin. "Aye."

Tressa strolled into the room at the top of the tower, a dark purple cloak wrapped around her body as her messy hair rested along her back. "What in the hell am I doing up at this ungodly hour?" She paused as her mouth hung open. "Oh my . . ."

The events that took place in the tower were no secret, but Tressa had never been up here before. The place was off-limits to anyone outside of Merrick or the other vampires. No one had lived to tell the tales of the grisly aftermath until now. Although the sight of blood was nothing new to her, the odor made her cringe, the horrid scent making her stomach stir. Tressa tiptoed barefoot along the side walls, avoiding the various splatters along the floor.

Lucas yawned as he entered the room. "What's goin' on?"

"Welcome," Merrick said happily, tossing a bloody piece of material into the lit firepit.

"What are we doing up here, Merrick?" Tressa halted as she spotted one of Merrick's robes covering something in the corner. "What's that?"

"Oh, that?" Merrick chuckled with a diabolical grin. "Go on, take a gander at it. See fer yourself."

Tressa hesitated as she pinched the cloth and slowly pulled it away, revealing the mutilated body of Camille underneath.

"Fuckin' hell!" Lucas exclaimed, horrified.

Tressa jumped back in surprise, dropping the robe unevenly across Camille's body. "What the hell, Merrick? Why did you kill her? We needed—"

"Because I do not take orders from you," he declared in a fierce, steady tone.

He sauntered over to her with his hands interlocked behind his back, his bloody footprints trailing along the floor as he circled around her.

Tressa's voice was shaky. "Merrick, I wasn't—"

"You have some serious notions questionin' me in my own home."

"Forgive me—"

"Silence. I would not speak out of turn again if I were you, Tressa. I'm in no mood fer your yappin' tongue, so you better watch it." The blood squished under Merrick's feet as he approached Lucas. "Now then, let this be a warnin' to you. Never, and I mean never, bring another person into my domain without my permission. Do you understand me, Lucas?"

Meeting Merrick's soulless gaze, he answered, "Yes."

"Pardon? I didn't quite hear you."

"Yes, sir."

Merrick patted Lucas's upper arm. "Well then, aren't we a good wee fella? Now, do you have anythin' to say before you are dismissed?"

"Where's Leif? Haydrin mentioned he was up here."

"Aye, he was. But he left. Anythin' else?"

"No, sir."

"Very well." Merrick flicked his wrist and waved him away. "You may go now."

Lucas glanced over at Camille's body as he rotated on his heels, observing the blood along her undergarments and multiple puncture wounds on her neck and inner thighs. "Wait, I have anotha' question."

"What is it?" Merrick asked with a flat, dismissive tone.

"Whaddaya gonna do with her?"

Merrick stared at him, drawing out his answer. "You should know the answer to that by now." Turning around, he added, "Dismissed, Mr. Fraye." He cleared his throat and directed his attention to Tressa. "Now then, are ya finished with your wee conniption?"

Tressa nodded as the sounds of footsteps retreated down the stairs.

"Do ya mind speakin' up? I didn't quite hear you."

"Yes, Merrick."

"Splendid. Well, you may have the floor then."

Tressa released an unsteady exhale before asking calmly, "May I speak freely without suffering any repercussions?"

Merrick contemplated, the long pause building tension in the room. "Sure, why not? I'm feelin' generous."

"Why did you kill her? We needed her magic. The whole point of all this is to get you as much magic as possible. Right? So, why waste a perfectly good source of magic, especially one you don't have yet?"

Merrick meandered casually throughout the room, circling around Tressa with a blank expression on his face and a calmness to his voice. "First of all, I did it 'cause I wanted to, and because I may do whatever I see fit. I do not need permission, nor do my actions need to be justified. Second, I found her to be a bit of a floozie, and ya know me, I've never been very fond of *easy* when it comes to certain things. And lastly, her magic was quite mundane. No real powers aside from borrowin' others. And frankly, she wasn't particularly useful to me outside of bein' a delicious meal." He halted, taking a step toward her. "All I need now are the Drolnogard's magic and his damn children's. Accordin' to the prophecy, those children have the most powerful magic, and I want it. And I want to control the dragons. So, I don't care about any other trivial or mediocre powers."

"What about Karramis? Her magic is—"

"I do not need her."

"But what about her fire magic? You still need—"

Tressa cut herself off as Merrick gave her a pointed glare, his pale blue eyes fading to black.

Tressa folded her arms across her chest as if to protect herself. "Listen, you need fire magic. And I really think you need her magic. I truly believe she is a lot more powerful than you think."

"I don't need her magic, Tressa. I would, however, like a taste of her."

"But why not have both? I mean, you can get both with the ritual."

Merrick exhaled. "Fine. If it will shut you up, we will move forward with your plan."

"Do I have your word?"

"Aye, you have my word. Karramis will not die by my hand until after I have consumed her magic."

Camille's body was in full rigor mortis and stuck in an unflattering position with her blue eyes frozen open. The young Echo's magic would have enhanced his powers, but Merrick's lust for blood had ruined the chances of being even more powerful. Merrick was never going to get all the magic he needed to make himself the most powerful entity ever if he did not stop killing out of spite or for sport.

Karramis had always been part of the plan up until now, and Tressa was unsure why Merrick was going against something they had been planning since they first learned Karramis was part of the prophecy. His motives and even more unpredictable nature made her worry, and not just about the future of their ultimate goal, but also whether or not she would still be around much longer.

Merrick stared over at Camille as the desire for flesh burned his insides. "I'm finished with this conversation. Is there anythin' else before you go?"

"Yes, actually. What about the children?"

"I'm tired of waitin', so we will go and retrieve 'em as soon as possible."

"No," Tressa pleaded, dropping her arms, "you can't do that."

"I beg your pardon," he announced with a sharp tone. "I can't?"

"No, I didn't mean it like that. It's just they can't possibly have all their magic yet, and if you take it too soon, you won't get all their powers. You need all of them, Merrick." She batted her dark brown eyes at him. "But I have a suggestion to help . . . Something that might help take your mind off of waiting."

He angled his head and scowled. "And that would be?"

She ran her fingers over his chest, leaning her body into his. "Well, it's more of a favor actually."

He grabbed her hand and squeezed, his face cold as ice. "What is it, Tressa? I'm in no mood to deal with your wretched attempt at seducin' me. It may work with the others, but it will not work with me, so stop wastin' my time."

"My apologies." She slid her hand out of his grip and backed away. "I . . . I think you should leave the realm for a bit."

"Pardon?" The request left him baffled and annoyed. "You want me to leave? Now? Well, I'm not goin' anywhere. I refuse to leave now that I know those children and Will are alive."

"Let me explain my request."

The hunger intensified as Merrick ran his fingers through his light brown hair. He paced, and a low growl rumbled from his throat. His skin sliced open along his arms and face, tiny cuts stretching longer and exposing rough, black flesh underneath. His eyes were wide, red specks appearing within his blue irises as his bones started to crack. Groans emerged with the growl as Merrick fought against the pain.

Tressa retreated closer to the door, the space between the two providing comfort. "Merrick, listen to me. Please, just breathe."

Merrick closed his eyes, huffing wildly through his nose. The rips along his skin sealed, and the room grew quiet as he opened his eyes, the light blue meeting her flustered gaze.

"Explain," Merrick said gutturally. "And I would hurry if I were you."

"Six months. Just give it six months. Then we can see how far they've come. Plus, it might do you some good to leave for a bit. I mean, when was the last time you went home to Ireland?"

"It's been a long time."

"See," she said, confidence rising in her voice. "I think maybe it's time you go home for a little while. Go enjoy yourself in any way you see fit. You've been so restricted lately, and I think it has you on edge."

Merrick considered. "Maybe you're right. It would be lovely to have a holiday and fully recharge." He paused. "I do rather miss havin' more options on the menu, and the hunt lately has been exceptionally dull and a wee bit unsatisfyin'."

"Great," Tressa said. "So, you'll go then?"

"Aye."

"Great. I really think it will be good for you. Oh! And I think Leif and Lucas should go too."

Merrick narrowed his eyes. "Why?"

"Well, because they've been working nonstop since the portals closed, and I think they deserve a break too. Maybe they can go see their family or something."

"Leif is almost a thousand years old, he doesn't have any family left. And I don't really know much about Lucas or if he even has a family."

"Maybe they can just go and relax somewhere. Get away from all the drama here. You all seem a bit tense, and it's clouding your minds."

Merrick narrowed his eyes, skepticism bleeding through his gaze. "And what about you?"

"Well, it's nothing personal, but . . ." She inched closer to the door and hesitated to finish. "Now, don't take this the wrong way, but I need a break from you. You've been on edge lately and haven't been yourself with me. Plus, someone has to stay put and keep an eye on Karramis and her family. Someone has to stay behind and monitor their progress, right?"

Merrick stared at her, intentionally making her even more uncomfortable. "Aye." He twisted over to Camille's body. "I think it's time for you to go now."

"Oh, yes. Absolutely, of course. I won't keep you." Tressa halted under the threshold. "When will you leave?"

"As soon as the sun sets this evenin'."

Stepping onto the landing outside the door, Tressa grabbed hold of the railing.

Merrick started to untie his robe. "Tressa?"

"Yeah?" she said from the shadows.

"When I return, I *will* be takin' what is mine. And if you get in my way, ya won't live to see another day. Do you understand me?"

"Yes," she said softly.

"Yes what?"

"Yes, Merrick."

"Right then. Dismissed."

Tressa made her way down the stairs. "Goodnight, Merrick."

The tower door above her slammed shut, and roars and guttural screams rumbled through the dark structure. Tressa traced her hand along the handrail as she made her way toward the moonlit opening at the base of the stairs. Exiting the tower, she glanced up at the window as a set of eyes burned into her back, the sharp stare making her skin crawl. A silhouette of a monstrous beast with giant wings perched high in the stone frame, the flickering light hidden behind Merrick's demonic body. His clawed hand grasped Camille's severed leg as his sharp teeth ripped the flesh from her bones. Keeping a close eye on Tressa, Merrick watched as she disappeared into the cold and dark winter morning.

~

Sterling Andralae awoke with terror on her face, her brown irises rolled back behind her twitching eyelids. The nightmare and summer heat drove her body temperature up as beads of sweat trailed down her forehead. Visions played back on a constant loop, flashing repeatedly over and over again in her mind. Words overlapped the images and echoed in her head.

Compelled by an uncontrollable force, Sterling slid out from under her blankets and wrote down another verse of the prophecy on her bedroom wall as the nearly full moon rested in the night sky outside her window.

To be continued in:

# Fate of the Unknown
### Magic of the Realm ~ Book Three

# *Pronunciation Guide*

## New Characters

Aayrah: A-RUH

Alfina: AL-FEE-NUH

Andralae: ANN-DR-UH-LAY

Cillian: KILL-EE-IN

Edrick: ED-RICK

Malena: MUH-LEAN-UH

Mariska: MUH-RISK-UH

Marryn: MARE-IN

Natomna: NUH-TOME-NUH

Niko: NEE-KO

Phosmeratae: FOSS-MER-AW-TAY

Raeth: RAY-TH

Randolyn: RAN-DOE-L-IN

Terramina: T-AIR-UH-MEAN-UH

Tiffasa: TIFF-A-SUH

Yaya: YAW-YAW

Refer to Book One for more pronunciations

# Translation Guide

*Au revoir* - Goodbye

*Bonjour* - Hello

*Ca c'était quoi?* – What was that?

*Chère* - Dear

*Enchanté* – Enchanted/Delighted

*Excusez-moi* – Excuse me

*Fy fån* – Dammit/Fuck it/For fuck's sake

*Jävlar helvete,* - Fucking hell

*Je ne sais pas* – I do not know

*Je suis* – I am

*Je vois* – I see

*J'étais* - I was

*Madame* – Madame/Misses

*Mademoiselle* - Miss

*Merci* – Thank you

*Merde* - Shit

*Mon amour* – My love

*Monsieur* - Mister

*Öga för öga* – Eye for an eye

*Ordinaire* – Ordinary

*Oui* – Yes

*Problème* - Problem

*Très bien* – Very good/well

*Va te faire enculer, connard* – Fuck you/Fuck off, asshole

*Nu går vi* – Let's go

# Content Warning

This book contains the following:


Death

Violence

Abuse

Mature Language

Suggestive Language

Miscarriage (Mentioned)

# *Acknowledgements*

First, I want to thank all the readers who have given this fantasy series and new author a chance. I hope you enjoyed the first two books and are looking forward to Book 3.

Second, I want to thank my children, Isabelle and Ian. Your love, support, encouragement, and enthusiasm help keep me going on this new journey. Thanks for being by my side and always making me smile. I will never be able to express how much you both mean to me. I love you so much.

Next, I'd like to thank my beta readers, Isaac Marraffino, Nathan Marraffino, and my daughter. Thanks for taking the time to read this story in its early stages. Your advice, suggestions, opinions, and corrections were a huge help.

A special thanks to my mom, Anna Gough, as well as Alexandria Heath, Jaime Heath, Stephanie Kittleson, and those who pledged on my Kickstarter to help fund *The Evil Within*.

Last, I would like to add a special acknowledgement to two very important men in my life who are no longer here to celebrate this dream with me. To my dad and big brother, I love and miss you both so much. Books one and two, first editions, were released on your birthdays and those dates will forever hold a special place in my heart. Please give Oliver, Papa, Nana, and Great Grandma a hug and kiss from me.